HEIRS
OF THE
CHAMPION
The Well of Magic, Book 1

M.G. KING

WRITERS REPUBLIC L.L.C.
515 Summit Ave. Unit R1
Union City, NJ 07087, USA

Website: *www.writersrepublic.com*
Hotline: *1-877-656-6838*
Email: *info@writersrepublic.com*

Ordering Information:
Quantity sales. Special discounts are available on quantity purchases by corporations, associations, and others. For details, contact the publisher at the address above.

Library of Congress Control Number:		2020936603
ISBN-13:	9781646202089	[Paperback Edition]
	9781646202096	[Hardback Edition]
	9781646202102	[Digital Edition]

Rev. date: 04/08/2020

I dedicate this book
to Liam Regan

Afelith , The Land of Kings

Thundering Heights

Dulangar

Forest of Death

Chillpeak

Winding river

Crosthill

Zeledon

Lasgaroth

Wildlands

Xemoor

CONTENTS

Prologue..xi

Assassination Plot 1

Blackshiv and the Grey Hawks................................... 19

The Escape 39

The Lightning Strikes 55

Newfound Power.. 75

Arrival at Zeledon 89

The Overseer 103

Trial of the Well... 119

Brothers' Reunion 137

An Ancient Prophecy 149

Wanted... 161

Darkness Returns... 175

Escape to Smuggler's Way 193

The King's Speech... 207

The Last Chapter 215

Epilogue... 229

PROLOGUE

CHAMPION OF THE KING

T HE WELL OF MAGIC. THE realm between realms. The source of all magic. The essence of life itself. It flows through every living thing. The Well of Magic has been used by wizards, kings, and everything in between for generations. Magic isn't used by everyone, but if you so choose to, you can create your connection with magic by taking the trial of the well, where the guardians of Zeledon will take you to the well itself and test your will. Magic can be used for many things such as for medical treatments to help heal faster or for destructive power. The possibilities are limitless. Each individual person has a different connection to the well. Some connections may be faint or weak, and some are naturally strong. With time and training, you can strengthen your bond with the well.

This tale takes place in the lands of Afelith. A country full of many kinds of peoples and cultures and creatures from around the world. The country does not have one ruler, as it is also called the Land of Four Kings.

Thulgran Ironfoot is the king of the dwarves. Dwarves are quite similar to humans anatomically, but most of them are no taller than four and a half feet. Stocky and muscular, the lot of them. The men often grow long beards and usually carry axes or hammers. For the dwarves that are not warriors, some are bounty hunters and sellswords, but they are well-known as blacksmiths, creating the best weapons in all of Afelith. Through the Forbidden Forest, his people reside in the north, in the mountains of Thundering Heights. The dwarves will keep to themselves, but they'll trade with elves and humans if it seems profitable.

Halamar is the king of the elves who live in the paradise city of Lasgaroth, to the east. Elves are generally tall, around six feet, with pointed ears. Many of them are marksmen with the bow, and some delve into using magic for healing. There are two kinds of elves in these lands, brown skinned and gray skinned. The grays are called dark elves. Halamar is a dark elf. The elves have a long-standing friendship with the humans.

Morock is the goblin king. Though they may vary in shape and size, generally goblins are small, gangly, green-and-brown creatures who dwell underground. The king is the biggest and strongest. Thieves, they are. Goblins like to sneak around in the dark and steal food and valuables from anyone. They aren't violent creatures, except toward the dwarves. Goblins and dwarves have a bloody history, constantly fighting under the mountain that lies across their borders. Goblins and dwarves have always fought for control of Thundering Heights. The dwarves have been victorious for the past hundred years or so.

Leandrol is the king of Cresthill, the human kingdom to the west. As his father's successor, he was a warrior prince. Along with the team he led, he completed covert quests under the Crown. Twenty years ago his team decimated a group of bandits that attacked an elvish settlement. Leandrol saved a small girl's life and adopted her as her parents were killed in the raid. She became his ward when he became king. Cresthill is a heavily fortified city with a large army, but all are welcome to visit.

The city in the middle of the desert to the south is Xemoor. There is no king in Xemoor. It's a marketplace full of the world's pleasures and treasures. Xemoorians are copper-skinned people with purple eyes and hair. For the most part Xemoorians are identical to humans, except they have three fingers instead of five. They are shopkeepers and weapons dealers as well as bandits and sellswords.

The four kings have been invited to Xemoor's gladiator arena, where prisoners are set to fight to the death. Only through victory do the prisoners regain their freedom. Each king elects a champion to fight in the arena, representing the Crown.

It is now the main event. King Leandrol of Cresthill has chosen Savas, a warrior who uses the dual-wielding sword style. He is fighting a golrig, a hulking creature with light-green skin and fangs and nearly eight feet tall. Golrigs are nomadic creatures who traverse freely across the lands. This golrig's crimes were committed in Afelith, and he was captured and set for execution. Originally, Savas was supposed to have two other men to help him take this creature down, but he felt there was no honor in it, so he insisted on fighting it one-on-one.

King Leandrol of Cresthill made his way toward the warm-up room of the arena to see his champion off before his match. He was a man close to forty years old, with long black hair and a long beard. He wore a red velvet cape, signifying his royal bloodline, with specially crafted silver armor trimmed in gold and a sword hanging off his left side.

Savas paced back and forth in front of his entrance to the arena, ready to go. Both of his swords are crossed on his back like an X. He was in his midthirties and childhood friends with the king. Instead of wearing his champion armor, he wore a traditional leather kilt with a left shoulder guard crossing his torso.

"Is it wise to enter the arena in this armor—or lack thereof?" the king spit out as he gripped Savas's shoulder.

"Wearing metal armor will slow me down. I can't afford to take a direct hit against a golrig. I must stay agile."

"At least put on the iron gauntlets and use that shield over there."

Savas sighed like a young boy being asked to do chores he doesn't want to do. "As you wish, sire."

"No need to be so formal. You know I'm just looking out for you. I can't let you make careless choices which would leave your young lads orphans now, can I?"

Savas quickly turned his head to face the king. "I will *never* leave my boys!"

"I know you don't intend to, but we both know you might be in over your head here. It is not dishonorable to have aid in this fight. Don't let your pride get in the way of coming home in one piece, home to your boys."

Savas had his back to the king. He unsheathed one of his swords and handed it to Leandrol.

"I am not without help. I have aid from an old friend."

The king had a smile on his face as he was handed this special sword. "It has been a long time since you two have worked together. I withdraw my previous concern for your safety."

The special sword the king held is an enchanted weapon called the Windblade. An ancient spirit lives within the weapon, and when held by a host, the spirit and master work as one. While on a quest many years ago, Savas found the Windblade in the sacred lands. He quickly bonded with the Windblade, and they have been partners ever since. These days Savas only calls upon its help when he is in a tight spot. He should have a considerable edge against the golrig now.

The king passed the Windblade back to Savas. "You still must take the shield with you." As he pointed to the corner of the room where it hung on the wall.

Savas sheathed the Windblade and picked up the shield from the wall. He decided not to use his second blade and dropped it on the ground. He put on his helmet, iron-plated with a red-dyed horse-hair Mohawk. He approached Leandrol, and both men locked forearms, a sign of brotherhood.

The king rested his left hand on his old friend's shoulder. "Be careful out there."

Savas nodded and headed to the gates of the arena.

The shouts of the crowd of the arena were deafening as Savas walked onto the sands. He always loves it. He unsheathed his sword and raised his shield as the crowd got even louder. The opposite gate opened up, and the golrig made his way to the center.

Facing a golrig was scary enough, thought Savas, but with dual-wielding axes and a helmet similar to his made it even more terrifying.

The golrig had fangs and two massive tusks protruding from the bottom of his mouth. One is chipped. It let out a loud roar, which momentarily silenced the crowd. Savas grabbed his sword tight as his legs trembled from fear and adrenaline.

Before the fight began the golrig crossed both axes on his chest and bowed to Savas. Confused, he responded with a bow of his own. Today was actually the first time Savas has seen a golrig. From what he has heard, they were savage beasts, though the one he faces today seems civilized. Maybe people have been wrong about them?

The golrig screamed out and charged toward Savas, both axes held at his sides. Savas stood his ground with his shield up. The beast raised one arm up and plunged his axe down as Savas rolled to the left side of his opponent and drew first blood on the golrig's ribs. The beast cried out, holding his stricken side. Before Savas had the chance to back up, the golrig grabbed his shield out of his hand and backhanded him with it.

Savas has never been hit so hard in his entire life, and he knew the golrig held back. His nose was certainly broken. Struggling to get back up, the beast gave him no time to recover as he tried to strike Savas on the ground repeatedly. All he could do was roll as fast as he could to avoid the shots. Too many were too close for comfort. Without enough time to be able to stand up, he flicked his wrist in his sword hand and slashed toward the golrig. The Windblade created a strong current that threw sand at the beast, creating and opening for Savas to stand up.

As he got up, he held his arm out toward his fallen shield and flicked his wrist toward himself as the Windblade created a current to bring the shield back to him. The crowd roared so loud the arena floor shook. Savas ran toward his opponent with his shield held high. The beast stood up and attempted to decapitate Savas on his way in. As the golrig struck, Savas leaned his head back, threw his shield at his feet, and used it to slide underneath the golrig and strike behind the knees of the beast.

The golrig fell to his knees in pain. It seems Savas was literally cutting him to size as they now stood the same height. He put all of his strength into cutting the golrig's left thumb off. Now, the beast couldn't hold a weapon in his left hand. The golrig dropped the axe out of his right hand and grabbed Savas by the neck, lifting him off the ground. The beast got back on his feet and punched Savas so hard in the ribs with his four-fingered hand while the crowd fell silent. He gasped for air, knowing a few of his ribs were broken. The beast threw Savas against the wall hard enough to crack the stone.

On the floor, separated from his sword and shield, with a broken nose and ribs, the golrig slowly walked toward Savas. He was bloodied and beaten. He shed a tear, realizing he will never see his two sons again.

I didn't think I was going to go out like this. I'm sorry, Caedus and Cedric. I failed you. I love you, my sons, Savas thought while the golrig towered above him.

"Admit defeat. I do not want to kill you. I only want my freedom, not blood on my hands," the golrig said.

Savas was in disbelief.

The beast reached his hand out. "Sons need their fathers!"

As a sign of surrender, Savas put two of his fingers up to the four kings. Leandrol and the other three kings nodded their heads to spare him. Savas reached his hand out as the golrig helped him up. The announcer declared the golrig the winner, giving him freedom and exemption from his past crimes. The man and the monster headed toward the exit of the arena together. Before they left, Savas stopped and turned around. While holding his broken ribs, he used his other arm to lift the golrig's hand up, signifying his opponent as the winner, and the crowd went wild. The beast smiled and raised Savas's arm showing there was no loser in this fight.

The warriors walked out of the arena together. The golrig helped Savas walk, as his injuries were more severe. Once in the barracks, the mashkiki, also known as medicine men, are ready to help the man with his injuries.

Savas was seated, still holding his side. The golrig was standing beside him. One of the mashkiki looked up at the golrig.

"Get out of the way, beast! You gained your freedom. You need nothing else. Now leave!"

"Hey! Show some respect. He can rip your head off as easily as breathing. He is in need of medical attention as much as I do!" Savas spat out angrily.

"It is quite all right, Savas. I can attend to my own injuries. I am also quite used to the ignorance of humans."

The mashkiki took a hesitant step back.

"I will leave you to get treated. This man will work better when I am not here." He started to walk out of the room.

Savas snapped his head back toward the golrig. "Wait! I never had the chance to ask...What is your name?"

The golrig turned around. "My name is Turog." He turned back and left the room.

I wonder where he will go, thought Savas. *How did he know I have sons?* He had a feeling he will see Turog again. He would still be in the room if it weren't for the rude mashkiki. He grimaced as the man attended to his wounds. It's going to be a while before regains his full strength. Breathing has proven to be more difficult since his nose is broken, not to mention his broken ribs on the left side. He finally took off his helmet and threw it across the room. His long dirty-blond hair fell around his face and shoulders as sweat trickled everywhere. Surely it made the mashkiki uncomfortable, which brought a smile to Savas's face.

King Leandrol came into the room with the elven king, Halamar. Beside them are two hooded figures who serve as bodyguards to Leandrol. They are quite mysterious. You can't see their faces, and they are transparent. They are spirits, balanced between life and death. When they were living, they went through some secret training to reach their current state of being, to serve Cresthill beyond the grave. Due to their transparency, they cannot be defeated in battle, though they can kill you with ease. As perfect bodyguards, they can walk through walls and people. They are simply known as faeds.

King Halamar put a hand on Savas's shoulder. "Savas, my boy, you sure took a beating. How are you holding up?"

"Well, I have seen better days. Thanks to the golrig sparing me, I'm thankful to be alive. I should be back on my feet in a few weeks," said Savas.

"This was your first loss in the arena, was it not?" the elf asked.

"Yes, my friend, it was. Thirteen fights in the arena, twelve victories. Surely any other opponent would have risen to glory today by killing me. But this golrig, Turog, is honorable. Not well-known among his kind. I don't think I would have given him the same courtesy. I am alive because of his mercy." Savas started to rise to his feet.

Leandrol put both of his hands on Savas's shoulders. "You had me worried for a minute. Cresthill is proud of you. I am proud of you. I'm sure your lads will be happy to see you when we return home. Are you ready?"

"I thought I might stay for another day or so, give Lennie a visit."

"In that case, please bring Victor with you," Leandrol said as he made a hand gesture to one of the faeds to retrieve Victor.

"I don't need a lad to protect me, Lee. I can take care of myself," Savas said quietly.

"Said the man who is barely standing up. Take it as an opportunity for Vic to experience the world beyond our home. It's an order, not a suggestion. He goes with you." Leandrol smacked Savas on the back hard enough to make him stumble and made his way toward the exit of the room.

Just before Leandrol made his exit, a man no older than twenty walked in the room with silver armor and a longsword across his back.

"You summoned me, sire?" the youth asked as he bowed with a smile on his face.

The king patted the young man on the shoulder. "Yes, my boy. I have a new assignment for you. Savas will give you the details." Then he took his leave with the faeds.

Halamar saluted both men and made his exit.

From the echo in the hallway, the king yelled out, "Give Lennie my best!"

Victor put his hands on his hips and smirked at Savas. "So what is this quest the king speaks of?"

"I decided to stay in town for another day or two. The king wants you to accompany me in the event of an attack. I hear you are quite the rising star in our army?" Savas asked as he sat back down.

Victor sat next to him. "I just want to do my part. Serve our great city while making the king proud."

Savas pet the top of the young man's brown-haired head as if he were still a lad. "You are a gifted young man, very disciplined and skilled in the art of the longsword. I think you will make a great leader one day."

The younger man smiled. "You really think so?"

"Yes, I do. You know, one of my sons, Caedus, looks up to you, sees you as a hero."

"Your words honor me, Savas. Since I was a boy, I always looked up to you as a hero. Part of the reason I joined the Cresthill forces was to be like you." The boy looked a little embarrassed when he said that.

Both men stood up. Savas put his arm out toward Victor. He answered as both men locked forearms, "Your words also honor me, young man. I see a bright future for you. But first, let's change out of this attire and go visit my old friend Lennie."

After leaving the arena, both men walked the dusty streets of Xemoor. Savas wore clothing of the common folk, a simple button-down white shirt with brown pants and boots, the Windblade sheathed on the back of his belt. Victor had his longsword wrapped in cloth across his back and wore a hooded leather armor.

Xemoor's market has the biggest selection of goods in the world. It was Victor's first time there, and he took in all the sights and explored some of the shops.

Savas made a gesture for Victor to follow him down one of the side streets. Toward the end of this street Victor saw a big sign of the building Savas was leading him to, which said "*The Desert Jewel.*"

As they went through the swing doors, Victor saw that it was a pub. Though small and dingy, it was still nice in its own way. The bar area starts to the right and some tables on the left. As Savas walked toward the back of the bar area, he patted some of the patrons on the back and asked how they are doing. He took a seat on one of the stools. Victor followed him. As they sat, a man came out from behind the bar. He was a tall Xemoorian with long purple hair in a ponytail and tanned skin. He had a scar on his right cheek and wore an apron. Victor knew he must be the barkeep.

Savas quickly stood up and walked toward an opening at the bar with his arms extended.

"Lennie! How are you doing, my old friend?"

A smile came across Lennie's face as he walked toward Savas with his arms out, and they embraced each other. Savas pulled back from the pain in his ribs.

"Savas, it's been a long time! I'm doing well, just the same old thing as you know. You look a little beat up there. Things didn't fare well in the arena?"

"Not as I had hoped, no, but I am alive and that's what matters. I have this young man with me to watch my back until we get back home." Savas pointed to Victor.

Victor stood up, headed toward the other two men, and reached his hand out. "Victor Vog. Nice to meet you."

Lennie shook his hand. "Nice to meet you too, young man."

"So how do you two know each other?" Victor asked.

Lennie gestured for the men to sit. He grabbed two mugs and poured them some ale. "As you know, he is Champion of the King"—he turned around to point at Savas—"and I was a sellsword for a time, a mercenary. Many times our paths had crossed as our quests had similar goals. I found myself getting slower and less effective in combat in recent years." He pointed at his scar. "I opened this place up and decided to retire from questing."

"Interesting," Victor said as he leaned on one side of the counter. "So you worked with the *Grey Hawks?*"

"On occasion, yes, but I didn't like to stay with one faction for too long."

Savas downed his entire mug of ale quickly and, when emptied, slammed it on the counter with a refreshing sigh. "I've always said it, your ale is the best in all of Afelith. I shall have another!"

Lennie smirked as he filled him up while Victor was still sipping his first one. The light that came through the doorway suddenly became a giant shadow. Someone huge approached, and the pub doors swung open. The figure was so big it had to bend down to get into the doorway. As it walked in, Victor stood up and everyone left the pub in fear. Savas looked over, and it was none other than Turog. He was so big that he sat on the floor to be at eye level with the other men.

"I told you our paths would cross again," Turog said with a smile.

Lennie had a slight look of confusion on his face. "I see you know each other," he said as he noticed the hulking monster had his left hand bandaged up with a missing thumb and bandaged knees and ribs. "So are you the one who gave Savas such a beating earlier today?"

Turog nodded his head. "Yes, and I have taken a beating myself, but I only wanted to win my freedom. No need for unnecessary bloodshed."

Lennie found the biggest mug behind the bar and poured an ale for Turog. It was more like a pitcher to fit six ales in for the normal man.

"You are a golrig, are you not? Your kind are known to be savage beasts with no regard for human life. You seem to have a sense of honor and wisdom, which has never been seen in your kind."

Turog gently grabbed his oversized mug. "Yes, I am a golrig. Most of the tales you hear are mere stories. True, in the past there were a few cases of golrigs who took pleasure in killing others not of its kind, but most of us like to keep to our clans and not involve ourselves in the world's troubles." In one giant sip, he finished the entire pitcher of ale.

Lennie gave him a refill. "Not much is known of your kind to the world of men and elves. Who knows what the dwarves know, they don't bother with anyone. So tell me, Turog, what crimes landed you in the arena, if you don't mind my asking?"

Turog downed the second mug of ale as Victor and Savas turned their heads to listen to what he was about to say.

"A fellow golrig in my clan, a man whom I considered a friend, betrayed me. It cost me everything. I did not expect to be blindsided by someone I trusted."

Savas slapped Turog on the back. "It's okay if you don't want to give us the details, my friend."

Turog's nostrils flared as he crushed the giant mug he was holding into dust. "The pain is still fresh, I don't want to tell the whole story. But the short version is, my former friend framed me for a crime he committed. I got so angry, I...I killed him. And I was taken in to face judgment in the arena. As you know I gained my freedom, only to be banished from my clan for life."

"Where will you go now?" Victor asked.

Turog looked over to face him. "I do not know yet. I may travel to find my new place in the world." He dropped a few silver coins on the counter and stood up. "Sorry about the mug. Great ale, by the way." Turog put his four-fingered hand on Savas's shoulder.

"Before you go, I must ask. How did you know I am a father? In the arena you said, '*Sons need their father.*'"

Turog smiled. "Because I am a father too." He nodded his head at all three men and made his way toward the exit.

Savas yelled out, "You are always welcome to visit Cresthill if you make your way there someday."

Turog turned his head and smiled. He waved good-bye and walked out of the *Desert Jewel*.

~~~

The night was getting late, and Lennie sent Victor and Savas to retire in a spare room he had above the bar. At first light they will make their way back to Cresthill. On horseback it should take about two weeks to get back home.

The next morning, before the *Desert Jewel* opened to the public, Lennie made breakfast and packed food for the Cresthill natives' journey home. Plenty of cheese and bread and water by the gallon for both men. Surely both men will engage in some hunting in the meantime for some meat on the road. The three men enjoyed some eggs and potatoes. They laughed and talked about past adventures.

Just before opening Savas and Victor packed the rest of their things and headed for the stables. Lennie walked with them and said his final good-byes.

He gave Savas a big bear hug. "May you have safe travels, my friend. Send a letter once you get back home."

Savas offered a half smile. "Yes, I will. I'll be back soon enough, you have the best ale around." He patted his old friend on the back.

Lennie now faced Victor and locked forearms with him. "It was an honor to meet you, young man. I see you becoming the greatest of leaders one day in this world."

Victor smiled. "The honor was all mine. Thank you for your hospitality."

"Anytime. Keep this man safe, he is getting slower with age." He jestingly slapped Savas on the back.

Victor and Savas put all their journey food and supplies in saddlebags and jumped on their horses. As they started to gallop away, Savas turned around and saluted Lennie. He responded with a wave until they were out of sight.

~~~

They rarely stopped on the way home, just to sleep at night. Every four hours one of them would keep watch after dark while the other one slept. Wolves and bears prowled around at night in this area of the world. The journey has been cut to a little over ten days instead of fourteen. Most of the way Savas talked about his fights in the arena and quests with the king years ago. Victor talked about his goals and ambitions to become the commander of the Cresthill army or to become Champion of the King himself someday.

On first light of the tenth day, they finally arrived to Cresthill. They made it home.

Victor walked Savas to his home just outside of the city, a nice little cabin away from the public.

Victor walked him to the door. "This is where we part ways. I must report to the king."

"Would you like to meet the boys? I know Caedus would love to meet you," Savas asked.

Victor look down toward the ground. "I would love to, but I must report back to his majesty. Maybe another time?"

Savas put his hand on Victor's shoulder. "You don't have to be so formal about the king with me. We go back since before you were born."

Victor smiled. "Thank you." He got back on his horse. "Until next time, my friend." He waved and galloped toward the city.

As Savas was just opening the door halfway, his sons tackled him to the ground in excitement. He yelled in pain from his ribs but also laughed because he is happy to see his boys again.

"Welcome home, Papa!" one of his sons named Cedric yelled out.

Coming from one of the other rooms is the babysitter Avaline, the advisor of the king. She was also one of the world's only two wizards who survived the mage rebellion a thousand years ago. She has white long hair and icy-blue eyes with the look of a woman in her early thirties, even though she has been alive for much, much longer. She was wearing a white hooded robe, loosely fit but also snug enough to see her athletic curvy figure.

"Okay, boys, give your father some space." She picked up her staff by the front door.

Savas slowly got up because his ribs are still broken. "Thanks for watching the boys, Ava. They love spending time with you."

Ava pressed one of her hands on his ribs, and it started to glow. It was healing magic to fix his ribs. Then she did the same for his nose.

"I'll spend time with the boys anytime. How do you feel now?"

"Still sore, but much better. Thank you."

Ava put her hands on his cheeks and smiled.

Savas responded by hugging her.

"I'm sure you are tired from your journey. I'll take my leave." She hugged the two boys and walked through the front door.

Savas sat on a stool next to the fireplace. The boys were lying on the bear-pelted carpet next to him. His boys were twins, ten years of age, but they did not look like twins. They looked very different. Caedus had short black hair, and Cedric had long blond hair, resembling his father. Both shared gray eyes.

Caedus looked up at his dad. "Who did you fight this time? You never came back hurt before."

"I fought a golrig. He was huge. Probably nine feet tall. We had a good fight, but he stopped it because he didn't want me to get hurt. He is a nice man."

Both boys smiled.

Cedric stood up and asked, "What's his name?"

"Turog."

Both boys looked at each other in amazement.

"I didn't know golrigs were real! That's so cool! Can we meet him sometime?" Caedus asked.

"I'm sure one day he will come to Cresthill, and I'll introduce you boys to him."

At the same time the boys both said, "Wicked!"

Savas stood up and put his hands on his waist. "Did you boys stay up all night to wait for my return?"

The boys looked down on the floor. "Yes." They looked upset.

Savas came down to one knee to be eye level with his boys. He grabbed both of their heads and gently pulled them closer to him. His forehead gently touched both of theirs.

"Do not be sad, boys. I am not mad. I looked forward to seeing you the whole way home."

The boys hugged him.

Cedric raised his head up. "We love you, Papa. We always look forward to your return."

Caedus nodded his head in agreement.

"And I will always return. I cannot lose in battles because I will *never* leave you boys alone."

They let go of the embrace, and Savas stood up.

"I'm sure you boys are tired. I am too. Let's rest for a few hours, then maybe later you would like to go to the city? We can get those toys you wanted."

Cedric yelled out, "Yes!"

"Rest up, boys. We will leave in a few hours."

The boys headed toward their room.

Caedus faced his father. "It's good to have you home, Papa."

All three fell asleep within a few minutes.

A few hours later Savas woke up and saw it was pouring outside. The sky was black, darker than it normally would be when it rains during the day. He looked out the window and saw Cresthill is clear of rain and darkness. Why is only his house being covered in darkness? He sensed dark magic and grabbed the Windblade.

He cracked the front door open to peek outside, and an unimaginable force pushed the door off its hinges and him across the room. Red steam filled the room, and a figure in hooded black cloak slowly entered the house. Caedus and Cedric entered the room to see their father on the ground and a strange man standing over him. Caedus ran toward his father, but before he can get to him, another man jumped into the house through a window, shattering glass everywhere.

Only it wasn't a man. It was a werewolf with yellow eyes and long black hair down its back. He wore torn pants and a vest, with claws drawn out and fangs. He stood before Caedus and put his arm up, warning him not to move forward. In fear he stayed back. The werewolf roared and leapt toward the dark man.

The dark man made a small hand gesture, and the werewolf flew out of the house as if an invisible force pulled him out. The dark man now looked toward Caedus. One of the dark man's arms turned into a purple beam of energy resembling a sword. Caedus couldn't see the man's face, only the glowing yellow eyes. Not like the eyes of an animal like the werewolves, these eyes were pure evil.

He raised his hand to slay the boy when Savas jumped on his back. The dark man only flicked his head back, and a shockwave of energy knocked Savas across the room. Just then Avaline appeared and spun her magical staff to throw a stream of fire toward the dark man. He put one arm up and blocked the path of fire in all directions and caused the house to catch fire.

Cedric held his brother's arm in fear of what was happening around them. The red steam had approached them, and it muffled the sounds around them. The dark man cast lightning from his hands and struck Ava off balance and knocked her into the wall. While she was down, he reactivated his purple blade, grabbed Savas by the neck, lifted him off his feet, and stabbed him through his chest.

Blood splattered everywhere. The werewolf jumped back in the house as the dark man shot out a blinding light. The werewolf shielded Caedus and Cedric with his own body.

While everyone was temporarily blind, Caedus couldn't feel his brother's touch anymore. When his sight returned, he saw his father on the ground, the dark man was gone, and Cedric was gone.

Ava lifted Savas's body up, and the werewolf lifted Caedus up as the house crumpled into wood and ash. The dark man stabbed Savas through the heart. He was dead.

When they were safe enough from the flames, Ava put Savas's body down and Caedus ran toward him. Tears streamed down his face as he screamed for his dad to wake up. His face was cold when Caedus touched it, and he started to shake. Ava pulled him back and held him to calm him down.

The werewolf looked toward Ava. "The attacker has taken the other boy. I can't follow his scent. The trail went cold after the dark cloud over the house."

Caedus screamed in anger and despair at the realization that his brother was also gone. He looked down at his father's fatal wound, the gaping hole where a portion of his chest used to be. He grimaced at the sight. Blood stained the grass surrounding his body. Above all else, as gruesome as it was, he couldn't bear to look at his father's face, pale and lifeless. Savas was his hero, his protector, his father. Now gone forever. It was too much for him to handle, and he ran in the opposite direction for a few steps before throwing up.

He held his stomach in pain and tried to get up. Avaline rushed to help and lifted him up to his feet. Caedus buried his face in her cloak as he started to sob. She gently held him for comfort while looking toward the werewolf.

The half-man half-beast groaned as the man half started to take control of the shared body, as the fight was over, at least for now. Caedus looked over to him and saw the hair all over his body fade away and the fangs shrink back to regular teeth. The claws were now gone, but his eyes remained yellow and he still had long hair from his head, which flowed down to his waist.

Now with the look of a normal man with the exception of the eyes, he bent down to one knee to face Caedus. "Are you okay, son? Are you hurt?"

The boy wasn't physically hurt, but mentally, it was something else entirely.

The man put his hands on the boy's shoulders. "My name is Therion. I was a good friend of your father's."

The boy looked up at him.

"I promise I will do everything I can to find who did this. We will find your brother. You just have to stay strong. Can you do that?"

Caedus nodded his head without saying a word. Therion stood up and headed toward Savas's body. He cradled his friend in his arms, stone-faced. He lifted him up and headed toward the city to bring him to the castle. Ava walked Caedus ahead of Therion so he didn't have to see his father's body.

Now at the gates of the city, the soldiers on watch saw the three arrive along with a body in Therion's arms. Everyone stopped what they were doing and moved to let them pass. Many whispered in confusion. Someone yelled out, "The Champion of the King is dead!" which made Caedus's lip quiver.

Avaline lifted her staff above her head and muttered the word *sylentwo*. He noticed he couldn't hear anything anymore except Avaline's voice.

"You don't have to hear what people are saying right now, child." She rubbed his back, and they quickened their pace.

Some of the soldiers from the watchtower saw them approach from afar and called for some mashkiki and the king. Guards flooded the streets and shoved civilians to make way for Avaline and Caedus. Therion followed slowly, now covered in his friend's blood while carrying him. Caedus tried to look behind him, but Avaline pushed his face forward.

As they reached the entrance to the castle, King Leandrol rushed toward the wizard and saw his champion's lifeless body behind her. He fell to one knee, holding his heart and a tear fell down the left side of his face. Two faeds materialized by his sides to help him up, but the king waved them away. Leandrol cupped his hands under Caedus's cheeks.

"Are you hurt, son? Are you okay?"

Caedus opened his mouth, but he couldn't bring himself to utter a word. Leandrol wiped the boy's tears away. Caedus reached out and wiped the tears off the king as well. He smiled. After suffering a tragedy, the boy still showed compassion for others. He rose up and grabbed one of the boy's hands with both of his.

"Stay strong, my boy."

Ava and Caedus headed into the castle, while a faed relieved Therion of Savas's body. The king touched the champion's forehead, only to find it as cold as ice. Therion grabbed Leandrol by the shoulder.

"I wasn't strong enough to help him. The wizard and I together weren't able to help."

Leandrol's eyes widened. "You must tell me everything! Leave out no detail. Follow me to the study." He whipped his cape behind him as he turned around.

Both men walked toward the castle, followed by the faed carrying Savas. The guards worked crowd control as the civilians started to panic. It's not every day a dead body was carried through the streets, leaking blood over the cobblestones and unsettling everyone in sight.

One of the captains gathered everyone around once they calmed down.

"Fear not, citizens of Cresthill! It is true, the Champion of the King has been slain. This was from an attack which took place outside the city. You are safe, but it would be wise to go back to your homes or at the very least stay in the city until we go through an investigation. My men will escort those who desire it."

Therion and King Leandrol walked fast toward the study. The assistant to the king, a tall and lanky man by the name of Gustaf, quickly rose to his feet as the other two men walked at a rushed pace.

"What has happened, m'lord? What's wrong?"

The king gestured for Gustaf to walk alongside of them.

"Savas has been killed. The faeds are moving the body as we speak. Oversee the transfer to the medical wing and meet us in the study."

Gustaf's eyes widened in disbelief. "Savas, the champion? How?"

"Examine the wounds yourself."

"I...I don't know what to say," the man said while he ran his hands through his red hair and started to sweat.

"Don't say anything! Please do as I say, then meet us in the study," the king spat out.

Gustaf bowed. "As you wish, m'lord." He started to turn around as the king gestured for him to stop.

"One more thing. Make sure the guards settle everyone down. We don't need a citywide panic."

Gustaf bowed and ran toward the guardsmen outside.

Therion quickened his pace to slam open the doors to the study before the king entered, nearly knocking the doors off the hinges. Once both men entered, Leandrol closed the doors and locked them. Leandrol took off his cape and threw it on the floor. He sat down on a red velvet chair, leaned back, and pressed his fingers onto his forehead as if he had a headache. Therion took his vest off and used it to wipe all of Savas's blood off his body, then threw it in the fireplace. Leandrol gestured for him to sit. He put a hand up to refuse and paced back and forth in front of the fire.

"What happened? *How* did this happen?" the king asked with some sadness and a small flare of anger.

Therion stopped pacing and turned toward the king. "Savas must have arrived home from Xemoor earlier today."

"Yes, Victor reported back to me about six hours ago. I had him accompany Savas on the way home because he took a massive beating in the arena."

"Really? This attacker may have known Savas was in a weakened state when he got home."

"Did you notice anything which could identify this murderer?"

"He was wearing a black hooded cloak. Not of these lands, the material was nothing I felt before. I couldn't see his face, but he had yellow eyes. It is the only feature I could identify about his appearance."

"Is he another werewolf?" the king asked as he bent forward to lean his arms on his knees.

"Not the eyes of the beast like mine. I think these eyes are from the taint of dark magic. His eyes were evil."

"From your point of view, start from the beginning."

Therion crossed his arms, then raised one hand up and cupped his chin. "I wasn't sure Savas was even home, but I sensed something heavy in the air. Some powerful magic, dark magic."

Leandrol had a confused look on his face. "Strange that I did not."

"It must have been because I also live outside the city like Savas. I am close enough to see his house from mine at the top of the mountain, as you know."

"This is true, but I meant the three of us are bound by the Phoenix. We both should have sensed the danger he was in. I was just in here doing research until you showed up with his body in your hands."

Therion sat down across from Leandrol. "I couldn't sense him in danger either. I only felt the crushing presence of this hooded man. After I felt a presence, I looked toward his cabin and it's surrounded by storm clouds. This was unnatural, so I decided to investigate."

"How did Avaline come into play?" the king asked.

"I felt increasingly uneasy as I came closer to Savas's cabin, so I transformed. I assume Ava sensed the darkness also because she was heading toward the front as I headed toward the back. As I got closer, I ran on all fours and jumped through the window." Therion stood back up and started pacing again. "I stood in front of his sons to warn them to stay back. I barely got more than a few steps forward before the hooded man threw me out of the window with unrelenting force. While I was outside, Ava must have used fire magic because the cabin began to burn. I ran back in and grabbed Savas's sons. The place was smothered in red smoke. I was only able to use my sense of smell to find the boys, and when it cleared up, I had only Caedus in my arms."

The king quickly stood up. "Did this hooded man *take* the other boy? With all of the chaos I did not realize that he was not among the rest of you!"

Therion looked down. "This is the only explanation I can think of. He was in my arms with the other boy and then gone. Vanished into thin air. When I lost the scent of the hooded man, I lost my touch with the other boy." He clenched his fists and shook his head. He flipped over the table he was standing by and let out a roar. "I failed him! I failed Savas, and I failed the boy, both of his boys!" As he started to get worked up, his fangs started to grow and his claws started to emerge.

Leandrol put a firm grip on his old friend's left shoulder. He struggled to keep eye contact as Therion kept shaking his head. "Hey! Hey!" Leandrol started to shake Therion with both arms now to get him to stop moving. "This is not your doing! Don't make yourself believe it is! It was the monster who just took our dear friend away." His lip started to quiver and his eyes watered. "Our brother."

Therion's claws and fangs retracted as the king let go of him. Therion finally made eye contact with him. "We will find this hooded man. We will find Cedric. We will bring this madman to justice."

They locked forearms and smirked at each other.

Avaline held Caedus's hand through the castle doors. His mouth was open in awe as he looked up at how high the ceiling was. He had never seen a room this big, and this was only the entrance. After a pause, some of the royal guards ran past them to calm down the crowd of common folk outside. Ava tugged him in her direction and led him to the throne room.

Once inside, Caedus saw a tall man with reddish hair with a twirly mustache and a sense of elegance about him run hurriedly past him and Ava. He was running toward where Savas was being sent to.

Ava looked down at Caedus. "That was Gustaf, the king's assistant. He makes sure everything stays under control in the castle."

The boy nodded his head. He looked toward the throne to see someone sitting cross-legged on it. It obviously wasn't the king; he and the werewolf stormed off in another part of the castle. It was a woman. This woman looked strange to Caedus. She had dark-gray skin and pointed ears. She was an elf! She stood up and walked toward Ava and him. The elf wore leather armor with black knee-high boots, metal shoulder plates, and a green scarf.

She bent down to one knee and put both of her arms out underhanded. Caedus let go of Avaline's hand and gently grabbed both of the elf's hands.

"My name is Alanna, the king's ward. How are you holding up, Caedus?"

The boy didn't know what to say. He blushed because he has never seen someone so beautiful and he was holding hands with her. On the left side of her face she had beautiful white lines intertwining in vertical motion from her forehead, through her eye, and down to the side of her mouth. It signified the elven clan she used to be part of. She had sparkling red eyes and beautiful scarlet hair leaning over her right shoulder in a braid.

Alanna stood up and grabbed Caedus's head and kissed him on the cheek. He was too embarrassed to look up. His face was as red as her hair.

Ava grabbed the elf and hugged her.

"What's the situation?" the elven woman asked.

Avaline tapped her staff on the floor twice and muttered the same incantation as before, *sylyntwo*. This time Ava and Alanna spoke among themselves.

Caedus was out of earshot, and he walked toward one of the steps in front of the throne. He sat down and put his elbows on his knees and rested his chin in his hands.

Who was the hooded man? Why did he take Cedric? he said to himself. *Why, why did he kill Papa?* His lip quivered. A tear streamed down his face. He punched the tile floor as hard as he could and hurt his hand, but he didn't make a sound. He rubbed it with his other hand when Alanna walked over to him.

"Avaline went to help Gustaf with matters around here. Would you like to accompany me?" Alanna asked.

Caedus stood up and looked at her. "I...I would like that." He had a hard time keeping eye contact with her because he would blush after a few seconds.

"Do you want to see the view from the top of the spiral tower?"

Caedus nodded.

"It's a long way up. Would you like to ride on my back?"

Caedus hesitated.

Alanna sensed Caedus isn't the kind of boy who would ask or want any assistance. "It's okay, Caedus. I'm stronger than I look." She got down on her knees, her back toward Caedus. She turned her head and smiled at him. She waved him toward her. He gently wrapped his arms around her shoulders and neck. She grabbed his legs and put them around her waist.

She walked to the small hallway behind the throne that led to a spiral staircase. Caedus looked up and was astonished at how far up the staircase went. It didn't seem to end. Alanna wasn't winded in the least. She went up the stairs faster than any normal human could go without making it uncomfortable for Caedus. She had a remarkable sense of balance and grace in her movements. Caedus smiled.

The top of the spiral tower is the highest point in the entire city. You can see for miles in all directions. When Alanna got to the top, she let Caedus down but held his hand. This beautiful view is her escape from reality, and she hoped it could be for Caedus also, at least for tonight. The sun was setting.

"The view is amazing, isn't it?" Alanna asked.

Caedus smiled. "Yes, it is! Do you come up here a lot?"

"I do. It helps me to clear my head." She pointed in the distance toward the edge of the mountains. "Is that where you live, Caedus?"

He nodded his head in agreement. "It's where I used to live. It's nothing but blood and ashes now."

Smoke was still rising from the ruin what earlier today was his home.

Alanna grabbed the top of his head and started gently playing with his hair. Her touch soothed Caedus. "Do you see the top of the small peak over there?" She pointed to the mountain where his cabin had been.

"Yes. What's up there?"

"We can't see from here, but at the top is another cabin. Therion lives there, the werewolf. That's why he was able to help you so quickly."

"He and Ava seemed to drive the hooded man away, but he took my brother," Caedus said as he looked down and got on to his knees, trying to stop himself from crying.

Alanna got on her knees also and grabbed his face with both her hands. "Hey, hey, don't cry. Let's change the subject. Where is your mother?"

Caedus was able to look at her now without blushing. "My mother? I don't know. I never knew her."

"Nothing? Your dad never talked about her? Did you ever ask him questions about her?"

"Papa never talked about her. A few times Cedric and I would ask where she is, but Papa always changed the subject."

"You have no memory of her?"

Caedus shook his head. "What about your parents? The king isn't an elf but you are. How come you live here?"

Alanna stood up and walked to the ledge, looking toward the city this time.

Caedus followed.

"Twenty years ago, my clan was raided by bandits. They asked for our riches, we had none. Elves value nature and family over material possessions. They thought we were lying. So they asked again, but each time one of us told them we had nothing of value, they started killing us one by one. They killed my father first. Naturally, I cried out."

Caedus reached out to hold her hand.

"One of the bandits grabbed me and put a knife to my throat and said he'll kill me if I made another sound."

Caedus looked up at her. "What happened next?" he asked.

Alanna smiled. "Three men came out of the woods and started to kill the bandits. The first one to die was the one holding his knife at me."

"Who were the men?"

Alanna looked down at him. "The king—at the time he was the prince—the werewolf, and your father."

Caedus's mouth opened up, and his eyes widened. "Papa fought off bandits to save you?"

Alanna smiled. "Yes, he did. The three of them took out the whole company of bandits, but not before they killed the rest of my clan. My mother among them."

"I'm sorry, Alanna."

She wiped a tear from her face and inhaled deeply before continuing, "It's okay, Caedus. It was a long time ago."

"How old were you back then?"

"I was six. Now I am twenty-six. When the bandits were killed, the king picked me up and brought me back with him. I had no family left, so he adopted me. When he became king, I became his ward. He has treated me with nothing but kindness and warmth."

"Did you ever go back to where your clan was? To say good-bye to your parents?"

She nodded her head. "Yes. A few days after the attack, Cresthill helped bury my clan and my parents with Halamar, the king of the elves. I go back there every year and bring flowers."

"That's nice. Do you miss them?"

"Every single day. You never get over losing someone you love. You are just forced to learn how to live without them." She put her hand on her heart. "My parents will always be with me in here." She patted her heart for Caedus to notice. "And your father will always be with you here." She put her hand on Caedus's heart.

The boy smiled. He put his hand on top of the arm Alanna was using to touch his heart, and she smiled. They heard someone coming up the steps. Gustaf appeared, drenched in sweat from sprinting the stairs, on top of everything else he was doing. He was already running when Caedus ran into him a little while ago.

He slicked his hair back, then leaned forward and put his hands on his knees. Still trying to catch his breath, he spoke.

"Alanna...young master...the king requested both of you in the study." He then sat on the stone ledge of the viewpoint.

Alanna put her arm on his shoulder. "Stay here and rest, Gustaf. We will make our way to him."

He grabbed her hand. "Thank you, m'lady," he said and smiled.

Caedus and Alanna made their way down the spiral tower and through the mazelike hallways of the castle, or at least in Caedus's opinion they were like a maze.

How could anyone know how to navigate this giant place? he thought, but Alanna seemed to know every turn and corner. Now, finally at the study, she opened the door to see the king and Therion sitting down by the fire and Avaline sitting behind one of the desks.

Caedus had never seen such an amazing room before. A fireplace big enough to have a person standing in it, roaring with fire that lit up the room. Luxury chairs surrounded the fire in a half circle with a small table in the middle. Behind the chairs was an entire library of books. Hundreds, perhaps thousands of books. *Maybe even more*, Caedus thought. The shelves were so high they each had their own ladder. A staircase leads to a second floor, also full of books and a wall full of maps of the world.

King Leandrol stood up to greet them.

"Alanna, my angel, and young Caedus, welcome to the study. We have a few things to discuss. Please find a seat to your liking."

Alanna patted Caedus on the back and sat on one of the chairs by the fire. Caedus sat on one also, in between Alanna and Therion. Leandrol sat back down in the biggest chair in the center of the half circle. Avaline stood up from behind the desk and in front of the fire, leaning on her staff. Caedus hadn't noticed Avaline's staff had a jewel at the top. He couldn't tell what color the jewel was because of the fire's glow that illuminated half the room. He didn't know if it was another one of her spells.

After a few moments of silence, Caedus stood up to get everyone's attention. "What's going to happen to me now?" His hands started to shake.

Therion reached over to grab his shoulder. "It's one of the things we are all here to discuss. Please sit back down and relax. Everything will be okay."

The man was physically intimidating. He stood a head taller than most, with scary yellow eyes, but his words brought comfort to Caedus.

The boy sat back down.

Avaline decided to speak next.

"As you know, Caedus, Therion and I were there trying to defend you and your father and brother. We failed to save your father"—she let out a deep sigh—"and your brother was taken from right under our noses."

Caedus grimaced. "Neither of you could have expected what happened. It's not your fault. It's *his*!" He clenched his fists.

Everyone in the room knew he meant the mysterious hooded man who killed his father and took Cedric away.

Leandrol looked at the boy. "We want you to know, son, I will use all resources and alliances at my disposal to find your brother and bring him back here safely. Also, we will find out who this hooded man is, his motive for killing your father, and we *will* bring him to justice!" The king was leaning on a gold-plated cane with a purple jewel at the top. His hands were visibly shaking while keeping the cane upright.

"Savas may not have talked about us much, but the three of us were best friends growing up." Therion pointed to himself and the king. "The three of us were even bound by magic up until tonight. We just want you to know you aren't the only one hurting. Everyone in this room loved your father, and we will do everything in our power to bring his killer to justice and to keep you and your brother safe."

Caedus buried his face in his hands and started to cry. "Thank you, everyone."

Therion walked toward Caedus and got on one knee to face him. Caedus looked through those yellow eyes. Therion grabbed the back of Caedus's neck with both hands and leaned his forehead against the boys. "We are all here for you, son."

Alanna covered her mouth, trying to hold in a cry.

The king was already crying but stayed as quiet as he could.

Avaline rarely showed emotion, but she had a look of sadness on her face. She must have seen thousands of people come and go in her long life.

Therion once again made eye contact with the boy. "Would you like to come live with me and my daughter? You will be loved with us."

Caedus was too choked up to even say anything, so he nodded his head and gave Therion a hug. The monstrous man squeezed the boy tight.

After the embrace, Caedus started to wipe his tears and stood up. "Before I go with you, I want to do one more thing here."

"What is it?" Therion asked.

"I want to see my father one more time."

The king raised his head. "As you wish. Come with me."

Once outside the study, Leandrol lead Therion and Caedus to where Savas's body was kept in the infirmary. Alanna and Avaline prepared to send ravens out to the elves and the Grey Hawks, a sellsword association, for aid in a search party to find Cedric.

Now in the infirmary, the king demanded the mashkiki and faeds leave immediately. The leading mashkiki, a man who wore a strange mask in the shape of a beak, whispered in the king's ear before leaving the room.

The king turned his attention to Caedus. "The medicine man informed me the fatal wound your father was inflicted with to the chest was instant. He likely didn't feel any pain on his way to the next life. I hope this information will bring some comfort to you." He patted the boy on the back. "It does for me."

Therion nodded his head. Both men placed one hand each on the boy's shoulders as the three of them walked toward Savas's body on the table. The mashkiki had covered his wounds and cleaned the blood.

Caedus tried his best to stay brave. The boy inhaled deeply and grabbed his father's cold hand. "We are going to find who did this, Papa, I promise. We will get Cedric back, and both of us are going to be warriors of legend, because our father was Champion of the King." Caedus had no more room for tears tonight. "I love you, Papa." He kissed Savas on the forehead, then backed away.

Therion and Leandrol bowed their heads as the boy spoke. Leandrol was still having a hard time believing Savas is gone. He and Therion grew up together with Savas and have known each other for as far as he could remember. Caedus lost his father, and Therion and Leandrol lost their brother.

Therion squeezed Caedus's shoulder and whispered, "Are you ready to come to your new home?"

Caedus looked up and nodded. The three of them made their way out of the infirmary to the castle entrance. The guardsmen had kept the citizens under control since they have last been out here; and for the time being, things are looking normal, with the exception of servants cleaning blood off the streets.

As soon as the king stepped foot outside the castle, two faeds appeared at his sides.

"Young Caedus, we will do everything we can to find your brother. That is a promise. In the meantime, settle in with Therion and his lass." Leandrol held out his hand to Caedus.

The boy quickly grabbed the king's hand and squeezed. His father told him you can see what a man is all about by his handshake.

"Papa always told me you were the most honest man he knew, and I believe it."

The king smiled.

Therion and Leandrol locked forearms and hugged.

"Since the seal of the Phoenix is broken, we need a new way to contact each other. Any word on the investigation, send a raven," Therion said.

The king started stroking his beard. "Ah, it has been decades since we haven't communicated telepathically to each other. This may take some getting used to, but so be it. I will send for you when the occasion arises. Good night to both of you. Safe travels."

The king bowed, as did Therion and Caedus, and they left.

Therion lived in a mountaintop cabin overseeing all of Cresthill. It was an easier route than Caedus thought it would be to get there. When they finally got to the top, the house and property were much bigger up close.

Therion put his hands on his hips and smiled. "Do you see the pit over there?" He pointed to a sand-covered area toward the back of the house.

"What is it for?" the boy asked.

"I train people in the gladiatorial arts. Your father, the king, and I basically lived up here growing up. We pushed each other to our limits constantly."

Caedus smiled. "Really? Can you train me too?"

"At first light tomorrow. You and my daughter Emilia will start together. Speaking of which, let's go inside so you can meet her." Therion patted the boy's back and led him to the door.

Before they were able to open the door, it swung open and a little girl came running out and hugged Therion fiercely.

"Welcome home, Pa." The girl had a huge smile on her face. She then looked at Caedus and gave him a huge hug as well. "My name is Emilia. What's yours?"

Caedus blushed and hugged her back. "I am Caedus. Nice to meet you, Emilia."

The girl had cute freckles across her nose and cheeks. She had blue shoulder-length hair. Caedus had never seen anyone with blue hair before. She looked about the same age as him. The three of them walked inside.

"How come you have blue hair?" Caedus asked.

She started to play around with it. "I'm half Xemoorian. Instead of having purple hair like them, it just came out blue, I guess." She pointed to her eyes. "Instead of having purple eyes, I have one blue and one purple."

"Wow, I like your eyes." Caedus has never seen eyes so beautiful before.

The girl smiled.

"Okay, children, the hour grows late. I think we could all use to sleep. Both of you be ready, I will wake you at first light for training tomorrow." Therion headed toward a room in the back of the cabin. "Em, show Caedus to the spare room." He looked over toward the boy. "And, Caedus, welcome home."

Caedus smiled.

Em grabbed his hand and lead him to the spare room, but instead of going into her own room, she went into his room and sat on the bed.

"Why do you want to train, Caedus?"

The boy sat on the bed next to her. "I want to be strong like my father, and I have to save my brother." He put his head down.

Em grabbed his hand. "I know what happened. I'm sorry, Caedus."

The boy had a confused look on his face. How could she have known if she was here the whole time?

"When you and my father got to the castle, he had a raven sent to me to let me know what's going on."

"Oh, okay."

"Ask me why I want to train, Caedus!" Em said with a smile on her face.

He looked into her different-colored eyes. "Why do you want to train, Em?"

"I want to be strong like my pa, and I want to help you get your brother back. We could defeat this hooded man together because we are family now."

Caedus didn't know what to say, so he hugged her. "Thank you."

After the embrace, she stood up. "From what I have seen when my father trains people, we will have to work as a team or else we will fail."

"What do you mean?" Caedus asked.

"You will see in the morning. Have a good night!" she said and walked to her own room.

It took no longer than a minute for Caedus to fall asleep.

The following morning Therion gathered the children to the sandpit in the back. He was not jesting when he said first light. The sun wasn't all the way up yet. Now in the center of the pit, Therion punched his open palm.

"Today we begin your training. The first task I have for you is simple. All you have to do is land a clean blow on me."

"Just land a clean blow on you?" Caedus asked.

"It's not as easy as it sounds. I am the fastest warrior in all of these lands."

Em nodded her head when Caedus looked over to her.

"Every day we will do this exercise, and if either one of you can't manage to hit me in one hour, you will scale the mountains with weighted packs. And when you come back, you will do my physical building workouts. Am I clear?"

Both children said in unison, "Yes, sir!"

Therion smiled and took off his shirt. "Good, now, both of you, come at me with everything you've got!"

Emilia and Caedus ran toward Therion and started swinging. Therion easily dodging everything they threw at him. Caedus threw a right hook too hard and missed. Therion backhanded him so hard he fell on the sand. Em threw a kick that he caught in midair, spun her around, and threw her onto Caedus while he tried to get back up. They clashed heads, and now blood trickled down the top of their heads.

"Don't the two of you want to take on this hooded man? He defeated me with ease, and you can't even hit me. You are going to have to try harder if you want to be a challenge for anyone." Therion raised his voice. "Now *get back up!*"

They helped each other back up. Therion looked into their eyes. These kids will not quit, no matter how beaten they are. He looked at Caedus. He had a fire in his eyes. He will be a fighter like his father before him.

I

ASSASSINATION PLOT

T EN YEARS HAVE PASSED SINCE the death of Savas and the kidnapping of Cedric, one of his sons. His other son, Caedus, was taken in by Therion, one of his father's closest friends. Therion raised Caedus with his own daughter, Emilia, to be one of the best in hand-to-hand combat as well as weapons training to any potential enemy. Soldiers from Cresthill would frequently come to train at Therion's mountaintop home alongside Em and Caedus.

Caedus loved training with the soldiers, but he looked forward to news on the investigation of his brother's kidnapping more so upon the arrival of the soldiers. Each time they had little to say. King Leandrol recruited help from the elves and a sellsword faction, the Grey Hawks, to help. After the first few months, the trail went cold. Even after, Caedus would go to the castle to check in on any updates once a month. He checked every month for five years, then he gave up on the investigation Cresthill was running. Technically, it was an open case but it wasn't a priority anymore. But it was Caedus's only priority. He was going to continue the investigation himself.

Shortly after Caedus and Emilia turned fifteen, Cresthill deemed the investigation a non-priority. The teenagers went to where he used to live, now an empty patch of land, and started looking for where the elves had previously found clues. The elves determined the hooded man used magic to accelerate his jump to a certain tree branch a hundred or more yards away. The accelerated jump left an indentation on the branch. From there, the hooded man must have run from the base of the tree to the Winding River, because a path from the tree to the river has a burned, straightforward direction into the river. The use of too much dark magic will bring unnatural properties. The hooded man's use of dark magic was so intense it caused nature around him to burn. He knew it, so he jumped into the river to throw off his trail. The trail had gone cold.

The trackers from the Grey Hawks then estimated many possible paths the hooded man could have taken, with no solid results. Victor Vog, the youth who accompanied Savas home from Xemoor, also trained with them. Over the years he and Caedus developed a special relationship. Caedus was the brother he never had, and Victor helped Caedus fill the void of missing his own brother. Up until about three years ago, Caedus had started to defeat all the soldiers hand-to-hand. The only one who could consistently beat him was Victor. They helped push each other to their limits.

Emilia and Caedus were hesitant to ask someone else for help in their own investigation on what happened to Cedric, though they finally decided to approach Victor to join them shortly after they turned seventeen. Without hesitation, he said yes. Victor considered Savas a mentor, no matter how brief it was. He deserved justice. Caedus deserved to be reunited with his brother. Victor revealed to Caedus he offered to lead the Cresthill investigation after it was deemed a non-priority, but the king refused because he didn't want one of his prized men to waste their time. Caedus understood where the king was coming from, but it still made him mad.

Since Victor had responsibilities to the kingdom, he was restricted as to where he could go so he used the king's study to research old maps for possible areas for the other two to investigate. If he found one worth checking out, he sent a raven to them with instructions on where to go.

Caedus and Emilia had searched to the edges of Afelith with no success. As painful as it was to him, he decided to give up. He had an uneasy feeling the hooded man would return for him. He felt all he could do was train as hard as he could until the hooded man came back.

Before Therion took Caedus as his own, Emilia's mother, Kashizu, moved back to Xemoor as she and Therion ended their marriage. Emilia still visited her mother though. It usually took about two weeks to get to Xemoor, and Therion would escort Em and Caedus to visit her for as long as a month before returning home. Caedus never had a mother before, but no one was more welcoming and heartwarming as Kashizu. The first time she hugged her, he cried. He never understood what a mother's love may have felt like until then.

As part of their training, Therion made them journey between cities by themselves since they were twelve years old. They shared a horse, but Caedus mostly let Emilia sit while he led the way on foot. They had to learn to survive and rely on each other. The first time they got lost it took them almost a month to get back. But each time became easier, and the last time they managed to shave a few days off the trip. At first Caedus and Emilia thought visits to her mother would be a break from their training. Little did they know Kashizu worked them ever harder than Therion ever did. The desert atmosphere did not make things any better either. Every other time they mentally prepared for her wrath on the way to Xemoor.

Now age twenty, three years after deciding to give up on his brother's disappearance, Caedus was told it was time to start training in the magic arts. He and Emilia wanted to start years ago, but Therion insisted they were not ready. They trusted his word without question. Therion told them the key to having mastery over magic is to have mastery of your own body. He trained both of them to the brink of hell and back to get them into the best shape as possible. Now was the perfect time for magic training.

After all these years Therion was still a giant compared to Caedus. He still made anybody look like a kid next to him. He stood about six and a half feet tall. The man with the eyes of a wolf, glowing and yellow. He was intimidating to most people, but Caedus and Emilia were used to him. When the full moon came out, he turned into a werewolf, but over time he had been able to control his wolf alter ego. He could transform at will if he needed to. To transform, he still had to look at the full moon. He had a moon tattooed on his right forearm with an enchantment, allowing him to transform when he looked at it. On any normal day he kept it wrapped in bandages so he didn't transform accidentally. He still wore his faded green vest unbuttoned, shirtless underneath, and brown pants worn by common folk.

Emilia was nearly six feet tall with shoulder-length, frizzy blue hair, and two different-colored eyes. She was half Xemoorian from her mother's side. Em's left eye was purple, and her right eye was blue. Full-blooded Xemoorians had purple hair and eyes. Being half human, she just turned out with blue hair and one blue eye. Her nose and cheeks were sprinkled with freckles. She thought they made her look cute. She wore brown leather corset armor with knee-high boots. With her athletic build, beautiful eyes, and freckles, Emilia became quite popular among the men of Cresthill when she made her visits. As she walked down the street, she would occasionally hear a whistle or notice smiles from passing men. Once, as she was buying food, a man checked her out as he passed by and got slapped by his wife for his wandering eyes. Emilia laughed.

Caedus and Emilia always argued over who was taller, but in truth, Emilia was about an inch or two taller than he was. Caedus's head and face were clean shaven. He was in excellent physical condition, stockier than his father was. He wore soldier's armor on his legs with the Cresthill banner as a loincloth with black boots and leather shoulder pauldrons with straps that crisscrossed his chest and extended to his waist, connecting on his back.

The three of them were on the porch of Therion's mountaintop home. The view never got old for any of them. They could oversee the entire city of Cresthill and the sea beyond.

"How does magic training begin?" Emilia asked.

Therion stroked his long black hair, now streaked with gray. Besides his hair, there was no indication of his age. One might think he is a strong thirty-five, but he was fifty.

"There is a specific way to go about it. Not everyone can have the ability to use magic. I don't see why you two can't." He looked toward Caedus. "Your father and I went through the trials together and came out with our magic powers."

"Didn't the king go through the training also?" Caedus asked.

Therion started to laugh. "Your father and I went first because Leandrol was afraid. He wanted to see if we were going to survive, and when we did, he took the trials after us."

"Really? He doesn't seem the cowardly type," Caedus said as he rubbed his chin.

"I jest you not. Over time the king had gained his courage, but just not back then. There were so many people who never returned from the trials. It was scary for us all, but he couldn't contain it like your father and I did."

Emilia had a worried look on her face. "Survive? Magic training could be fatal?"

Therion folded his arms across his chest. "Oh yes. It has to be taken very seriously. Which is why I didn't want you to start until I thought you were absolutely ready. I think now is the time."

Emilia didn't feel any safer hearing this, and she sighed, "As you say, Father."

Surprisingly, Caedus had no reaction. Em thought he would show the slightest bit of emotion but his face was stone. He stood up next to Therion. "What consists of these trials you speak of?"

"I cannot say specifically. One person goes at a time, and through magic your personal fears manifest. Once they do, you must learn to overcome them. If not, you are condemned to insanity and sometimes even death."

"Have you ever known anyone to have failed?" Emilia asked.

Therion put his head down. "Yes," he said softly. "As you know, Leandrol, Savas, and I were a team. We were competing against another team of three for the right to be bound by the Phoenix. Two on the opposing team never made it out. Your mother was the only survivor, Em."

Emilia shot her eyes toward her father. "Mom? If she failed, how is she alive and sane?"

"She passed the trials, but her team failed. She was devastated to lose them. That's when we fell in love, your mother and I. I was there for her when she needed someone most, and the rest is history."

"Do you know what her fears were manifested?" Em asked.

Therion sat back down. "I do, but you can just ask her yourself the next time you visit."

Em nodded her head.

"We can get started once we get to the city. Avaline is the teacher for the magic arts. She will be pleased to start on you both."

The three of them stood up. Caedus put on a brown hooded cloak, as did Emilia. They headed down the mountain toward Cresthill.

Today was rather crowded in Cresthill, for the annual feast day is coming up. Some elves and even a few dwarves were in town. The feast is something to behold, and dwarves never miss a chance to attend a feast. The elves often bring many different varieties of wine, and the dwarves bring ale. The dwarven women are known to be excellent cooks as are some of the human women. To gather the meat needed for such a feast, Cresthill had a hunting event called the Baccus Run. The baccus was a legendary creature, a form of deer or elk. Most people think it is only a legend, but every year people go looking for one. According to Avaline, the last baccus who was killed and cooked was over six hundred years ago. The meat of the baccus is supposed to increase one's magic power. Each year since then, everyone settled for chicken, deer, and boar meat, though one year someone hunted a griffin. It fed half the town.

With Therion lurking behind, Caedus and Emilia walked through the crowded cobblestone streets toward Cresthill's castle. From the front gate of the city, the main road to the castle heads uphill and with a slight turn to the right, creating the look of a giant moon crest, hence the name of the city, Cresthill. If you look to the right from the main gate, you see the castle towering above you, but all must walk through the crest to reach it. Along the way, many travelers were peddling goods from distant corners of the world. Xemoorians sold clothes, goblins sold trinkets, elves sold jewelry, and some dwarves sold jewels they mined from under the mountains.

Among the crowd is King Leandrol. Caedus hadn't seen him in nearly five years, since he blew the candle out on Cedric's investigation. He didn't know how to feel about approaching him after all this time. King Leandrol was showing his age, with a few strands of gray in his hair and beard. He was accompanied by his assistant, Gustaf. He hadn't aged a day since Caedus first met him ten years ago. Victor was also with them. He was now Champion of the King and the commander of the Cresthill army. He goes by Commander Vog these days and also sports dark-brown hair, about a month passed a shaved head, with a bushy mustache. He looked like an experienced veteran.

As Therion looked around the crowd with determined eyes, he sensed something was off. He grabbed Caedus and Emilia by the shoulders. "Keep your eyes open, something doesn't feel right."

"Like what?" Caedus asked.

"I don't know, but keep your eyes on the king. He is vulnerable here." He patted both of their backs. "Now, separate."

They knew better than to question him, so they separated into the crowd. Caedus felt his bones rattle. He looked around frantically for the source, and there it was. A man in a purple hooded cloak with purple eyes. But it was not a man, he noticed, it was a woman. A beautiful woman. He can't tell why, but something doesn't feel right about her, and she was eying the king too often. As he watched her pace quicken toward his majesty, he saw a dagger hidden in her sleeve. Caedus ran toward her, pushing people over in the process. He created unwanted attention on himself, which gave this hooded woman room to move closer to the king.

Leandrol turned around as Caedus ran toward him in an aggressive manner, but he didn't know it was Caedus. He was wearing a hood, and the king hadn't seen the young man in years. Gustaf and Victor pulled their swords out and stood before the king. While their attention was on Caedus, the hooded woman held her dagger tight and thrust toward the king's back. Just before landing the deadly strike, Emilia kicked the woman's arm and she dropped the knife.

The crowd panicked and started to run away. Amidst the chaos, the hooded woman tried to escape as Emilia tackled her to the ground. She was shrugged off as the king's attention turned toward the two women. Victor and Gustaf forgot about Caedus and rushed the king toward safety inside the castle. Caedus ran to help Emilia. The hooded woman smiled, like she would prefer a challenge. She held her arms out with her palms facing up. She wanted to take them on at the same time. Em attempted to kick her again, this time in the chest. The hooded woman let her leg get close enough for her to swipe Emilia's leg to the side to expose her back. She grabbed Em in a choke hold and dared Caedus to do something. He knew if he made the wrong move, she would snap Emilia's neck.

Emilia thrust her elbow into the woman's stomach, loosening her grip on her. She was able to wriggle her way out. She pushed away as Caedus came toward the woman. She threw a few punches his way. He dodged a few with simple head movements, though he couldn't believe how fast she was. She grazed his cheek with the last blow and drew blood. She thrust a front kick to try to throw Caedus off balance, but he caught it and twisted her ankle, which managed to turn her body around so her back was to him. Holding her leg bent behind her, he wrestled her to the ground. She groaned in pain, but it didn't make Caedus loosen his grip in the slightest.

"Who are you?" Caedus yelled out.

Before the hooded woman got a chance to say anything, three faeds appeared before them, the king's bodyguards. They pulled out their blades and pressed them against their necks. Caedus let go of the woman. A deep indistinguishable voice came from the one behind Emilia.

"By order of King Leandrol, you three are hereby under arrest for the assassination attempt on his life."

Caedus and Emilia know of the tales of faeds. They are not to be reasoned with. You must obey or be killed. It seemed the hooded woman also knew, and she put up no resistance. The three were escorted to the castle while Therion lurked behind them.

The faeds escorted the three to the castle dungeon. Instead of being thrown in cells, they were instructed to sit in three chairs next to each other in an open room. Once seated, their hands were bound behind their backs with rope and then the faeds disappeared into the air. They must be going to get someone to interrogate them.

Caedus sat in the center chair, the purple-eyed woman sat to his left, and Emilia to his right.

The purple-eyed woman looked toward both of them. "Who are you two? You ruined my plan."

Caedus grimaced. "Who are we? Who are *you*? You just tried to kill the king, and now they think we tried to help you."

The woman flicked her head back to brush off her hood. She had purple hair and bronze skin. She must be Xemoorian.

"I did not try to *kill* the king. I was instructed to take his weapon by any means necessary."

Emilia rose her head up. "You mean his sword? Even if you meant to take it, you tried to stab him in the back. Why is his sword so important?"

The Xemoorian woman looked at her. "As I said, by any means necessary. Stabbing him in the back may or may not have killed him. The king's sword is a weapon enchanted with magic. My master desires such weapons for his plans. Now I fear, since I failed, my master will have me killed."

Caedus snapped his head toward her. "Who is your master? Does he have yellow eyes?"

She nodded her head in agreement.

"And he also wears a black robe similar to yours?"

Again, she nodded.

"Your master killed my father and kidnapped my brother, Cedric. Do you know him?"

The woman made eye contact with him. "Yes, I know him. You must be Caedus! Cedric always talked about you."

Caedus's eyes widened. He dragged his chair in front of the woman and faced her directly.

"Cedric is alive? Is he safe? What does your master want with the two of you? What are his plans with the enchanted weapons?"

She put her head down. "I don't know what he wants from us or the weapons. Ten years ago he showed up at my house in Xemoor, killed my family in front of me, and took me with him. Cedric was already his disciple when I got there. We lived in a cell together. There were two others with us as well. We were trained in body and magic by our master."

"Four of you?" Caedus asked. "Who are the other two? Why is your master using you? To what end?"

Emilia moved her chair to face both of them. "I am sorry to interrupt, but what is your name?"

The woman looked shocked. No one has ever cared to ask what her name was. Even her master only ever called her *girl*. She looked into Emilia's eyes.

"My name? My name is…it's Sheska. My name is Sheska."

While she looked into Sheska's eyes, she saw fear hiding behind them. Em realized she was most likely a victim in all of this. She didn't have the choice to become an assassin or whatever she was. It was forced upon her and Cedric.

"My name is Emilia. Under the circumstances, it is still nice to meet you."

Sheska smiled. "Nice to meet you too, both of you."

Caedus smiled also. "Your master, what is his name? Can you take us to him?"

"Be patient, Caedus!" Emilia spat out. "We aren't going anywhere." She shook her arms showing that they were all still tied up.

Sheska closed her eyes and shook her head. "My master sees everything. I can't take you to him. He will kill both of you—and me. I always talked about escaping, but my fear of him outweighs my courage. Cedric always talked me out of trying to leave."

"If you are here, what compels you to go back to him? Why not just run away?" Emilia asked.

"He can find us. He will always find us. We cannot betray him. We cannot. He may even kill me just for talking to the both of you. I've already said too much." A tear slid down her right cheek.

Even though his hands were bound, Caedus leaned toward Sheska and wiped her tears away with his hood. "We are friends with the king. We can explain what has happened and help you. Let us help you, and help me reunite with my brother. Please."

Emilia caught Sheska's attention with a look. "If your master is going to kill you, what do you have to lose? We can do everything in our power to protect you."

Sheska smiled. "I appreciate your concern for my well-being, but I'm afraid your efforts would be futile against my master."

"There must be something we can do," Caedus said. "I have spent the last ten years preparing to face your master. I *will* kill him, even if it's the last thing I do!"

The seriousness of his words and a determined look on his face gave Sheska and Emilia the chills. He truly believed he will do it and will stop at nothing until he does.

While looking at Caedus, Sheska asked, "I sense the two of you haven't even started training in the magic arts. How could you possibly believe you will be a match for him?"

"How can you sense if we can use magic or not?" Caedus asked.

"Once you start training in magic, you will know what I mean, and not before then." The Xemoorian turned her head away.

"As you say, I guess. Either way, it doesn't matter how long it takes. Your master's day will come. It would be easier if Cedric could help. From what you say, he must be very powerful now. I'm sure he would help, if I get the chance to see him."

"He is not the little boy you once knew. He—"

Before she got the chance to say more, the three faeds reappeared and straightened their chairs to the way they were before they moved around. The door swung open, and three men walked in— King Leandrol, Gustaf, and Victor. The king stepped forward toward his captives while the other two leaned against the wall near the door they came in.

Leandrol made a hand gesture to the faeds to pull off the captives' hoods. He took another step forward.

"It has been some time Caedus, son of Savas, and mistress Emilia. I imagined our eventual reunion would not be like this. Explain to me what has happened today in your point of view."

He stood in front of Caedus with his hands behind his back.

Caedus raised his head. "The three of us, Therion, Em, and myself were heading to the castle to seek out Avaline. We needed her help to start training in magic. Earlier, in the crowd in front of the castle, I spotted her." He gestured toward Sheska. "I felt something was off about her, so I watched her closely. She pulled a knife and headed toward you, so I started to run. I knocked a few people over, and it made the crowd uneasy. It may have looked as if I were running to attack you."

Leandrol stroked his graying beard. "Hmm…interesting." He glanced at Sheska's eyes. "Please continue."

Caedus looked toward Emilia. She continued story.

"I kicked the knife out of her hand, which drew her attention on me. Then you were rushed back into the castle for safety. Caedus and I took her on, and when he pinned her down, then your faeds apprehended us."

"I see," the king said. "Your father gave me his perception before we came down here. As I see it, you and Caedus are free to go." He glared at Sheska. "But *she* will remain here for the time being."

The faeds untied Caedus and Emilia, and they stood.

Caedus put his hand on the king's shoulder. "This woman is not entirely at fault. She is being controlled by the man who killed my father."

Leandrol took a step back. His eyes widened. He grabbed Caedus by the arm and pulled him to the corner of the room where no one else could hear. He whispered into the young man's ear, "If what you say is true, then this is what we need to find your brother."

"I know. She knows Cedric. She said she grew up with him. They were raised and trained by their master, the man we are looking for." Caedus glanced back at Sheska, then to the king. "I believe her. She was explaining things to us before you came down here. It was real. She is genuinely terrified of her master."

"I see. Do you think she can take us to him?" the king asked as he crossed his arms.

"I'm not sure. She is afraid her master will kill her if he finds out what has happened here. She has to believe we can protect her."

Leandrol turned and walked toward Sheska. "Caedus tells me you fear your master. Tell me, could you at least take us to Cedric?"

Sheska looked into the king's eyes. "Yes, I can. There is no doubt Cedric would come to my aid if I needed. The trick is to meet him where our master cannot see, but he sees *everything!*"

"I can consult my advisor about this. She is a wizard and may have a counter to your master's looming eye."

"A wizard? They aren't real. The stories of them are just stories."

The king unclipped his sword and leaned it on the ground, using it as a cane. "How wrong you are, young one. No matter, her actions speak for themselves."

Sheska kept her eyes on the sword.

Caedus stood between her and the king. "Your sword is what she was after. Her master needs it for his plan."

Leandrol threw his sword away from him. Before it hit the ground, a faed caught it and left the room.

Victor pushed himself off the wall and stood next to the king. "If he needs your sword, your master must be after the other enchanted weapons as well."

Sheska nodded her head in agreement.

Victor grabbed Sheska by the shoulders. "Tell me, did you come here alone? Did you come to Cresthill alone? Did you?"

She put her head down, ashamed. "No. Cedric is here too."

Caedus and Leandrol stepped back.

Victor looked at the king. "She was just a distraction. The map which leads to the world's enchanted weapons is in the study. We have to go there now!"

The king pointed his finger toward Sheska and gestured for Gustaf to come toward him. "Do not let her escape. Throw her in a holding cell. Have two faeds accompany her at all times."

During the chaos of the assassination attempt, Cedric snuck into the castle with no problems. The guards' and staffs' attention was focused on the king's safety. Cedric lurked in the shadows as he looked for the study. After searching some of the massive halls, he peered through a cracked door and saw a giant bookcase. The study must be in there.

Two guards protected the entrance. These men are huge compared to him. Cedric stands six feet tall, thin, with an athletic build unlike his stocky father and brother. He had high cheekbones with long blond hair in a topknot. He wore a red loose-fitting robe and had glowing yellow eyes like his master. The eyes of dark magic and evil.

The two guards were big, close to his height, ironclad in armor, both holding quarterstaffs on their sides. There was no way around these two without a fight.

May as well go head on, he thought. He jumped in front of them and drop kicked one. He slammed against the wall while he attacked the other. The guard poked the spear end of the staff ferociously at Cedric once, twice, three times, four, five, and six. None hit their mark. Cedric was too fast, dodging with ease.

The guard put power into another thrust. Cedric pushed the blade down to the ground and used the staff as a ramp to kick the man in the face. The guard's helmet flew off, and blood spewed out of his mouth along with a few teeth. He hit the ground hard and dropped his staff. Cedric quickly picked it up and slit the guard's throat. Blood spattered everywhere. The man held on to his neck as his life drained away. Cedric stabbed the other guard in the head before he had the chance to get up.

Cedric threw the quarterstaff next to the bodies and headed into the study. The room was a lot bigger than he imagined. Two floors of books, but he was looking for a map. A map that contained the locations of the world's enchanted weapons. His master wasn't interested in the map itself but only one of the weapons, the lightning blade. The blade Savas previously owned, the Windblade, was now in Cedric's possession. The Windblade would be able to tell which symbol to look for on the map, which contains the lightning blade.

"Surely, master could have come here himself to look at the map. Now Sheska has been caught. I wouldn't have been caught if our roles were reversed. Master has foreseen it. It's always another test with him, to see how we will overcome the situation. Now I must stage an escape, but first, the map."

He looked around the room, through some of the many aisles of bookshelves. No luck so far. Toward the back of the room, he saw an elegantly carved wooden desk. It must be the king's. Behind it was a large map with many glowing dots placed all over Afelith. Cedric reached under his robe to unsheathe his blade. He held it up toward the map and let it guide his movements. After a minute or two, the point of the blade lightly touched a blue marker on the map, on the border of Lasgaroth, the elven city, and Thundering Heights, the dwarven mountains.

He looked closely at the blue marker. It's a small zigzagged line symbolizing lightning.

"There it is! I will break Sheska out, and we will retrieve the lightning blade."

"You aren't going anywhere!" a man said while blocking the entrance.

Cedric quickly turned around, clutching the hilt of the Windblade. This man towered over him. The man took off his hooded cloak and threw it on the ground. Musclebound, long black hair, and yellow eyes, not like his, more like an animal.

"You, you were there when my father was killed ten years ago, weren't you?"

The man walked closer. "So the second son of Savas returns. You must be Cedric. The name is Therion. You were snatched from my arms as I was trying to protect you all those years ago. It doesn't seem to me you are a captive anymore. You are no stranger to dark magic. The man who killed you father, your *master*, you are his disciple?"

Both men started to pace in a circle, keeping eyes on each other.

"It's not so simple, even you know that. You think I chose this path?"

"I understand. We have your companion in our custody, and you killed those two men outside. I can't let you leave."

"I have somewhere to be, and so does my companion. If we are not on our way, my master will *not* be happy. You must release her and give her to me."

Therion pointed at the younger man. "You are in no position to give orders. If we keep you both here, your master will come to us."

"I cannot allow it. Sheska and I have been given specific instructions. If we don't fulfill them, my master won't come here. He has other ways of getting things done. We are not his only disciples. He won't so easily fall for whatever trap you plan to capture him with. Your efforts would be futile."

"There are more of you? How many more?" Therion asked. He sounded calm, but the fact that there are more users of dark magic made him very nervous. He can feel Cedric is very powerful. Too much power for someone his age to possess.

Cedric had a face of stone. "There are two others. A total of four disciples under Lord Mathis."

"Lord Mathis, huh? The name doesn't ring a bell. He must have proclaimed himself. What is he the lord of anyway?"

"This conversation grows tiresome. Will you let me pass, or are we going to fight?"

"Like I said before, you aren't going anywhere."

Therion stopped pacing and readied his fighting stance. Cedric wasted no time and used his blade to force Therion back with strong wind. Therion crossed his arms and was pushed back only a few feet. A normal man would have flung across the room.

He is using the Windblade as an extension of himself! Therion thought.

Cedric rushed toward him and threw a flying kick to his opponent's stomach. Therion caught it and flung the younger man toward one of the bookshelves. It knocked him right through it and slammed into a wall. He slowly got up. Therion was already upon him. He put some power into a punch, which narrowly missed Cedric's head. His hand was stuck in the wall now.

This was an opportunity Cedric couldn't pass up. He quickly used a leg sweep to knock Therion to his knees and threw a right hook, which landed hard on Therion's cheek. It seemed to not affect the older man. It snapped his head back a few inches but showed no indication it hurt. It actually hurt Cedric's hand more than anything. Therion wriggled his hand out of the wall and grabbed Cedric's face with both hands. He lifted him up off his feet and headbutted him.

Before he slammed his head against the younger man's, Cedric quickly blocked the force of the blow with his arms. He surely would have been knocked unconscious otherwise. Therion threw his opponent to the ground. Cedric's arms were numb. The situation wasn't looking good for him. He did his best to shake it off and stood back up. Therion gave him no time to recover and charged toward him again.

Cedric used his weapon to slash heavy winds continuously toward Therion, enough to push him back against the wall. The moment his back hit the wall, Cedric used Therion's own body as a stepping stone to jump and land a massive kick to Therion's face. After the kick landed, Cedric spun around and landed a second kick with his other leg before hitting the ground. He drew first blood against Therion.

The older man winced as he touched the gash on his cheek. "It has been some time since anyone has been able to land a blow on me, let alone draw blood. It's time to end this little warm-up."

Warm-up? He can't even feel his arms because of the strength of this man. His body ached. He realized he was in over his head against

Therion. Was he really just being toyed with? Before Cedric he could blink, Therion was already behind him.

I have never seen anyone this fast before, Cedric thought. Before he could react, Therion had him in a chokehold so tight if he resisted, he would die.

"Yield!" Therion yelled.

Cedric didn't make a sound or move an inch.

Therion kicked the back of the younger man's legs and grabbed his neck tighter. "Do you yield?"

Cedric simply tapped the older man's arm, signifying giving up.

Therion released him and let him fall to the ground. Cedric gasped for air and softly rubbed his neck.

Therion took a few deep breaths as the door to the study slammed open. The first through the door was Victor with his sword out, followed by the king, as well as Caedus and Emilia.

Cedric looked up and noticed the young man with his shaven head. "Caedus?"

Caedus pushed the others out of the way to get a closer look.

Therion pulled the young man's hood off.

Cedric? He changed so much, twisted by dark magic, but he had the same face as he remembered when they were kids. A tear fell down the side of his face.

"Cedric? Is it you?"

II

BLACKSHIV AND THE GREY HAWKS

THERION LIFTED CEDRIC TO HIS feet and dug his long nails into his neck so he wouldn't try anything.

Caedus rushed toward his long lost brother and grabbed his shoulders.

"Cedric, it's really you! You have no idea how long I have waited for this."

Therion loosened his grip on the young man.

His yellow eyes made contact with his older brother. "Caedus. My brother. It has been far too long." His eyes flickered from yellow to his original gray, then back to yellow. That seemed to cause him a tremendous amount of pain, but he hid it well. He closed his eyes and embraced his brother forcefully.

Caedus held on tight. He couldn't believe the moment he'd been waiting for was finally here. The brothers released the embrace but held on to each other's shoulders.

Suddenly, four faeds entered the room with their blades drawn and pushed Caedus away from his brother. They crossed their blades together around Cedric's neck, so if he moved in any direction, he'd cut himself.

One of the faeds spoke out. "Son of Savas, you are under arrest for the murder of two royal guards and as an accomplice to the attempted assassination of the king."

King Leandrol walked up to the young man. "Young Cedric, I never thought this day would come, but killing two of my men is not something to forgive." He gestured to the faeds. "Take him to the dungeon, farthest from the entrance. Do not let him near his companion. Keep an eye on him at all times." Leandrol picked the Windblade off the floor and held it in front of Cedric. "I never thought you would use your father's own weapon as a tool to murder your own people. Take him away."

Everyone made way for the faeds to escort Cedric to the dungeon. Therion stopped them for a moment for a quick word. He put his hand on the young man's chest.

"You fight hard but you lack experience."

Cedric grimaced.

"Who are the other two disciples of Mathis?"

Cedric smiled. "It matters not who they are. I'm sure you can ask them when they come for me and Sheska." He shoved Therion's hand off him as he was taken away.

On the lower end of the city sat the famed Lunas Tavern. Not luxurious but quaint and loved by locals and travellers alike. It was windy out, so most people sat inside by the fire, except for one, a bronze-skinned elven woman with a hooded turquoise cloak and beautiful silver hair. Her hood was down as she avoided eye contact with anyone. For the most part she felt like a loner.

She raised her hand to get the barkeep's attention, and he walked over with a jolly smile.

"Good afternoon, young mistress. How may I help you on this fine day?" the man asked. The barkeep is a plump fellow, surely from having access to the kitchens whenever he wanted.

The woman raised her head up. "I will have some Lasgarothian wine."

"Ah, good choice. White or red, my dear?"

"Red, please. Thank you."

"No bother, young lady."

Just then a giant figure walked into the place and momentarily caught everyone's attention. A man in a brown cape walked in with a snarl on his face. He had short brown hair, almost like a soldier's, with a clean-shaven face. He was so big and muscular, he might have been mistaken for a golrig to some. Certainly the biggest human most of these people had ever seen. The man bowed toward everyone by the fire, then walked to the elven woman's table and sat down next to her.

The barkeep's eyes widened by the size of the man. "A drink for the gentleman?"

The giant man raised his head and smiled. "I will have a Xemoorian ale and two of your Baccus brews."

"All at once?" the barkeep asked.

"Yes."

"Right away. Lasgarothian wine, red, and three ales, two Baccus, and one Xemoorian."

The woman shook her head in agreement and smiled.

"May I ask the both of you, are you here for the feast day? I have never seen you before. You must be travelers."

The woman raised her head up. "Yes, we are looking forward to our first feast day." She quickly grabbed her companion's hand to show a little affection. Maybe to show off to the barkeep that they were romantically entangled. "We came early to explore the city for a few days."

The barkeep smiled. "Wonderful. Anything in particular you are looking forward to?"

"The fireworks," the giant man said.

"It is surely a sight to behold. I shall be back in a moment with your beverages."

The barkeep walked away.

The woman leaned back in her chair and looked toward her companion. "What have you got, Brock?"

The giant man, Brock, looked over at her and smirked. "It seems Sheska has been captured."

She smiled. "She is always getting herself into trouble. I'm sure Cedric will break her out. He has a softer spot for her above the rest of us."

Brock smiled and leaned closer to her. "Giselle, I wasn't finished yet!" Then he remained silent for a moment.

Giselle sighed. "Don't leave me in suspense. What is it?"

Brock was trying his best to hold in a laugh. "The golden boy has been captured as well. It's up to us to save them and gain the upper hand!"

Giselle's jaw dropped. An opportunity will never come up like this again.

"This is great news, Brock! Master will be displeased with them, and he will praise us on saving the job! It's a good thing we already have drinks on the way to celebrate!"

The barkeep returned with all four drinks on a silver tray.

"There you go, young masters. Enjoy, and just wave if you need anything else."

"Thank you, we certainly will," Giselle said.

The man started to walk away, but he turned around to face them again. "Oh, and welcome to our great city of Cresthill." He then smiled and went back behind the bar.

Brock downed his first brew in one sip like it was nothing. "There is one more thing, Giselle," he said while wiping ale off his face. "What Cedric found, the blade that master wants, he found the location. I saw it on the map while eavesdropping. Do you think one of us should retrieve the sword while the other breaks them out?"

Giselle took a sip of her wine. "If we retrieve the sword and break them out, we will certainly make an outstanding impression on master. It's risky, but I think we should do it."

"Who will do what?" Brock asked.

"I will retrieve this lightning blade. You can do what you do best. We shall meet back at home, the four of us. Maybe after this we will be master's new favorites."

Brock smiled and finished his remaining ales. He grabbed Giselle on the shoulder. "Please be careful. We don't know what lies in the sacred lands. Rumors have been circulating about a guardian."

She touched his hand to ease his concern. "Thank you, I will. Don't worry. Just be careful with breaking them out. Things could get messy really quick."

He patted her on the back and nodded his head, then walked out of the tavern.

⤨

Caedus and King Leandrol were in the throne room. Leandrol sat on the throne while Caedus paced back and forth. He picked up the pacing from Therion. He always did it when he was nervous. Caedus picked up more than a few characteristics from the man who raised him, mostly out of admiration. He simply couldn't sit still after seeing Cedric after all this time. He was sweating on the forehead and palms. His hands were also shaking. His adrenaline soared.

He walked faster toward the king, pointing at him. "You have to let me see him! Let me talk to him!"

"Must I remind you to whom you are speaking to?" Leandrol snapped.

Caedus put his head down. "I'm sorry, I didn't mean to get so hostile."

"It's quite all right, boy. Your situation is most unusual. You may see your brother, but first you have to do something for me."

"What must be done?" He didn't care what is was, he would do anything.

Leandrol paced, his hands behind his back. "As you heard, Cedric had two more allies out there. I fear that they will attempt a breakout, and we need some outside help. All you need is to go to the headquarters of the Grey Hawks and tell them I am calling in my favor."

"That's it? Can't one of your messengers do that?"

"Not exactly. The leader of the Grey Hawks, a man by the name of Blackshiv, won't come here unless you were to do something for him."

"What kind of Baccus chase are you leading me on?"

Leandrol gave him a disapproving look.

Caedus put his hand on his head, wiping off some sweat. "I apologize once again, King Leandrol."

"Don't worry about it, you don't have to run an errand for him or anything. I am not sending you on a senseless chase. He is going to want to test your fighting abilities. If you pass his test, he will come back with you willingly."

Caedus stroked his bald head. "And if he doesn't come willingly?"

The king raised his head and lifted up his right arm and yelled out, "Deth!"

Just as he put his arm down, one of the faeds appeared before the king and kneeled. "You summoned me, sire?"

"Yes, you are to accompany this young man to the Grey Hawks compound. If Blackshiv refuses to come back here, you will take him by force. Is this understood?"

The faed rose its head. "Yes, my king. Consider it done."

Leandrol looked into the faed's hood and only saw the darkness of an empty void. He always wondered if these faeds were anyone he once knew, for they were living people at one time.

"I will be awaiting your return," Leandrol said as he sat back down on the throne.

Caedus and Deth bowed and walked out of the throne room side by side.

"So your name is Deth?" Caedus asked.

The hooded figure looked in his direction. "Deth is my alter ego. I cannot reveal my real name."

"How come?"

"One of the conditions of becoming a faed is to hide your identity, for if you reveal it, the devil himself will hunt me down and take my soul for judgment."

"Seems a little harsh, don't you think?" Caedus asked with a smirk on his face. *This guy must be jesting*, he thought.

"When someone dies, their soul is brought to judgment immediately, to see if they are worthy to go through the gates of heaven or fall through the pits of hell."

Caedus stopped for a second.

Deth turned around to face him.

"Hold on a minute. Those stories of heaven and hell, it's just rubbish. Don't tell me you think the goddess and the devil are actually real?"

Deth reached under Caedus's pauldron and grabbed his left shoulder hard, a lot harder than Therion ever had. He couldn't move a muscle. He felt his shoulder burning.

"Trust me, boy, it is all real. It is a mortal sin to hide your soul after death. I will serve the crown for the rest of time, or if I am found out, I will spend the rest of time in hell. Never to return."

"I don't understand. How does one hide his soul from the gods, if they even exist?"

Deth dug his nails into Caedus's shoulder hard until he drew blood. "*Don't* test me, boy! If you don't believe me, ask Avaline about the gods."

Caedus was powerless to shrug Deth's hand off him. "Fine! Just let go of my shoulder."

Deth released his grip. "I apologize if I hurt you." He turned away, and they continued walking. Deth didn't walk; he just levitated above the ground.

"It's okay, just a minor wound," Caedus said as he rubbed his shoulder, wiping some of the blood off. "You still didn't answer my question. How does one hide their soul from the gods?"

"That is not a story for today. If everyone knew how to hide their souls, the realms would be off balance."

"How many realms are there?" Caedus asked.

"I…I am not sure. I myself have been to two of the realms. Avalene may know how many there are in total."

The faed seemed to stroke his chin, which Caedus couldn't see.

"Interesting. Emilia and I need to start our training in magic, now more than ever it seems, since new enemies have arisen. Where is Avaline anyway? I thought I would have seen her by now."

"She will return soon. She left town accompanying mistress Alanna and Queen Amaya."

Caedus snapped his head toward the faed. "The queen? On a quest?"

The faed looked toward the young man and shook his head. "Oh yes. Amaya never gave up questing even after she became queen. Her fire for adventure still burns bright."

"That's good. What is the quest they have taken on? It must be something big to have a wizard and warrior princess along."

"You may ask them upon their return. We have an assignment of our own to attend to."

Both of them had reached the entrance to the castle, where they bumped into Emilia.

"Where are you two going?" she asked.

Caedus grabbed her hand so she would follow them. "The king is sending us to the Grey Hawk's base. We must deliver a message to their leader and bring him back here before his highness."

"Can I come?" Emilia asked.

Caedus gave the faed a curious look.

"She may come along. She can prove useful."

The three of them walked out of the castle and through the streets.

"This Blackshiv, the king said he won't help us unless we are tested in our combat abilities first," Caedus said.

"Oh, I see. For what purpose though?"

"Apparently, he is always looking for new recruits for his organization."

"Oh, okay."

"Where is Therion?" Caedus asked.

"He personally wanted to keep an eye on your brother, so he escorted him with the other faeds to his cell. He is staying there to thwart any escape attempts."

"What about Sheska?"

Em smiled at the mention of her name. "She is kept in another room so she and Cedric can't make any contact."

"Two of my kind are watching over her," Deth added.

Caedus made a curious face and gazed at Emilia. "You smiled when I said her name. Do you like her or something?"

Emilia started to blush. She tried to cover her cheeks to hide it. "I…I don't know. We have a task at hand. We should try to concentrate on that task. Daylight is burning." She raised her head up and walked at a faster pace than the other two.

The Cresthill dungeon was in the basement level of the castle. In the farthest room from any entrance or exit was Therion, who was sitting in a chair backward, to lean his elbows where someone would normally lean their back, facing the young man in the cell, Cedric. Cedric's hands were bound behind his back and tied to a post. Therion didn't want to take any chances with him.

The older man brushed the gash on the side of his cheek, which was almost healed. "No one has been able to land such a blow on me in a very long time."

Cedric raised his head up. "Maybe you are slowing down in your old age?"

"I don't think so. I don't age like normal humans do. Us werewolves live twice, maybe three times, as long as a normal human would."

"I assume you have healing abilities as well? Your cheek opened wide when I kicked you, yet the wound is almost completely gone as if we fought a week ago."

"Yes, my fast healing is the trick to having a longer lasting life. I am immune to all sicknesses and diseases. I can only die of old age or succumbing to a fatal wound."

"I see. Are there more like you out there? You are the only one I met."

Therion stood up and kicked his chair out of the way. He sat on the floor cross-legged, facing Cedric with only the iron bars between them. "Enough about me. Tell me about you."

"What about me?" Cedric asked.

"Everything. Tell me what has happened to you from when this Mathis ripped you out of my arms ten years ago up until now. Everything."

Cedric smiled. "It seems you intend to have a long conversation. I don't think I will be here long enough to finish my story."

Now Therion smiled. "Don't get cocky there, *boy*. You worry about telling me your story. I will worry about the rest. Before you start, tell me, out of the four of you disciples of Mathis, who is the best?"

"Well, me, of course. I have been there longer than the other three, and my use of magic is the strongest. As you can tell, I also have a natural gift in hand-to-hand combat."

"You're too arrogant for your own good, Cedric."

This made Cedric angry. His face turned red. "*I* am not arrogant! It may seem so, but I am not. The other three disciples would agree on my superiority. It is not arrogance if it is all true."

Therion put his hands up and made a stop motion. "Okay, okay. I didn't mean anything by it. Start from the beginning."

Cedric leaned back on to the post he was tied to and let out a deep sigh. "When I was taken, it was all a blur until we arrived at his hideout. I was blinded by fear. When we got there, I was thrown into a cell. He didn't even say anything to me and left me there until the next morning's sunrise."

"Where is this hideout?" Therion asked.

Cedric let out a laugh. "You think I'm going to tell you? Even if I wanted to, which I don't, I can't tell you."

"And why is that?"

"My companions and I, we physically cannot tell anyone where our hideout is. Our master put an incantation on all of us. If we began to tell where the location is, our throats tighten to the point of not being able to speak."

Therion stroked his chin. "Interesting. I have heard of similar magic in stories but never being used in real life. Maybe Avaline can dispell you."

"She may, but like I said before, I'm not going to tell you."

"So be it. Continue," Therion said with a sliver of annoyance.

"The next morning he brought me breakfast, I asked him why he took me. He said I was special."

"How so?" Therion asked.

"He always told me that I was like no other. But after I ate, he left, and came back with a girl. My partner, Sheska. She told me he killed her family in front of her and was brought there. I was in pain too from losing my father. All I could do was try to comfort her. We ended up comforting each other. I never knew what happened to Caedus until today. Never knew if he lived."

"It must have been a relief to see him today, was it not?" Therion asked.

Cedric smiled. "It was. It's a relief to confirm he is alive. I came back to my home to find it a pile of ash some years ago. I assumed Caedus died with my father."

"I took him is as my own. He was raised with my daughter. I love him like a son. My daughter loves him like a brother. We are a family."

"At least one of the sons of Savas had a good upbringing. The disciples and I were raised in pain and misery, but it's what makes us strong."

"And you are okay with that?"

"It doesn't matter if I am okay with it. It's what has already happened."

Therion looked deep into Cedric's eyes. "No, I sense your pain and misery hasn't ended."

"Oh yeah? What do you know, old man?" Cedric snapped.

Therion hit one of the metal bars, which made a loud clanking sound. "I know a great deal, boy! You are not the only one who can sense things through magic. I sense your feelings, your inner conflict. I have experience. It would be wise to heed an elder's advice!"

"Everyone has an inner conflict of some sort."

"True, but not as deep as you."

Cedric grimaced and leaned his head back.

Therion moved from his cross-legged position to lean against the opposite wall with his legs stretched out.

"How do your other two companions factor into this? Were they also raised with you?"

"No. The whole first year, it was just me and Sheska, then came Minerva, another human. But she was already an adult when we were kids. Last was Brock. Human, but he is from the neighboring country Alexandria, beyond Thundering Heights."

Cedric lied about Minerva. She doesn't exist, but Lord Mathis insisted on never revealing all of his comrades' identities. He never outright admitted it, but he always implied to never speak of Giselle to anyone. For what reason? He does not know. It could be she was the stealthiest of them all. She was the most likely, out of all of them, to not get caught.

"What does Lord Mathis want with the four of you?"

Cedric smirked. "The four of us, the disciples of Lord Mathis, we are his tools to obtain four of the legendary enchanted weapons."

"What does he want with them?" Therion asked with great interest.

"If he controls the elements, it's the first step to controlling everything. He wants to shape the world in his vision.

29

After about an hour-long walk, twisting and turning through the streets of Cresthill, Caedus, Emilia, and Deth reached the Grey Hawk's compound. It was nearly as fortified as the castle. It is a huge building surrounded by a wall with archers at the top to make sure potential intruders or suspicious people would think twice before getting any closer.

Caedus looked back toward Deth with a puzzled look. "Why do we have to come here if the king has an army to protect the castle?"

Deth got closer to him so he wouldn't be overheard. "In this time of peace, the majority of the army has been disbanded. We have royal guards and the men you regularly train with under Vog's command. That's about it. Now we must lean on the sellswords for the time being."

"Ah, I see. Let's get on with it then."

The trio approached the massive exterior door, but before they got close enough, two archers drew their bows.

"Who goes there?" one of the bowmen asked.

Emilia and Caedus had their hands up. Deth just stood there, for arrows could not harm him.

Caedus looked up at the man who spoke. "King Leandrol sent us here on an errand. We must speak to Blackshiv."

The man lowered his bow. "What proof do you have?"

"Is my presence not enough?" Deth asked in annoyance.

"You never know. Many forms of trickery in the form of magic these days."

Caedus pulled the king's letter out of his pocket slowly. The royal seal was big enough for the guard to see.

"Open the gate! We have important visitors. Inform Master Blackshiv at once!"

The door opened up, and the three of them walked in. Deth doesn't walk; he just hovers above the ground. He doesn't have any visible feet to speak of. After the bottom of his cloak is just air.

They were escorted by two men, one on each side of them. Caedus noticed no two men were wearing the same uniform, for they have the freedom to choose which armor makes them comfortable and which weapons are best for them. At first glance they seemed like a ragtag group of men, these Grey Hawks, but they are a well-trained brotherhood. Each member bears a tattoo on the back of their right hands. A tattoo of a gray hawk.

In the first room was the quest board. A wooden board with notices nailed all over it. After completing a quest, you are rewarded by the person who made the request. It's how the men of the Grey Hawks make a living. Many from all over the world come to the questboard for jobs.

They passed through many hallways that led to bedrooms, dining halls, and, of course, its own pub. Most of the men hit the pub after a job. Some even spend all of their earnings in one night on drinks. Walking past one of the bedrooms, you can hear one of the men who have spent some coin on a prostitute.

There were many beautiful paintings everywhere they turned in the great halls. Most were of landscapes and battles of legend, but one of them stood larger than all the rest, a portrait of a man. This man had slicked-back black hair down to his shoulders, a clean-shaven face, and brown eyes. He had a black fur coat over his shoulders with golden laced black armor and a dagger on his belt.

I wonder who it is, Caedus thought.

Before turning to the next hall, a red-bearded muscular man stood in their way with no intention of moving. He smiled and stared up and down Emilia's every curve, without trying to hide it. She grimaced at him. The man reeked of wine and ale.

"Damn girl, that's some body you got there. Let's go back to my room!" Before she could react, he grabbed her butt and squeezed. She kneed him in the crotch. He shouted in pain, and as he fell on the ground, she punched him in the face so his head slammed on the ground.

Two other men of the Grey Hawks took notice and helped their man off the ground.

The bearded man had a cut on his head from slamming onto the marble floor. After getting back on his feet, he pointed at Emilia. "The wench attacked me. Let's get her!"

Caedus and Emilia stood ready, as well as their escorts. Before a fight broke out, a sound echoed through the hall. It made all of the Grey Hawks stop what they were doing. The sound was the bottom of a cane hitting the floor. It was a signal in the organization for undivided attention. Caedus couldn't find the source. He and Emilia frantically looked around.

Coming from the farthest room from the hall, they saw a man walking toward them, slowly. He was the one slamming the cane on the floor. All of the men in the building lined up against the walls, as if making a grand entrance for the man. As he got closer, they realized he was the man from the portrait they just saw.

Deth leaned into Caedus's ear. "There is the man we seek."

"Blackshiv?"

Deth simply nodded his head.

Now he was before them.

"I suppose I should introduce myself. I am Blackshiv, headmaster of the Grey Hawks. First off, who are you to make a commotion in my hall?"

One of the men who escorted them from the gate spoke up. "Dominic started with the lady. They didn't cause this."

Blackshiv looked at Dominic disapprovingly.

The bearded man pointed at Emilia angrily. "She is the one who hit *me*. I haven't done anything wrong."

Emilia grabbed his collar aggressively and got in his face. "You mean grabbing my butt wasn't uncalled for?" She was furious. She threw Dominic against the wall and rushed toward him again. After raining a few punches down on Dominick's face, Caedus grabbed her by the waist to hold her back.

Blackshiv slammed his cane so hard the ground shook.

"Enough! Dominic, get patched up. I don't want to hear any more from you."

"We have important matters to discuss," Deth spouted out with impatience.

"Very well, follow me to the courtyard."

Blackshiv sent the men, escorting the trio back to the wall.

The courtyard was in the center of the entire fortress. It was surprisingly well-kept for being in the middle of a place where drunks and shady individuals resided. Emilia's face lit up from all of the beautiful flowers scattered over the edges. Against the far wall were weapon racks for training purposes. Whenever two men had a grudge in the Grey Hawks they took it up in the courtyard. There was only one reason Blackshiv took Caedus and Emilia there, to issue a challenge.

Caedus put his hand on Blackshiv's shoulder to stop him.

"I know why we are here. The king informed me you want to test our skills, but can it not wait until we go back to the castle? We have pressing matters which require your help."

Blackshiv shrugged Caedus's hand off him. "First, do not touch me without permission, and second, I will help you. But first, I want to see how the son of Savas and daughter of the wolf hold up against four of my best men."

"How do you know who we are?" Emilia asked.

Blackshiv turned around to face the three of them. "What animal has the best eyesight?"

"How is this relevant?" Caedus asked with impatience.

"A hawk. Hawks have great sight. I am the leader of the Grey Hawks. I have eyes everywhere. I had my eye on the two of you for a long time."

"I see. We can talk about it later, but we are here on urgent business. We must go back to the castle."

Blackshiv put his hand up in a stop motion. "Patience, young man." He turned his head toward Deth. "You there, faed. Can you take a dozen of my men to the castle? Take them from the dining hall. Tell the king I will arrive shortly with these two and even more of my men."

Deth nodded and looked at Caedus and Emilia. "Don't hold back," he said, and he disappeared.

Blackshiv smiled and wrapped his arms around the other two. "Are you ready to take on some of my men?"

Caedus smirked. "If we must. Let's get this over with, shall we?"

Emilia nodded her head.

Blackshiv put his mouth close to the handle of his cane and spoke into it. "All trainers, to the courtyard immediately."

Caedus and Emilia took a few steps back in shock. Blackshiv's cane must be enchanted by some form of magic. When he spoke into it just now, it amplified his voice. He must have been heard across the entire compound. They had never seen anything like it. Enchantments usually amplify a weapon's abilities but uncommon to be used on ordinary objects.

Four men walked into the room all wearing similar garments, black leather armor with metal greaves and bracers. All were sporting hair down to their shoulders, one with a beard and the rest with a bit of stubble. The four of them lined up next to each other.

"These four men are my trainers. They teach martial arts and weapons training. They are among the elite of the Grey Hawks. They will come at both of you two against one. If you manage to defeat them all, I will owe you a favor, and believe me, being owed a favor by me is big!"

"What if we lose?" Emilia asked.

"Then the two of you will owe me a favor. Fear not though, I am an honorable man. I will not ask you to do anything you don't wish."

"So be it. Let's get started," Emilia said with a smile on her face.

Caedus smiled also.

The trainer with the beard, the eldest of them all, stepped forward.

"Weapons? Or hand-to-hand combat?"

Caedus and Emilia looked at each other and said in unison, "Hand-to-hand combat!"

The man bowed and made hand gestures to position his men. Caedus and Emilia stood back to back in their fighting stances. Their opponents circled around them, surrounding them.

One of the men closer to Emilia rushed toward her. She kicked him in the chin while flipping backward. Her attacker fell from the momentum for the kick. She leaned on to Caedus's back, which caused him to lean forward. She then somersaulted backward, which allowed them to switch positions.

The man who was kicked quickly rose up, now angry. He rushed again, now toward Caedus. At the same time one of the other men started raining punches at Emilia. She blocked a few of them, but got hit with a few. She threw a hard knee at his stomach and headbutted him so hard her head now hurt. The trainer grabbed his head with both of his hands where the headbutt landed, wincing in pain. Emilia jumped up and landed on the man's shoulders, then forced her body forward, causing the man's head to slam onto the hard floor. He will not be getting up anytime soon.

One down, three to go. The man Emilia kicked tackled Caedus to the ground head first. Caedus underhooked to create a choke hold around the man's neck. It didn't stop him from falling to the ground. He squeezed the trainer's neck to make him pass out. Before he succeeded, the third trainer kicked Caedus in the stomach, which forced him to let go of the choke.

The barely conscious man rolled off Caedus to recover while the other man was trying to stop him from standing back up. Emilia quickly jumped on top of the man who was recovering from the choke, punched him in the face to daze him even more, and twisted his arm so far back until she heard a snap. The man screamed in pain. Two out of the fight, two to go.

Caedus couldn't stand while his attacker hovered over him. He kicked the man behind the knee, and he fell, and the tables turned. Caedus quickly got back up and jumped onto the man, throwing down punches. He was hitting the man so hard his head was bouncing off the pavement, causing cuts to open and blood to pour everywhere. With one final blow, Caedus knocked the man unconscious. Three opponents down. The last man never moved. He stood and watched Caedus and Emilia take out his men.

"Good work. Those are some of the toughest men we have, but I will prove to be much more of a challenge. Prepare yourselves!" the last man said while stroking his long beard.

Emilia helped Caedus up and wiped some of the blood off his chest. "I took out two, and only one for you. I thought you always boasted you were better than me?"

He grimaced and tightened his fists while looking at the last man standing. "Time for all that later. Let's take this guy out together. The same way we fought your father."

Emilia rested her arm on his shoulder. "I see, no messing around today. I got your back. Lead on."

The last man stood with his arms out, open and ready for attack. It's obviously a trap, but Caedus and Emilia have a plan of their own. Caedus rushed forward and threw very fast, precise punches to the man's body. He blocked most of them. Just as he started to block the blows, Caedus threw an uppercut, which landed on the man's chin. He shook it off, but before he knew it, he saw Caedus fall to one knee. Emilia used him as a step to jump and throw a hard knee, which landed straight onto the man's nose. It was surely broken now. Blood started to stain his beard and neck. He grabbed his nose with both of his hands momentarily, but didn't have much time because the other two put relentless pressure on him.

If you take away his breathing pattern, the battle is half won, Therion always used to tell them.

Caedus and Emilia ferociously threw punches and kicks his way. Surprisingly, all were blocked. The man seemed to be fighting better since they broke his nose.

Blackshiv stood with a smile on his face while leaning on his cane. In the meantime he called some mashkiki to tend to the three of his men that were down.

"You disrupted my breathing, very smart. You have excellent teamwork, but do not think this means you will win against me," the bloodied man spouted out.

Caedus threw a front kick to push him back. Not as far as he hoped, but far enough. Caedus then rushed and kicked the man's knee, which caused him to fall on his leg. Then Emilia threw a powerful cross to the cheek, landing perfectly. Before being able to throw a second, he caught her arm and threw her against the closest pillar. He then threw a hard knee to Caedus's stomach. He winced in pain. Cross-uppercut-cross combination he landed on Caedus, followed by another knee. Blood sprayed out of his mouth as he fell to the ground.

Emilia got back up and jumped on the man's back, choking him. She wrapped her legs around his waist so it would be harder for him to shake her off. She doesn't think she can finish him with a choke, but she will try to weaken him. The man used both arms to try to loosen her iron grip on his neck. He can't breathe out of his nose; he can barely breathe out of his mouth now.

Caedus quickly got back up and started another attack. He threw everything he had into four monstrous uppercuts to the body followed by an elbow to his forehead, which caused a huge gash to open. Emilia let go of her choke and kicked in the inside of his knees.

The last man fell to his knees, blood pouring from his nose and head. His vision was blurred by the blood seeping into his eyes from the forehead gash. Caedus jumped and wrapped his legs around the man's neck and one of his arms, pinning them together to cut off circulation. The harder Caedus squeezed, the more effective it became. If the man doesn't escape, he will pass out.

Caedus forced the man on to his back so his bodyweight put more pressure on his neck. The one arm the man had free could potentially be used to escape, but Emilia hyperextended his elbow with her hips, ready to snap.

"Yield! Or pass out. Either way, we have you!" Caedus yelled out.

The man gurgled, nearly choking on his own blood.

"Shake your head if you yield!"

The man slowly shook his head. Caedus and Emilia immediately let go of him and helped him back up.

From across the room, Blackshiv stood with a smile on his face, clapping loudly. He walked toward them. "Well done, you two. I'm very impressed. Therion taught you better than I ever hoped he would. You beat the best men my organization has to offer."

The last man bowed at both of them. "Well fought. My name is Hamoon. It was a pleasure for me to test my skills against you."

Emilia gave a small bow back. "It's nice to meet you too. To be fair, if Caedus and I weren't teamed up, we surely would have lost."

"This may be true, but you both have shown some of the best teamwork I have ever seen. Are you linked telepathically through magic?" Blackshiv asked.

"No, not at all. We have just trained together every day for the past ten years. We don't have any magic abilities yet, we came to the city to find Avaline to start today. She seems to be out of the city with the queen. So we were sent here for your help."

"I see, well, we should be on our way to the castle." He looked at Hamoon. "Get yourself patched up. In my absence, you can run things here. I don't know how long I will be."

Hamoon nodded his head and turned toward Caedus with a smile. Caedus acknowledged.

"Do you want a mashkiki to look at you two before we head out?" Blackshiv asked.

"I am okay. I don't know about Caedus though. He took more of a beating than I did," Emilia said with a sly smile.

"Very funny, but I am okay also. Let's head to the castle. I will update you on the situation."

"Very well, lead on."

Emilia led while Caedus and Blackshiv lingered behind. Six of his men stayed behind the three of them.

Little did they know during the entire fight, a figure in the shadows was watching. It bypassed all the guards and snuck in, staying in the shadows. A figure in black armor with a bow on its back. Not one of the disciples or Lord Mathis, but something else. The armored figure continued to trail the three as they left the compound.

Once the castle was in sight, Emilia smiled. "We are almost there."

Blackshiv smiled.

"Is it your real name?" Caedus asked.

"What?"

"Blackshiv. That cannot be your real name? It's just the color of a blade. Is it an alias?"

Blackshiv grimaced. "My real name matters not. Another time perhaps. But don't use my favor to you to ask what my real name is."

Caedus simply nodded his head.

The ground started to shake, and a loud bang erupted. It came from the direction of the castle. They looked over and saw burning and smoke. There was an explosion in the castle!

Caedus's eyes widened. "Cedric is trying to escape. We must hurry!"

The three of them sprinted toward the danger as the common folk ran away in fear.

III

THE ESCAPE

GISELLE STOOD ON THE FAR side of the winding river, facing Cresthill, which was miles in the distance.

The landscape is so beautiful from here. This view would make a beautiful painting, she thought.

Giselle had always enjoyed art, paintings and sculptures, but being a disciple of Mathis, there wasn't time for such things. Maybe when all of this is over she can have a life of enjoying the arts and other things the world has to offer. Not likely, but there is hope. Even for the bad guys.

Instead of Cedric, I will be the Master's favorite, after I attain this weapon for him.

She saw smoke rising from the very top of the hill, where the castle stood. She smiled.

"Not much time now before the other three head this way. I must get my hands on the lightning blade first."

The escape has now begun.

⁓⊗⁓

A few minutes before

Brock scaled the mountainside of the city to reach the dungeon walls where Sheska and Cedric were being kept. Since the dungeon was under the castle, he had to break through part of the mountain itself to get into the cells from the outside. For cell airflow, there were very small window openings through the rock at the top of the wall. All Brock needed was a small opening to get started.

Sheska was the weakest of the four disciples, both in mind and will. Her lack of confidence was, and always will be, her biggest issue. Brock would have to help Sheska escape. Cedric can take care of himself once he breaks through the cells.

Brock heard muffled voices through one of the windows. He carefully peeked inside. Cedric's back was to him, with his hands tied behind him. He was talking to a big man with long hair. Brock had never seen anyone close to his own size before. This man talking to Cedric might have been just as big as he was.

He is someone I do not want to get tangled up in a fight with, Brock thought. *I have to steer clear of him if this escape is to be successful.*

With Cedric located, he began to look for Sheska. He scaled the mountainside, looking through every window. Most of the cells were empty, save for a few petty criminals. Brock found Sheska on the opposite end of the dungeon, in the very first cell. He wondered why they were kept so far apart. *The job must get done regardless.* Sheska's hands were not bound like Cedric's. *At least they were smart enough to realize who was more dangerous of the two.*

Cedric was guarded by the huge man he was talking to, but why wasn't Sheska guarded? She was dangerous enough to lock up, but not to guard? Something was out of place. Brock had an uneasy feeling about this whole thing now, but he mustn't let fear dictate his actions. He took a deep breath and then another. He wiped the sweat off his forehead and headed back toward Cedric's cell.

The four disciples of Mathis all have the ability to use magic. Cedric's specialty is the power of the wind, using air currents to bend to his will. Brock, on the other hand, had the ability to combust any inanimate object. He can turn anything he touches into a bomb. He was going to use his power to cause the cell walls to explode so his companions can escape.

Behind Cedric's cell, Brock touched five areas, four corners and the center, to blow a hole big enough for Cedric to escape through. He had to touch something in place for about five seconds before it was able to explode. Before he detonated, he climbed back behind Sheska's cell.

Brock snapped his fingers, and the walls exploded, creating a big hole under the castle. The explosion alerted everyone in the dungeon. Cedric anticipated the eruption, so he dodged what he could. The man guarding him was not so lucky, the force of the blast pushed the bricks and cell bars toward him with devastating force. The pole that Cedric was tied to broke just enough for him to be free of it, but his hands were still bound behind his back. He inched his hands under his legs as he sat down to bring his knees to his chest to free his arms from his backside. He was still bound but now with more freedom to move since his arms are in front of him now.

Brock looked into Sheska's cell to see she was being guarded by invisible men with hoods on.

They must be the faeds from the legends, he thought. *They both disappeared after the loud bang. Did they head toward the chaos, or are they invisible? No time to think about it now. Time to remove Sheska.*

Sheska knew from what was going on that Brock had arrived, and he was heading her way. She put her palms together and crossed her legs to summon her magic power. As she did, a bubble if ice surrounded her body, to serve as a barrier for the impact Brock was about to create to get her out. He used his power to break through the second wall, this time with less intensity so he wouldn't accidentally hurt Sheska. Her ice barrier did little to help as the rubble shot toward her fast and struck her in the head.

Just before Brock jumped inside the second open cell, he saw Cedric leap out of the first one. Cedric turned as he fell and made eye contact with Brock. He nodded his head as a sign of gratitude. As he fell, Cedric held his bound hands in the air and his sword, the Windblade, flew to him and freed him of his ropes, then landed in his arms.

Cedric shared a mental connection with the Windblade, for it was a spirit of one of the legends of centuries ago. With just a mere thought, Cedric could call his weapon to his side from any distance. He fell hundreds of meters before he used the Windblade to ease his fall and land on his feet without getting injured.

"Showoff," Brock whispered to himself.

Surely the faeds would be on him in a few moments. He turned around, picked Sheska up, and slung her onto his shoulder. She fell unconscious from getting hit with the debris. A big bruise covered a portion of her cheek and a cut on the top of her head with blood trickling down her face. He jumped down toward where Cedric landed.

Brock landed so hard he created a crater in the cobblestone. Cedric could have softened Brock's fall, like his own, but out of curiosity he wanted to see if someone as big and strong as Brock could survive the fall, and he did.

Brock knew he would survive the massive drop, but he thought Cedric might have lent a hand because he was holding Sheska. Cedric and Sheska had the closest bond of the four of them, just as Brock and Giselle were close. Since they have formed their bonds, Mathis picked up on it and continuously pitted them against each other to see who would come out on top. Rather cruel, but the strongest always survived. In the majority, Cedric and Sheska would gain the advantage over Giselle and Brock. It made Brock furious, feeling inferior to someone younger and much smaller than himself, but at the end of the day, the four of them were like siblings.

No time for bickering. They were still in the heart of the city, and too much attention has been drawn to them. They landed in the middle of the heavily populated marketplace. Shopkeepers and patrons ran away in fear.

Cedric looked up and saw three of the faeds in pursuit of them. They glided down from the holes in the mountain, approaching them fast.

"We must make way—and fast. It's not going to be easy to shake them off," Cedric worried.

Brock frantically looked around the shops. He saw a garment seller at the end of the street.

"Hurry, over there! We could shed our cloaks for new ones."

Cedric agreed. "Not a bad idea. Now give Sheska to me and create a distraction."

Brock nodded, and they split up. Cedric carried Sheska on his back and zigzagged through alleyways while Brock poured his magical energy into random walls and objects to throw the faeds off their trail.

The first area he detonated was a wall on the far end of the street, away from their destination. As it exploded, the faeds moved faster toward it.

Cedric entered the garment shop from the back as Brock went through the front. They threw their cloaks off and looked for new ones. Every few moments Brock snapped his fingers to make something else explode to throw the faeds off.

Cedric put Sheska down, removing her cloak. Brock looked through the window to see the faeds were getting closer.

"We must hurry. They are almost upon us."

Cedric threw him a hooded robe with the Grey Hawks' symbol covering the back, silver and black. "Put this on. You must burn our old clothes."

"Don't worry, this whole place is coming down," Brock said with a smile.

Cedric chose a simple brown robe and looked more like a beggar, which may help this situation. He found something similar to wrap around Sheska. Brock picked her up again. This time he held her in his arms.

Cedric looked up at his massive companion. "I can create a wind current strong enough to carry us to the river. Are you ready for this?"

"Let's do it."

Cedric twirled the hilt of the Windblade around above his head and lashed out toward the river. The current was so strong it nearly pulled the three of them away.

Just as they were ready to jump, the faeds caught up with them.

"Don't move! There is nowhere you can hide from us," the faed in the lead bellowed while pointing his blade toward them.

His voice made Brock's bones rattle. He jumped into the current with Sheska while Cedric stood facing the faeds. He attempted to push them back, but it was futile, as the wind had no impact on these otherworldly creatures. Since he made no difference, Cedric backflipped into the current and was dragged by the river.

Before Brock landed in the water, he snapped his fingers one last time and exploded the shop with the faeds inside.

Hopefully I got 'em, or at least took them off our trail for now, Brock thought.

As he landed, he made sure his back was to the water while he held Sheska tight, bracing for impact. Shortly after he hit the water, Cedric arrived.

As Sheska hit the water, she jolted awake. Her arms were wrapped around Brock's shoulders, and she was neck deep in the river. Her eyes widened. "Where am I?"

"We escaped Cresthill, but we may not be out of danger yet," Brock yelled as he struggled to keep his head afloat.

A few minutes after the first explosion, Giselle headed along the riverbank, toward the border of the sacred lands. Without looking back, she heard two more explosions minutes apart, the last one she actually felt. She decided to look back once more and saw unusual movement coming toward her in the river. Not the natural movement of fish, but something else. As it came closer, she noticed three people in the water on the verge of losing consciousness. Not just any three people though.

Is that Brock? Yes, it is. Sheska is leaning on his shoulders. She looks hurt, and there is Cedric behind them.

She saw a cracked tree nearby, as if lightning struck it in the past. She reached out with her arms and closed her eyes, summoning her magic. She can manipulate nature, sometimes making things grow or wilt at an abnormal speed. She concentrated on the tree, and it grew strong branches far enough for her companions to grab on to from the water.

Brock quickly climbed above water with Sheska still on his back. When Cedric reached the tree, Brock picked him up with one arm and threw him toward Giselle. She helped him sit up, then reached to help Sheska back onto land. Brock managed to get himself out. He lay on the grass with his arms and legs spread out.

Giselle put her arms around Cedric and Sheska. "Are you okay? What happened? I was able to see the destruction from here."

Cedric held her hand on his shoulder. "We are okay. Sheska was hit on the head with some rubble on the way out."

Sheska put her hand on Cedric's knee. "I will be okay. Just a small cut on the top of my head."

Cedric turned her head to see the cut. "Are you sure? You were out for a few minutes."

"Yes, I am fine. I am more worried for you and Brock. You expended a lot of magic back there. Especially Brock. I'm surprised he is even awake."

"Barely, but awake." Brock burst out from behind all of them, out of breath.

Giselle leaned back and cupped her hands around Brock's face. "I think we should go back home. We will be safe there in the event you are still being pursued. You guys are spent."

"I do not think it wise to return home, at least not yet. I think we are being followed. They would want to know where we are hiding out," Cedric said in a quieter tone. "After what transpired today, we will be Cresthill's most wanted. Bounty hunters will come looking for us. We have to be careful about what we do next."

"I see," Giselle said, "What do you suggest we do?"

"I do not think we are far from the weapon master wanted me to retrieve. Let's go together. The four of us."

Giselle smiled. "Sure."

Cedric and the two ladies stood up, but Brock was still lying on the ground.

"Wait a second, jumping in the river was a last resort to escape. How did you know we were going to be out here?" Cedric pondered out loud.

Giselle had a look of worry on her face, and Brock quickly stood up behind her. She looked up at him.

"Should I tell him?" she asked Brock.

"Tell me what?" Cedric asked angrily.

Brock raised his hand for Cedric to stay where he was. "When you found the location of this lightning blade, I was spying on you. I sent Giselle to retrieve it while I helped you escape, so master would be in our favor for once."

Giselle put her hand on Cedric's chest. "Don't be upset. I didn't make it there yet, but we are close. As you said, let's find it together. I don't want us to fight over this."

Cedric didn't try to hide the intense anger on his face. His yellow eyes glowed with fury as he turned his back on his companions. He took a few steps forward and unsheathed his blade from his back. He threw the blade with such force toward some trees, it knocked them all over with the intense wind. As he threw his blade, he let out a loud scream.

Giselle and Sheska took a few steps back. Brock stood in front of them in case Cedric tried to attack them.

Cedric turned back around, looking much calmer. Brock still blocked the way toward the girls. Cedric lifted his left arm above his shoulder, which called his blade back to his hand. He let the power of his blade ran through his body, becoming an extension of the weapon. Now in front of Brock, he simply put his right hand on Brock's stomach. A flowing sphere of energy materialized in his hand, and it pushed Brock back several meters and knocked him on the ground.

"Don't worry, big guy, I'm not going to hurt anyone," Cedric said as he sighed.

"What did you just hit me with?" Brock exclaimed.

"I used the Windblade to channel strong current into a small center point in my hand, and I released it into you."

Giselle grabbed Cedric's right hand with both of hers, as if inspecting it. "I had no idea your power had matured. Now you and the Windblade can work almost as one?"

"It seems so. I never knew I could do that until just now. It just came to me, I guess. It felt natural."

"You are starting to become more like…*him*. I don't know if it's good or bad," Sheska said worriedly.

Cedric looked toward her with a slight smile. "Don't you worry"—he grabbed both of her shoulders—"I am not like him."

Brock stood back up. "You may not think so, but the scary thing is, you have been becoming more like him in recent days. It was only but recently your eyes share the same yellow glow as master. It's unnatural."

"It is not my intent, but worry no more. I will never hurt you three. We are family."

"Your words are sincere," Giselle said. "But master pitted us against each other for so long, what's changed?"

"Mathis has always turned us on each other as a game. He wanted us to compete to see how far we would be pushed to become better. It could be the wrong way to go about it, but we are who we are because of what he put us through. But after all this time, we have proven today that we are at our best working together."

"You're right," Brock said as he put his arms on Cedric's and Sheska's shoulders. "Mathis molded us into who we are now, but let me propose this. If the four of us work together, do you think we can take him on? Can we defeat him and finally be free?"

Sheska and Giselle's jaws dropped in shock. Cedric had an emotionless face of stone. Sheska made eye contact with Brock.

"I...I don't think we can defeat him, even if we fought together. We should not speak of this. He could be listening to us now!"

Before Brock could respond, a faed from the city flew toward them faster than anything they had ever seen. Its hand reached out toward them. It grabbed Cedric on his right shoulder. He screamed in pain and was brought to his knees. The faed's hand burned into his skin as if he was being branded with its hand. Smoke rose from his shoulder.

"You are not getting away so easily!" the faed exclaimed in a deep voice.

Brock shook with fear. He barely moved, but he managed to stand in front of the ladies so from the point of view of the faeds, it was only him. He was so big that you couldn't see if someone was behind him at all. Out of nowhere, a portal opened up behind them, with an arm reaching out. The arm of Lord Mathis pulled his four disciples through the portal. When the four of them fell through, he immediately closed it so the faed couldn't get through.

Hidden far within the Forbidden Forest was the ancient Castle of Dulangar. One thousand years ago this was the castle of the mages before they were all wiped out. It was a city once, but now only the castle remains, surrounded by rubble and wasteland. Back then it was discovered that humans couldn't contain magic for very long; otherwise, they would go mad. Elves, on the other hand, were magical creatures. They could withstand magic without mental side effects. Humans are fragile in nature and cannot withstand more than one magical ability at a time.

Mathis and his four disciples had been able to stay hidden for so long because no one dared to go to the Forbidden Forest. Travelers steered clear and would rather go around. It has always been a dark, dank place. Swamps and dead trees everywhere. There had also been many recorded cases of people killing themselves in the forest. Many believe it was haunted by the people who died there.

A decade ago when Mathis arrived in this land, he created a barrier that only he could pass through. Since then he gave his disciples the ability to freely pass through. No one from the outside could get in, but no one has ever tried to go into a city of ruins anyway.

On the top floor of the castle was where Mathis spent most of his time. He secretly created links with his "children" that they do not know about. He can sense where they were and what they were doing, no matter how far away they were. He was sitting on his throne, while eavesdropping on their conversation, and suddenly he felt a sense of pain. It was very strong, one of his disciples was screaming in agony. It was Cedric. He reached out with his enhanced senses. All four of them were together? A few weeks ago when they left for Cresthill, they left in two pairs, not all together. Brock and Giselle always partnered up, as well as Cedric with Sheska.

The pain he was sensing was getting more intense, so he decided to pull the four of them back home to the castle. He stood up and walked to the center of the room. He raised both arms outward and made a clockwise motion with both arms, creating a circle in the air. His left arm circled upward while his right arm circled downward. Once his arms eventually crossed, he moved his hands in the center of this magical circle and pressed forward. As he pressed forward, a portal opened up and he saw his four disciples. Sheska, Giselle, and Brock had their backs to him while Cedric was being attacked by a faed.

Mathis reached his left arm out and made a snatching motion back, which pulled all four through the portal quickly enough to throw off the faed. His disciples were yanked as if attached to puppet strings. Once back in the castle, he quickly flicked his wrist and the portal disappeared.

Brock landed on his back, Giselle fell on top of him, followed by Sheska on top of her. Brock groaned as the immense pressure hit his midsection. Cedric fell next to them, his shoulder still steaming from the faed's brand, too afraid to touch it.

Mathis turned around quickly to face his four and folded his arms. He took his hood off to get a better look at them. Over the past decade he had been showing signs of age. He had crow's feet around his eyes, and his long hair and beard were sprinkled with gray, unlike the dark black hair he had when he found Cedric. His eyes were glowing yellow, but recently, his iris was surrounded by a bright red. The disciples had wondered why, but never had the courage to ask. In no way Lord Mathis was to be taken lightly just because he has gotten older. He may even be more powerful than he was ten years ago.

The girls scrambled to get to one knee to bow to their lord, as did Brock. Cedric struggled to just sit upright, without trying to bow. He sat cross-legged while tentatively holding his burned shoulder.

Mathis took a few steps forward with his eyes on Cedric. "How bad is it? Let me see."

Cedric moved his arm away and leaned his shoulder forward so his master could see. It was clearly a brand but in the shape of a hand. It seemed faeds could burn anyone with only a touch. Faeds were largely unknown in the kind of things they can do, in combat or otherwise. This scared Mathis to a degree. He had no way of knowing how to fight a faed. No one has and lived to tell about it.

"On your feet, Cedric," Mathis said quietly.

Without replying, he stood up next to the older man. Mathis lightly grabbed Cedric's arm to get a closer look. He waved his hand over the burn and whispered, "Noapai."

Cedric instantly felt relief. "The pain, it's gone! How did you…"

"You should know better than to question my abilities!" Mathis snapped.

Cedric bowed his head. "I apologize, my lord. I just never knew you had healing magic."

Mathis grimaced. "As you can see, I do. You just never needed to see it. My depth of magic is beyond what the four of you could ever think possible." As he spoke, he snapped his head toward Brock. "If the four of us work together, do you think we can take him on? We can defeat him, and finally be free?"

Brock's face was pale, his mouth wide open. His hands started to shake, but he tried his best to hide it. "I...I..."

Mathis walked toward the taller man. "Isn't that what you just said a few minutes ago? Right before I decided to save you from one of your worst fears?" His voice got louder as he got closer to Brock.

"Master, I didn't mean..."

"Didn't mean what?" Mathis grabbed Brock by the neck and hip-tossed him to the ground. Mathis put his knee into the center of Brock's chest. "You didn't mean to say you think you have what it takes to *kill* me? The only one of you who had a voice of reason was Sheska. She knows the truth. She knows I cannot be defeated."

Giselle and Sheska didn't know how to react, they didn't know what to do. Cedric clearly had anger brewing inside him. It showed on his face. Mathis had a grip on Brock's neck. Brock held Mathis's arm with both of his hands. Mathis was a man of slight build, but he was physically stronger than Brock. He never realized just how strong Mathis really was until now. He always counted on his own physical prowess against opponents. Brock understood now that his strength was nothing compared to Lord Mathis.

"What shall I do to you now?" Mathis said with a smirk. He enjoyed the fear he struck in Brock's heart. Mathis started to squeeze Brock's neck, choking him. Suddenly, a powerful sphere of wind swept toward Mathis, who deflected it with ease. Cedric caught the sphere with his hand and crushed it, which created a small blast of forceful wind in every direction. The blast knocked the girls off balance.

"You dare—"

"It was only to stop you from hurting him. Now get off of him."

Mathis paused, still holding Brock to the ground.

"It was not a request, Lord Mathis. Get off him *now!*" Cedric yelled angrily.

Mathis's eyes widened. He forcefully pressed his body weight into Brock while getting up, inflicting one last bit of pain. As Mathis walked toward Cedric, the girls rushed to Brock to see if he was okay. Brock had never been more embarrassed in his life. He tried to brush off the girls, but he was so fearfully shaken. He could barely stand. Giselle and

Sheska stood by his side and kept him upright. Brock couldn't stop his legs from shaking. He tried in vain to hide it.

Mathis was just a meter from Cedric. "You dare defy me? To what end?"

Cedric looked beyond Mathis, toward his companions. "Hey, all of you get out of here! Take Brock downstairs." Staring into his master's eyes, he continued, "I must speak to Lord Mathis alone."

Mathis was fuming in anger.

Before they left the room, Giselle gently touched Cedric on the shoulder. "Will you be all right?"

"Yes, now go, please."

She turned and left. Mathis and Cedric were alone.

Mathis walked to one of the massive windows overlooking the ancient city. He clasped his hands behind his back. "I see your powers have grown, my boy."

Cedric stood next to the older man and folded his arms across his chest. "It seems they have. I can't explain it, but my bond with the Windblade has been growing, thus creating more power I can channel with it, as if we are one."

"I see," Mathis said as he looked at Cedric from the corner of his eye. "I remember the feeling. The power made you feel unstoppable, indestructible, but do not let it consume you, as it almost did with me."

Cedric didn't physically respond, but he was surprised. "You have had enchanted weapons before?"

"Yes," Mathis said, shaking his head. "Once upon a time, long before you were born. Over time I had multiple enchanted weapons. A sword, a bow, and an axe. Each with their unique powers. I pushed myself too far with them, suffering dearly for it." He put his arm on Cedric's shoulder. "You must not. Work together with your weapon, and you will be okay."

"I will."

Cedric started to walk toward the center of the room, away from his master.

Mathis didn't turn away from the window, and his voice echoed across the room. "What gave Brock the sudden idea to stand against me?"

Cedric turned around, facing the older man. "He was only excited about seeing my new powers. He knows it is an attainable level the four of us can reach, and when they do, no one could stop us. He may be right. If we all worked together, we would be a challenge for you."

Mathis quickly turned around, clearly angry. "And what makes you so sure?"

"It is just speculation, but if you treated Brock the same way you treated me, he wouldn't think of leaving."

Mathis folded his arms. "You may be right. We will see. I shall talk with him later."

Cedric started to pace between the throne and the center of the room. A trait he shared with his brother, but never knew.

"What's on your mind, boy?"

"What?" Cedric snapped back.

"You are pacing. You are nervous. Spit it out."

Cedric stopped. "I saw him today."

"Your brother?"

"Yes, my brother." He put his head down as if ashamed.

"And? What happened?"

"I didn't want to run into him. What must he think of me now? He saw my eyes, and when he did, he actually stepped back a few paces. He must think I'm a monster."

"What happened then?"

"He still embraced me. It has been far too long since we have been separated." He gave a sharp look toward the older man, silently challenging him, for it was he who separated the brothers.

Mathis noticed the glance. Did Cedric really believe he could challenge him, the great Lord Mathis? He decided to ignore it for the time being. Baiting Cedric, Mathis threatened, "What do you intend to do about it?"

"I know he wants to talk to me, and I with him, but now is not the time. I am not ready yet."

Cedric knew Mathis was testing him, but he wouldn't fall for it. Mathis secretly wanted him to take the bait so he could put him in his place, the same way he did Brock earlier.

"What will you do now?" Mathis asked, his patience restored.

"I will retire for the night, and at first light tomorrow the other three and I will retrieve this lightning blade."

Mathis smiled. "Good, good. You finally found a way to work together as one. But make no mistake, no more talk of *defeating* me. I will know of it. Do you understand?"

Cedric did not answer. He just gave Mathis his stone-faced stare and walked toward the door to exit the room. Before he did, Mathis pulled Cedric toward him like a puppet on a string once again. He grabbed Cedric by the neck with one hand, while digging his sharp fingernails deep into his cheek with his other hand. He dug so deep, he penetrated Cedric's mouth.

"I do not believe you heard me. Let me repeat myself. There will be no more talk of trying to find a way to defeat me. *Do you understand*?"

Cedric was in so much pain he couldn't move. Blood was pouring onto Mathis's hand and the side of Cedric's cheek, and life was being choked out of him. He faintly nodded, and Mathis released his grip and pulled his nails out of his cheek.

Cedric had one last comment before he left the room. He held the side of his pierced face. "Make no mistake, Lord Mathis. I will do what you ask without question, but don't for a moment believe I am afraid of you."

Mathis smiled. "I would expect no less of my best student. Now get out of my sight. Do not come back until you have what I want."

"As you command," Cedric painfully replied as he walked out of the room.

Now alone in the throne room, Mathis sat down, grinning. "Once I get my hands on the lightning blade, I will be one step closer to my goal." He bellowed menacingly, rattling Cedric down the hall.

IV

THE LIGHTNING STRIKES

C AEDUS AND EMILIA, LED BY the headmaster of the Grey Hawks, Blackshiv, ran into the smoke-filled castle. A few moments ago two explosions erupted under them. The headmaster turned his head enough to see the other two behind him.

"They may not have gotten far. We must retrace their steps. We can catch them before they leave the city."

Caedus nodded his head fiercely. "Let's go!"

Caedus led the way as they navigated through servants and some soldiers in disarray. Some were blown back by the explosions, with wounds from rocks flying in all directions. None looked life-threatening though. The Grey Hawks who were escorted by Deth were attending to the wounded when Blackshiv arrived.

Finally, in the cells, they saw a huge hole in the wall of the first cell, big enough for someone to jump through. Blackshiv stood over it.

"Check the last cell. Therion is there. See if he is all right."

With Caedus close behind, Emilia ran through the cell block looking for her father.

How does he know my father is here? Emilia thought. *He was with us the whole time.*

Therion was barely visible, hidden by a boulder and the bars from the cell door on top of him. Emilia quickly threw everything off him to sit her father in an upright position. Caedus noticed the wall behind

55

Therion had a huge impact hole. The explosion must have pushed him back so hard that he almost fell through the wall.

Emilia got him up sitting upright. "Papa! Are you okay? Wake up!" She shook his shoulders lightly.

Caedus got on one knee next to her. "Wake up, old man! You're stronger than this," he yelled. Then he lowered his voice to a whisper, "I know you are."

Blood covered half of the older man's face and arms. If he didn't block at the point of impact, he might have died, any ordinary man would have. It looked like his forearms may be broken though. He inhaled deeply, and his eyes opened wide. He began to cough.

Emilia couldn't hide her excitement that her father was okay. She disregarded his injuries and squeezed his head on to her chest and began to put her fingers through his hair.

"I thought I lost you for a minute there, Papa. Don't scare me like that."

Caedus put his arm on Therion's shoulder and smiled. "What happened?"

Therion was still disoriented, but he shook it off quickly. He tried to stand, but his broken arms couldn't hold his weight, and he fell to the ground.

"Your arms are broken, Papa. Let us help you," Emilia said.

Both of his children lightly wrapped his arms around their shoulders and slowly got him up.

Therion looked at the hole in the wall where Cedric jumped out of. "Your brother escaped through there."

"By himself?" Caedus asked worriedly.

"No, he wasn't alone. Someone else came to his rescue. The entire time we spoke, he knew someone was coming for him. I thought he was bluffing. I was wrong."

Emilia and Cedric looked at each other.

"This man that orchestrated the escape, he has immense destructive power. It looked like he used his bare hands to blow through the walls."

Some of the Grey Hawks ran into the cell. Some ran to the hole. Two others took over for Caedus and Emilia, helping Therion walk. One of the men at the hole bent down and looked with interest at what was below. "Young Caedus! Look here!"

Caedus ran to the hole and bent down alongside the man. "What is it?" he asked with great interest.

"Look at the marketplace two levels below. There they are. We could still catch them!"

Caedus's face lit up with excitement. He saw a giant man holding someone over his shoulder. It must be Sheska. The big man was following someone. It was Cedric!

"They won't escape me." He grabbed the sword out from the other man's sheath and jumped out of the hole in pursuit of his brother.

Therion disengaged from the two men helping him and ran toward Caedus's jump-off point.

"Caedus! No!" He fell to his knees. He was too late.

Caedus couldn't survive such a fall, but he quickly noticed why his boy took the other man's sword. He stabbed one of the banners in the market to soften his fall and landed safely. The faeds were already in pursuit of the fugitives, but it was still too dangerous for Caedus to be there. Therion turned back and faced his daughter.

"I'm sorry, Em. I have to help your brother."

Before she could even react, her father already jumped out to meet with Caedus. She ran to see them. Therion landed hard on his feet, cracking the stone.

Caedus quickly turned around. "You're hurt, you have no reason to come with me until you are healed."

Therion's broken forearms was searing with pain. He winced as his legs were wobbly from his jump, but he managed to grab Caedus on the shoulder.

"I may be, but I am not letting you attempt to capture opponents more powerful than you are by yourself. I am with you until this is over. Healing can wait."

Caedus smiled. "Just take it easy. Stick to the kicks for now."

Therion nodded. Both men looked up to see Emilia looking down at them. Both men saluted to her and ran toward the fugitives. She clenched her fists at her sides.

"Those two! I can't believe how reckless men can be!" She shook her head. The man next to her was the owner of the sword that Caedus borrowed before he jumped off. "What is your name?" Emilia asked the man.

"My name is Bastion. Nice to meet you, m'lady." He put his hand out toward her.

She grabbed his hand. "Likewise." *He sure doesn't seem like the other savages in his organization*, she thought. "What do you say? Do you want to help me go after them?"

Bastion nodded. He brushed his long reddish-brown hair to the side. "Of course, follow me."

They ran to the front of the dungeon where Blackshiv resided. He was leaning on his cane, waiting for them to get closer. "I see that foolish father and brother of yours jumped down to the market."

Emilia rolled her eyes and folded her arms across her chest. "Yes. Bastion and I are going down to help."

Blackshiv nodded. "I will not stop you, be on your way."

As they ran past him, he patted their shoulders on their way out. He also pointed at three of his other men and gestured to follow them.

Down in the marketplace Caedus and Therion walked side by side. One of the faeds gestured for them to stop as a sign to not get involved. As much as they didn't like it, they had to respect the faed's command.

Caedus noticed one of the stalls pushed to the side. Cedric must have landed there. Therion saw a small crater near where he landed. The man who helped them escape must have landed there.

He must be massive in size if he could do that. He may be as big as me, if not bigger, Therion worriedly thought.

As the faeds looked around for the escapees, different areas of the market began to explode. The first one was the knocked-over stall Caedus was near. It knocked him back but didn't do much besides scare him. Therion helped him up. The faeds quickly glided over to where they were to investigate.

As the five of them huddled together, a second explosion erupted about fifty paces ahead, destroying a brick wall to one of the shops. Two of the faeds went to check it out while one of them stayed by the burning stall.

Suddenly, random objects—potions, banners, wine bottles—from all around started to erupt all at once. They were trying to create chaos to ease their escape. The faeds were a bit disoriented. They didn't know where to look.

Therion closed his eyes and stood very still. He concentrated, to see if he could sense where they were through magic. They obviously knew how to cover their tracks. They were good. What they didn't count on though was that Therion had superhuman hearing. His hearing was magnified, thanks to being part wolf.

Across the marketplace was a garment shop. Therion heard faint whispering from inside.

"Hey!"

The faeds immediately looked toward Therion.

He lowered his voice. "In the garment shop. They are trying to blend in to escape!"

The three faeds quickly glided over to the front of the shop. Just before they got to the entrance, Caedus and Therion noticed a giant gust of wind formed from behind the shop. Therion looked at Caedus. "They must be using the power of the Windblade to jump."

Caedus's fist clenched. "They must not escape!" Disregarding whatever the faeds wanted, he ran toward the shop with Therion close behind.

"Don't move! There is nowhere you can hide from us," Therion heard one of the faeds yell out.

Coming from the castle, Emilia and Bastion came running toward the garment shop as well, with three more Grey Hawks. Just as they converged to the entrance of the shop, the entire place blew. Emilia was closest. In an act of desperation, Bastion shielded her from the blow as they flew back. Caedus fell into Therion. Their heads clashed, and both of them fell to the ground unconscious.

One of the faeds flew in pursuit of the escapees outside of the city while the other two faeds and Grey Hawks unaffected by the fire helped the others on the ground. It seemed Caedus and Therion were all right.

One of the faeds leaned them upright against a wall next to each other until they woke a few moments later. Therion woke up first and shook it off. Caedus, on the other hand, was in a lot of pain. His head throbbed from clashing heads with Therion. He cupped his face in both hands and groaned.

Therion purposely leaned on Caedus to get his attention, since the pain from his arms intensified. "You all right there?"

Caedus looked up to make eye contact. Therion was able to tell he was still clearly in a lot of pain he was trying to hide.

"Better than you." He smirked. "Let's get those arms checked out. I'll be okay."

Both men used their backs to inch up the wall they were leaning on to stand up.

"Let's get your sister," the older man said.

Halfway down the street, Emilia was barely moving on the ground. Lying on top of her, Bastion was unconscious. Even if she wanted to, she couldn't move. His hair was covering most of her face, and his weight was crushing her as she started to panic. The other three Grey Hawks helped get Bastion off her. Relieved, she took a few deep breaths before attempting to get up. The faed offered a hand.

"Thank you," she said to the spirit.

It simply bowed in return.

She walked up to Bastion and the three men who helped him off her. He still wasn't awake. She didn't realize how much damage he sustained as he saved her from the majority of the blast. His entire back and parts of his legs were seriously burned, quite possibly permanent damage. One of the men placed two fingers on Bastion's wrist checking his pulse. There was none.

"What's wrong? Is he going to be okay?" Emilia asked.

One of the men stood up and faced her. His eyes were watery. "He… he didn't make it." The man's hands shook.

Emilia's eyes watered, and a tear fell from her sparkling bright-blue eye. She grabbed the man's hands to stop them from shaking. *He must have been friends with Bastion. I couldn't imagine the pain.*

The man started to cry, and Emilia instinctively embraced him. He buried his head in her shoulder and cried out. She couldn't hold her tears back. After a few moments they let go of each other. As he began to turn away, Em grabbed his hand once more.

"I'm sorry!" she cried out. "He put himself in harm's way just to save me, a stranger. I am so sorry." She fell to her knees and cried aloud. She dug her hands in her face, feeling ashamed.

The man got down on his knees too and put his hands on Emilia's shoulders. "This was not your doing, my lady. Bastion saved you because that's the kind of man he was. He was selfless, to the end. He exchanged his life for yours, and that's worth something."

Emilia wiped her tears away and breathed in deep. "Thank you. How did you know him? You must have been close."

"Yes, we met years ago when we were put on a quest together. We got along so well. We ended up doing countless other jobs together. He was like a brother to me." The man looked down and grabbed Bastian's now cold hand.

"I never asked what your name was. How rude of me," Emilia said.

"Don't worry, I take no offense. My name is Gaius." He reached his arm out to help Emilia stand.

She smiled and grabbed his hand as he pulled her up.

Just then Therion and Caedus ran toward them. Therion grabbed Emilia's face with his massive hands. "You okay, baby girl?"

"I'm fine, Papa." She looked down at Bastion's body. "This man, Bastion of the Grey Hawks, sacrificed himself for me. I would have been dead if it weren't for him."

"I'm so sorry," Therion whispered to Emilia and the other men. "Losing a brother in arms is not easy."

Gaius put his hand on his chest. "Your words honor me, wolf of the mountain."

Therion grimaced. "Is that what they call me these days?"

"I'm not sure, but that's what master Blackshiv refers to you as."

"I see. Well, the name's Therion, kid." He held his hand out.

Gaius tried to hold in his excitement and shook Therion's hand. The wolf was a legend, and he was standing before him. He was very tall, though not the ten-foot-tall monster he was believed to be.

"It is truly an honor to meet you, sir."

"It's all mine, kid. Say, would you like some help carrying your friend back to the compound?"

"I appreciate the offer, but my comrades and I can handle it."

"As you wish," Therion said as he patted the younger man's shoulder.

"It is time we will be on our way." Gaius faced Emilia. "If you would like, m'lady, we will notify you of the funeral arrangements."

"Thank you, Gaius. Actually, can I accompany you to the compound?" She covered her mouth with both of her hands to hide her face in the event of rejection.

"Of course, you may." He smiled.

Gaius and his two comrades picked up Bastion, and Emilia followed behind them. She looked back at Caedus and Therion. "I will be back soon."

Caedus put his hand on her arm. "I'm glad you're okay, Em." He smirked.

She cupped her hand on his cheek. "Likewise, both of you." She then turned around and caught up with the other men.

Therion and Caedus turned and headed toward the castle.

Caedus rubbed his head. "We have to find out where they are going."

"In time. We must first see the mashkiki and report to the king."

"Every moment we are here they are getting further and further away."

"One of the faeds went after them, most likely to tail them and report back their location. Have faith, we will see them again. Sooner rather than later, I suppose."

Therion could see Caedus did not want to hear any of this and wanted to continue the chase.

"I—"

Therion raised his voice. "Caedus! Have patience. For me, get checked out and wait for the faed to report back. Can you do that?"

"Yes. I'm sorry, I just…I need answers from Cedric."

Therion wrapped his arm around the younger man. "I understand, my boy. Do not worry, I will be with you every step of the way to find him and his companions in due time. Try not to stress over it."

"I'll do my best, I suppose, but finding them is only the beginning."

"I know this Lord Mathis is planning something. I know no one wants to stop him as badly as you do. I am with you, so is Emilia, and all of Cresthill. I know it's not your strong suit, but please, *please* have a little patience. This fight is far from over."

"As you say, I will do my best." Caedus smiled.

"That is all I ask." Therion smiled back.

The men are escorted on both sides by faeds as they slowly made their way to the castle.

Gaius led the way back to the Grey Hawk's compound. Once inside, everyone made way for Bastion's body to be safely moved. Some came to help relieve some of the stress from holding his body up from Gaius's other two companions. Emilia lingered behind them with her arms crossed, trying to hold in her tears.

She didn't know what to think. A good man died to save her. Would the other hawks turn on her, blame her for what has happened? It was a little too much for her to take in. She started to feel dizzy. Her legs started to wobble. She got down on one knee to stop herself from falling. She started to sweat and panic.

Gaius snapped his head back and ran to her. "Emilia! What's wrong? Are you all right?"

Emilia couldn't even bring her head up to make eye contact. "It's my fault he is dead." A few tears hit the floor.

Gaius lifted her head. "Someone will get you a glass of water. Breathe in slow and deep. I will come back to you once I see to Bastion's body."

"Hamoon."

"What?"

"Hamoon. Please bring him to me."

"As you wish. It will be but a moment until Hamoon is before you."

"Thank you." Emilia tied her best to smile.

She found a bench to sit on down the hall as she waited. Only a minute or two until Hamoon showed up with a glass of water. He sat next to her and handed the glass. She slowly grabbed it and started sipping slowly.

"Young Emilia, what troubles you?"

"Bastion…he…he saved my life, at the cost of his own." She faced downward. "He died because of me."

"What has happened to young Bastion is a tragedy. He had such promise. He was on his way to becoming a great leader."

"And it has all been taken away because of me!" Emilia yelled as tears rolled down her face.

She managed to look at him when she yelled and noticed that he now had bandages across his nose from when she and Caedus broke it earlier today in their fight. He seemed okay otherwise though. He rubbed one of his arms because earlier Emilia almost snapped it in half. He rubbed some kind of ointment on it. It made his dark-brown skin glisten. She could almost see her reflection.

"I knew Bastion. I am sure he didn't die because of you. Tell me what has transpired."

Emilia proceeded to tell Hamoon what happened since she left the compound earlier today, and he listened with great interest.

Hamoon put his hand on her shoulder. "There was no way to predict what was about to happen. Bastion saw it before you did and acted accordingly. He shielded you from the fire and paid the ultimate price, and dare I say, I know if he had another chance to do it all over again, he would have done the same thing."

Emilia wiped away her tears. "Thank you. I am glad I met him, despite how brief."

Hamoon smiled. "He must have seen something in you to want to help you."

She rolled her eyes. "I guess so. Did he have any family?"

The older man stroked his beard. "Yes, he has an older brother by the name of Dominic. He is here."

Emilia's eyes widened. "Dominic? Big guy? Reddish hair and beard?"

Hamoon had a curious look. "Why, yes. Do you know him?"

Em winced. "Kind of. Before I fought you, Dominic was a little too handsy with me, so I smashed his face against the floor."

"Really? I apologize, I had no idea. Do you know how long I have been trying to get him off the ale and wine?" She shook her head. "A very long time. But now, learning what just happened to his brother, it may push him over the edge."

"Where is he now?"

"After he got patched up by your apparent beating, he passed out in his chambers. It is best to wait for him to sober up before I break the news to him."

Emilia stood up. "If I may, can I tell him?"

"If you so wish. But from what you told me, it seems that he wouldn't take any news well from you."

"I know, but I feel responsible. He deserves to know the truth, and since his brother saved me, I feel that it should come from me as well."

Hamoon nodded his head. "I admire your sense of honor, young lady. So be it. When Dominic wakes up, you can break this unfortunate news to him, but under one condition."

"And what's that?"

"I will accompany you, in the event that he tries to get violent. For your safety, of course."

Emilia smiled. "Agreed."

Both of them locked forearms.

"In the meantime, I would like to check on my father and Caedus. Can you send a raven to my home when Dominic comes to?"

"Absolutely, my lady, until then." Then he bowed.

She put her right hand on her chest and bowed as well and ran toward the castle.

At the castle's infirmary, Caedus and Therion sat down on separate tables. More attention was given to Caedus since Therion healed at a superhuman rate on his own. The medicine man wiped the blood off Caedus's forehead and closed the cut. Once the man finished putting a few stitches in, he focused on Therion and both of his broken arms.

Caedus managed to take his left pauldron off as his shoulder was bothering him. He looked down and saw a handprint. It looked like it was branded on him. It must have been when Deth grabbed his shoulder earlier today when he dismissed the existence of the gods.

The mashkiki turned around and saw the mark. "Where did you get that? That is a serious burn! Why didn't you show me when you walked in here. Quick, put this on it."

The man picked up a small bottle of ointment and handed it to Caedus. He opened it and rubbed a layer over the entire burned area. It didn't really hurt Caedus. It was just kind of there. He didn't think Deth wanted to hurt him intentionally.

"Have you ever seen anything like this before?" Caedus asked.

"I have not," the medicine man said. "This may be something beyond my skill to heal. That ointment may help a bit, but that mark will most likely stay with you for the rest of your life."

Caedus nodded silently.

"If you so desire, the faeds or the king's advisor Avaline may know more of this other worldly subject."

"Thank you." Caedus now pointed at Therion. "What are you going to do about his arms?"

The mashkiki cupped his chin and smiled. "You know, over the years I must have treated this clumsy fool a hundred times. At this state, his natural healing would have him back to normal in about a week or so."

Caedus made a curious face. "Is your healing really that fast?"

Therion smiled. "Yes, my boy, it is. One of the perks of sharing this body with the wolf."

"I guess that's why Emilia and I have never seen you really hurt before today."

Therion pointed at Caedus, but pain coursed through his arm by his quick movement, and it showed on his face. "I am not really hurt, a little pain, but nothing serious."

"You still have to take it easy for a few days, you big oaf!" the mashkiki yelled out.

Therion glared at the man. "Settle down, Ezio. We will go home after we report to the king."

"As you should," Ezio said with a sly smile. "No training of any kind for five days, is that clear?" He stared intently at Therion.

"As you say."

"Good! You are both free to go. Take that ointment with you, young man. It should last a few days. If you want more, you know where to find me."

Caedus shook Ezio's hand. "Thank you, sir."

Both men make their way to the throne room, where the king waits for them. You can tell Gustaf has been doing a good job keeping everything under control. He and Blackshiv have overseen the wounded being tended to and getting the men to begin repairing all the damage the castle and marketplace suffered today.

Caedus approached Blackshiv and leaned into his ear. "One of your men didn't make it in the marketplace, I'm sorry."

"Who?"

"I believe his name was Bastion."

Blackshiv's face immediately showed sadness. "Oh no. He was such a bright young man."

"Emilia and Gaius took him back to your compound."

Blackshiv looked to the floor. He didn't move for a few moments, then he looked at Gustaf.

"It's okay, I have things taken care of here. Go to your men."

Blackshiv didn't say a word. He patted Caedus on the back and walked out.

"The king is just inside. He is expecting you," Gustaf said as he swung open the doors to the throne room.

Therion simply nodded, as did Caedus. They walked in the throne room as Gustaf shut the doors behind them quickly. Inside was not just the king, but Queen Amaya; Alanna, their elvish ward; and Avaline, the king's advisor and a wizard.

Therion calmly walked toward them while Caedus lagged behind. He hadn't seen any of them for nearly five years. He was a bit nervous, especially to see Alanna. Ever since the king gave up on Cedric's disappearance, Caedus kept his distance from everyone at Cresthill, except for Victor. Caedus always had a crush on Alanna. To him, she always looked like a beautiful angel, even when she was not trying to impress anyone. To him she was always just so stunning.

King Leandrol noticed them walking toward the center of the room. "Ah, here you two are. I have been expecting you."

Both men kneeled before the king and newly returned queen.

"No need to be so formal, on your feet the both of you," the queen said with a smile. She gave Therion a hug. "It has been far too long, Therion. How long has it been?"

Queen Amaya was a tall woman, about five foot eleven inches. She had bronze skin like a Xemoorian and long black hair tied back. She had a few smudges of dirt on her, one on her cheek and some on her legs and arms. They had only just arrived from their journey before Caedus and Therion walked into the throne room.

Therion smiled. "It's hard to say. It seems lately when I have been coming around, you are off on some grand adventure. A few years maybe?"

"I am not sure either, but I see that you have a few sprinkles of gray in your hair now. The kids too much for you to handle?" Amaya said as she ran one of her hands through Therion's long hair.

Therion put his arm around Caedus. "They are a handful, but they are also my pride and joy."

Caedus smiled. He was a bit embarrassed.

"Is that really you, Caedus?" Alanna asked.

Caedus blushed. "Yes, m'lady." Caedus lowered his head as a small bow to her.

She lifted his head with her light touch and gave him a hug.

He had a delayed reaction, then embraced her all the same.

"I see that you have grown up to be a fine young man."

"Y-you flatter me, m'lady. You are as beautiful as ever."

This time Alanna blushed. She was better at hiding it than Caedus. "Thank you very much, Caedus."

Behind Alanna and the queen was Avaline with a big smile on her face. She jogged toward Therion and Caedus and grabbed both of them with one arm each, pulling their heads toward hers. "Oh, how great it is to see you both. It has been so long."

"The pleasure is all ours, I assure you," Therion said with a smile.

It's strange that Avaline is centuries older than anyone here, but she doesn't look that much older than Caedus.

"Just before the two of you walked in, His Highness was catching us up on all that had happened today. It seems the two of you have the last piece to report."

Caedus put his hands behind his back and postured up. "Yes, Lady Avaline. I regret to inform you that the two fugitives escaped with the help of a third party. They escaped the city, but one of the faeds is currently in pursuit." He tried his best to hide the emotion from his face.

"We know this must be hard for you," the king said as he rose from the throne. "Your brother is now the enemy, as are his companions. With the murder attempt on me, the murder of two guards, escaping imprisonment, and massive destruction across the city, they will now be the three most wanted individuals in these lands."

Caedus looked down to the floor. "I understand. I ask but one request."

"And that is?"

"That I be with whomever you send to bring them in. Whatever fate may befall my brother, I just want to have a little one-on-one time with him. That's all."

Leandrol stroked his beard and nodded. "So be it. Reasonable enough. I must warn you though, you must not let your emotions cloud your judgment."

"I understand."

The king put his hand on the younger man's shoulder. "We are with you. Don't worry."

Both men smiled. As Leandrol sat back down, one of the faeds appeared before them. It was the one who chased Cedric and the others.

"Your Highness, I have urgent news on the fugitives."

"Yes, what is it?" the king asked.

"I had them pinned down a few miles down the river when a portal opened up and dragged them inside. I was able to see a little bit of the other side. I may know where their hideout is."

Caedus stood between the king and the faed. "Where? Where is it? We must go there now if he knows where to look."

"What did I just tell you, Caedus?" Leandrol said softly. "You must calm yourself."

Caedus turned around to face the king. "If we know where they are now, we must not waste any time!"

"Mind who you are talking to, boy! We will find them, with a plan and with patience. Do you understand me?"

Caedus grimaced. "As you say."

The king focused his attention to the faed again. "If we are not to be interrupted, you may continue."

"The portal, I was able to see the other side. It was—"

"Wait!" Leandrol interrupted. "It may be wise for Caedus to walk out of the room now. He doesn't need to hear this yet."

"Are you serious?" Caedus said, flaring with anger.

"Very. Now please leave. You will be summoned later. You need to cool your head."

Therion nodded in agreement with the king.

Caedus walked out with fists clenched, shaking his head. He made his way out of the castle to one of the nearby balconies that overlooked most of the city and some of the landscape beyond. The sun was setting, and the view was beautiful. Caedus thought today had to be one of the longest days in his entire life. He heard footsteps behind him and a shout.

"Caedus! Caedus!"

He turned around to see who it was. It was Alanna running after him.

"What are you doing here, m'lady?" he asked with a bit of concern. "Is everything all right?"

"Quite all right, Caedus. I just wanted to see if you wanted some company. You must have a storm of emotions going on in your head right now."

"Yes, it has definitely been a long day."

"I am here for you if you would like to talk about it. Get some of what you are feeling off your chest?"

Caedus was not the type to share his emotions to anyone, not even Emilia. But with Alanna, he felt like he could tell her anything.

"Sure, I would like that. May I ask you something?"

"Anything," Alanna said with a hint of excitement.

"Ten years ago today was when my father died. Would you like to accompany me to his grave? I visit every year on the anniversary." He was a bit nervous. It was a strange thing to ask someone. What if she says no?

"Yes, I would love to!" Alanna smiled.

Caedus smiled. The graveyard in Cresthill lie on the ground level, so it was the furthest point from where they were. It was a long walk, maybe an hour and a half, but Caedus didn't mind since Alanna was with him. They started to make their way down one of the main streets.

"Isn't the anniversary of your parents' death coming up as well?" Caedus asked.

"Yes, in six weeks. Why do you ask?"

"I...I don't want to impose, but if you would like, since you are accompanying me tonight, maybe I can join you when you visit your parents' resting place?" Caedus began to sweat a little. He quickly wiped it away. "It's okay if you don't want me to."

Alanna was a few inches shorter than Caedus. She had to tilt her head up to make eye contact with him. "I would really like that."

Both of them blushed and turned their heads away to try and hide it. Just before one of them could continue the conversation, they ran into Emilia.

"Is that you, Em?" Alanna asked with a smile.

"Alanna!" Emilia ran over and hugged Alanna fiercely. She even jumped on her, but she knew Alanna was strong enough to hold her up.

"Were you heading to the castle?" Caedus asked.

"Yes, I was going to look for you. We couldn't end the day without going to your father's grave. Is that where you two are heading?"

"Yes. Alanna has agreed to come as well. I was afraid that you weren't going to make it."

"I have never missed a year, and I never will. I always go with you to visit your father. Nothing will ever change that." She reached over to give Caedus a hard squeezing hug.

He squeezed her just as hard.

Alanna loved how great those two always got along, not of blood, but family all the same.

The three of them made their way to the graveyard. Emilia told Alanna about the fight they had against the Grey Hawks earlier in the day. Once at the cemetery, they weaved through hundreds of gravestones, for Savas's stone was almost in the back, reserved for royalty for when they pass. Savas was not royalty, but he was like a brother to the king and an influential man in the city, even in all the land.

Now at his father's grave, Caedus got down to one knee and stared at the stone.

Here Lies Savas
Champion of the King
Loving Father

Alanna and Emilia both put their hands on one of his shoulders while he was on his knee. He was facing the ground, then he looked up and noticed something strange.

"Do you see that, Em?"

"See what?"

Caedus stood up. "The top of the stone, there is something different about it."

He walked up to it. It had three handprints on it. The middle print had no mark, but the two outer hands had two suns imprinted in the middle of the palms. He looked back at the other two.

"My father always told me I was his right hand, and Cedric was his left. This handprint on the right is meant for me."

"And the left one is for your brother?" Alanna asked.

"I suppose, but after all these years, this has never been here. I don't know where it came from."

Caedus stretched his arms to his sides and shook them when he put them back down. He nervously put his right hand on the handprint he suspected was for him. Once he did, the ground started to shake. It shook so violently that the girls fell down, and Caedus's hand was stuck on the stone. He couldn't move it.

The sky turned pitch black, and lightning started to strike all around them. Thunder roared over all the lands. Alanna grabbed Emilia's hand. Both of them grabbed on to Caedus. As they did, the black sky opened up and a giant lightning bolt of red struck Caedus. It knocked them off of him while he was still stuck in place, now screaming in pain.

The lightning strike never stopped. It was continuously pouring down on him, going into his body. Emilia quickly got up and tried again to get Caedus free, but this time she burned her hand trying to touch him. The screaming never stopped, and it was breaking Emilia's heart, falling into despair. Alanna didn't know what to do; she was fear stricken.

After another agonizing minute, it finally stopped. When it did, a mysterious force pushed the girls back a few feet. After experiencing the worst pain in his life, Caedus somehow never felt better. The massive lightning strike did not burn him, but steam rose from his body. He turned around to see Emilia and Alanna on the ground.

There was a strange feeling. Fear. He can sense fear, like it was alive. He felt it where the girls were on the ground. At first he felt confused, but quickly discovered that he was sensing that the girls were feeling fear. He looked at the palm of his right hand, where the mark of the sun was on him just like on the stone. Did this lightning strike grant him the power to sense emotions? Was this the power of magic?

V

NEWFOUND POWER

EDRIC DIDN'T SLEEP THAT NIGHT. After his encounter with Lord Mathis, Sheska sewed up his puncture wounds after their master dug his nails through his left cheek. His neck was also a bit sore; Mathis grabbed on to it pretty tight. Cedric took a lot of deep, slow breaths.

He, of course, wouldn't admit it; but when Mathis had a hold of him, he was terrified. He wasn't the best role model for sure; he was hard on all of them. But last night was the first time Mathis actually tried to hurt him. In the past Mathis always beaten them mercilessly in training, but this was different. As of late, Lord Mathis's eyes had a tint of red surrounding the yellow glow. Something he had been doing in his lab was causing him to change. The disciples didn't know if it was good or bad.

After he was patched up, he went to check on Brock and Giselle. Brock took a long hot bath to clear his head and wash off his nerves, metaphorically, of course. Cedric told him to sleep it off, and tomorrow is a new day. Shortly after sunrise, they were going to work together to obtain this lightning blade.

Out of all of the disciples, Cedric was the only one with the courage to stand up to their master. Mathis always secretly enjoyed his confrontations with Cedric, but the younger man pushed him over the edge this time. Beginning talks of possibly defeating him? Overthrowing him? It was unthinkable. Lord Mathis ruled them with an iron fist, and now it was time to increase the pressure.

In all honesty, as angry as he got, he welcomed the challenge of his disciples. He would beat them into submission, and there would be no more whispers of disobedience. He had new special assignments for them.

Mathis rarely slept. He spent most of his time in his laboratory, where nobody else was permitted. None of his disciples attempted entry. Even if they did, the entrance was warded to keep intruders out. After he sent Cedric away for the night, he made his way to the lab.

The throne room was on the top floor, and the lab was in the basement level. Mathis always took his time on the walk down. The basement was dark and dank, with cold stone surrounding him. The torches on the walls lit automatically as he passed by them.

Now in the hallway that lead into the lab, he walked through a transparent blue barrier that kept all others out. Once inside, he headed toward the room on the left. Beyond the barrier, the lab was straight ahead a hundred paces and halfway up were two more rooms. To the left was a room that contained only a giant red glowing stone floating in the center of the room.

He grabbed the stone and carried it to the room to the right. This room was his personal chambers. Once inside he discarded his robe on a chair to the left of the doorway. The bedchamber consisted of his bed, the bed of a king, with beautifully crafted wood posts and enough pillows to bury someone. The only other things in the room were a shelf of trinkets he had collected over the years and the chair to his left.

He put his hand on one of the shelves as he looked at his collection. Sometimes he had a hard time believing he was a few hundred years old. Life has been a long winding road, he was being kept alive through his immense connection to magic, otherwise he would have been dead for decades. There was much more he needed to accomplish before his death.

He turned around and sat on his bed. He threw the red stone in the air. It began to hover over his body as he started to lie down.

"I can't believe I lost control tonight. My condition is getting worse. I must use the stone to recharge myself."

Two bolts of energy came from the stone and grabbed at his temples. He grimaced in pain for a moment, then drifted to sleep.

Alanna and Emilia looked up at Caedus from the ground, confused on what just happened. Steam rose from his body, but he seemed otherwise unharmed. He turned to face both of them and lifted his right forearm. He still had trickling red lightning on his fingertips.

"Is this the power of magic?" he whispered to himself.

The lightning faded as he clenched his open hand into a fist.

Alanna quickly rose up and ran toward Caedus, grabbing his hand.

"Caedus, are you all right?" she said with tremendous worry.

Caedus seemed a bit disoriented, scanning in all directions.

Alanna grabbed his face with both of her hands.

His attention was fully on her now. "I…I feel great. In fact, I have never felt better."

"What happened to you?" Emilia asked as she got up from the ground.

Alanna let go of Caedus's face, but she continued to search his body for wounds.

He focused his attention on Emilia. "The lightning ran through my entire body. I never felt more pain in my entire life, but when it stopped, I felt…I still feel great."

"This surely wasn't normal lighting. This was red, and you seem unaffected," Alanna said as she continued to search for injuries.

Emilia was beginning to think that she was using this as an excuse to feel around Caedus's body.

Caedus acted as if she wasn't touching him at all, as if both of them were not even there. He stared into the distance again. Emilia slapped him in the face with force. It was so loud, it echoed. Her handprint was now on half of his face. Grabbing his face in pain, his attention wasn't wandering anymore.

"What did it do to you?" Emilia yelled out.

Alanna couldn't believe what she just saw. "By the goddess! You didn't have to go that far!"

"It's okay, Alanna." Caedus grabbed her hand and put his other arm on Emilia's shoulder. "When I got hit, I think it gave me power. I think I have the power of magic coursing through my body."

"How can you be sure?" Alanna asked.

"What did you feel when I was getting struck?"

"I was afraid for you," Alanna said.

"As was I."

"I know, I was able to somehow sense it, feel it."

Emilia put her hand on Caedus's face where she previously slapped. Lightly rubbing it as a gesture of apology. "I don't understand. What do you mean? Feel what?"

"When you were on the ground, I was able to feel your fear. I don't know how to explain it, but it seems the lightning strike gave me the ability to sense emotions. I think it's an attribute of magic."

Alanna crossed her arms. "I see, I hope we don't have to go through pain like that to get our magic. We should seek out Avaline immediately."

Emilia made a curious face. "You don't have magic yet?"

Alanna smiled. "Not yet. Elves usually don't use magic for the first hundred years of our lives or so. We are taught to be able to live without relying on magic. Since I had been raised by humans, I have adopted some of your customs, such as starting magic at an earlier age."

At the entrance of the graveyard, two figures appeared. Since it was dark, it was hard to tell who it was from that distance. As they got closer, Alanna was able to see it was Avalene. She used one of the faeds to teleport to their location.

"What happened down here? Is everyone all right?" the wizard asked.

"We are all okay," Caedus said as he stepped forward. "You saw the lightning from the castle?"

"Yes." Avaline folded her arms and walked closer to him. "Something is different about you, young Caedus. Your presence feels stronger than before."

"I was struck head on. I touched my father's grave, and I couldn't take my hand away. Then the sky darkened, and I was hit with intense energy. I think it granted me the power of magic."

"How can you be sure?"

"For example, I was able to feel their fear when I got struck," he said as he pointed at Alanna and Emilia. "And I sense a great deal of confusion from you."

Avaline gave Caedus another curious look. "I have no doubt what you are sensing is magic, but what confuses me is, I have never seen anyone receive powers by a lightning strike. We've only ever known the way to attain magic is to go through Zeledon and pass the trial of the well."

"The well?" Emilia asked.

"The Well of Magic. It is the world's source of power, for good and evil. It keeps all of the realms in balance."

Emilia simply nodded her head, as did Caedus and Alanna. The faed hovered to Caedus and hesitated to make physical contact, its arm was outstretched, almost touching his branded shoulder.

"Young Caedus, I apologize for your injury. It was not my intent."

"You must be Deth then. Is there any way to tell you faeds apart?"

"Y-you are not angry with me?"

"No, if it was not your intent, then it's okay, really." Caedus reached over to touch its shoulder and his hand went straight through. He forgot faeds cannot be touched by living beings, if they do not wish so. "I am sorry, I forgot..."

"It's okay, young Caedus." Deth materialized his hand enough to grab the younger man's, and pressed it against his now touchable shoulder. Caedus smiled. Deth slowly put his hand on Caedus's shoulder as well but made sure to not hold on for long. Even though its face wasn't visible, Caedus was able to tell that Deth must have been smiling.

"It has been a long day for everybody. Let's retire for the evening. Tomorrow we should begin magic training with the three of you," Avaline said, leaning on her staff.

Everyone headed out of the graveyard and toward the castle while Deth lingered behind. He saw the three handprints on the grave as they started to fade away. He leaned down and put his hand on the name of Savas engraved on the headstone.

Caedus turned around. "I sense...sadness from you. Did you know my father?"

Deth looked up at the young man. "A long time ago, yes. He was an honorable man. He would have been proud of the man you have become."

Caedus smiled. "Did you know him while you were alive?"

"No, I was in this form when he was the champion. I'm afraid that is all I am allowed to reveal, young Caedus."

"I will ask no more of you then. Let us make our way back to the castle."

Deth nodded his hooded head. "I will...find a way for you to recognize my appearance in the future."

Caedus nodded and ran to catch up with the others.

Deth looked back at Savas's grave, then turned to look at Caedus. "Savas, my old friend, if you were here today you would be proud of the man that your son is becoming."

⚂

It has been a long day for everyone in the Kingdom of Cresthill. Hopefully, tomorrow will be a better day. Caedus didn't sleep a wink; too much was on his mind. Therion never returned home that night, which was normal when he visited the king. He also didn't want Caedus to know he now knew the location of Cedric's potential hideout. Once they got to the castle, Avaline retired to her quarters for the night. Alanna decided to accompany Emilia and Caedus on the climb to their mountaintop home. Once there, Caedus built up a fire in the back and simply sat cross-legged for most of the night.

Emilia rarely showed affection toward Caedus, but since it has been a trying day for everyone, especially him, she kissed him good night on the cheek before she went to bed. Alanna did the same before sleeping in Caedus's unoccupied bed for the night. It didn't feel right for her to leave without making sure Caedus was more at ease.

Just before the sun came up, Therion arrived at the house. He went straight to the back to see how Caedus was doing.

"You were always quiet. We could never hear you. But I can sense your presence now, old man."

"So it is true? Avaline told me you have magic senses now."

Caedus got up and turned around. "Yes, it appears so. Is this what it feels like with everyone? Can you sense everyone?"

"No, that would be too overwhelming. People with magic can sense other magic users. If anyone has a strong emotion, magic or not, you can sense their feelings as well."

"Yes, I was able to sense fear from Em and Alanna when I was struck by lightning last night."

"Are you hurt?"

"No. Actually, after getting struck, I have never felt better, physically. I feel like I might be stronger—and faster too."

"Would you like to test this newfound power?" Therion asked with a smile.

Caedus didn't have to answer; he was already in his fighting stance. Therion smiled. He didn't hesitate and directly went after Caedus. He jumped in the air and raised his fist to punch Caedus in the face, but he dodged it and got behind Therion. The older man quickly threw a kick that Caedus barely blocked. Before Therion was able to pull back, Caedus grabbed his leg. He was never quick enough to catch Therion, ever. He really was faster.

Caedus attempted to trip Therion, since he was standing on one leg, but quickly realized it was a faint. Caedus let go of the older man's leg and hit him straight in the jaw. Caedus had hit him before, but not this powerfully.

Both men stood straight; the sparring match was over.

"You were able to feel it too, couldn't you?" Therion asked while massaging his jaw. "You are faster and stronger, not by much, but it is a decent improvement."

"Right," Caedus said quietly.

"Not to mention that you are exhausted. You didn't sleep, I can tell. You need to rest, Caedus."

"I will when we catch Cedric and the others."

"You can't do this to yourself, son. Don't let this consume you. We *will* catch them. We just can't go in blind. Who knows what kind of traps and tricks they may have conjured up wherever they are hiding."

"So you still don't know where they are?"

Therion let out a sigh, reluctant to what he was about to say. "The faed told the king and I where they could possibly be, yes."

"And you would not tell me?"

"For now, I will not tell you. It's for your own good." He put a hand on Caedus's shoulder.

The younger man inhaled deeply before talking. "I know. I just can't…I can't just wait around. Cedric is out there. He is alive. I need answers."

Both men walked to the back porch and sat down.

"You know when I was talking to him yesterday, when he was still in that cell, I could tell he was conflicted."

"Is it possible to break away from dark magic?"

"It's all up to the person who wields it. It could be easier for Cedric or his companions, but a man like this Lord Mathis, he may be irredeemable."

"When I saw Cedric yesterday, I looked at his eyes. They were yellow from his dark magic, but when he saw me walking into the room, his eyes briefly turned back to normal."

Therion smiled. "That is good. There is a chance at saving him then."

"Sheska too. When Emilia and I were tied up with her, she didn't seem evil. In fact, she is terrified of Lord Mathis. She wants to get away. She never crossed the lines that Cedric has, at least for now it seems. Only Cedric shares the eyes of this Mathis."

"I see. It's a tricky situation. We don't know what the intentions are with the other two under Mathis. We will figure all of this out, together." Therion reached his hand out.

Caedus smiled and reached for Therion and locked arms with him.

"Stand up. You're not too old for a hug," the older man said.

Both men wrapped their arms around each other. Both of them winced since they were still sore and exhausted from the day earlier. They simply just laughed together.

The back door opened. It was Emilia.

"You two look happy."

Therion opened up his arm for her to join in as a three-way hug. "Come here, Em."

She put her arms around both of them and smiled.

"How are you feeling?" she whispered to Caedus.

"A little better." He smiled. "Did Alanna leave?"

"No, she is still sleeping. You should wake her up."

"Me?"

"She was worried about you. She didn't want to leave until you felt better."

Caedus smiled.

"She is in your bed."

"Mine?"

Emilia nodded her head and smiled. She shoved him toward his room. He breathed in deep and walked into the house. Down the hallway he entered his room to see Alanna curled up with her back to him without a blanket on. He sat on the side of his bed and touched her arm. It was cold. He massaged her arm to gently wake her.

She started to rub her eyes and shook her head. She looked up at Caedus holding her arm.

"Oh, Caedus, I must have dozed off. What time is it?"

"The sun just rose a few minutes ago. It's still early." He continued to hold her arm. "You feel so cold. You must have fallen asleep before putting the covers on."

Alanna sat up eye level to Caedus. "Yes, I never meant to fall asleep. I periodically looked in the back to make sure you were all right, and I must have dozed off a while ago."

"I am okay. Thanks for thinking of me. It means a lot, but you look exhausted."

Over the years Alanna always had her hair in a braid or tied up, but now her hair was down. Caedus ran a few fingers through it.

"I've never seen your hair down before like this. You look great."

Alanna finally got caught blushing. There was nowhere to hide when they are face-to-face. She smiled, and it caused Caedus to blush as well.

"Thank you." She put her hand on top of his. His hands were warm from being by the fire all night. She moved his hand and grabbed his other one and put them on both of her cheeks. "Your hands are warm. Is it always so cold up here?"

"Sometimes. It's certainly colder here than in the city, but you'll get used to it. The fire is almost gone, but would you like to sit by it? To warm up?"

"I'd like that." She lay back down and dragged Caedus to lie next to her, side by side. "Just give me a minute."

As soon as she spoke, both of them fell asleep while holding hands.

Emilia passed by the room to see them sleeping, so she covered them up with a bear pelt and closed the door.

Cedric started to get ready for his journey to Zeledon. He was mad that he had to abandon his robe during his escape from Cresthill. He needed to change his outfit from the stupid brown cloak he wore last night. He put on simple black pants and boots with a white button-up long-sleeved shirt and a dark-brown duster.

He attached a scabbard to his back, leaning toward his right side for the Windblade. The slight curve to his blade made it difficult to unsheathe at times, but he had gotten used to it over the years, with endless hours of practice. Before he left his room, he reached for a black wide-brimmed hat to wear. He and his companions are wanted criminals now, so anything to hide his face was a help. Not to mention he now has five small scars on his left cheek. Earlier, he packed a bag with food for a few days, which he slung on his back.

On the roof of the Castle of Dulangar was a dragonling, in other words, a baby dragon. About two years ago Cedric and Brock travelled as far as Alexandria, the country to the north, and found a giant egg. Brock knew something was alive inside, so they brought it back home with them.

After it hatched, Cedric was the first thing it saw and considered the boy his parent. The dragon was gentle for what it was, a dragon. It acted like a pup more than anything. It wagged its tail and licked Cedric or Brock sometimes. The girls were afraid of it, and Mathis didn't care for it. Even though it was still a baby, the dragon was eye level with Cedric. It was big enough for him to ride on its back. That was his plan today, to ride the dragon to Zeledon to get past the guardian.

Just like faeds, the guardian of Zeledon was a legend. No one knows how true the stories are, but the guardian was supposed to have terrifying power.

While passing the throne room, Mathis caught his attention.

"Cedric! Come in here, please."

Before he was visible in the doorway, he stopped. "I thought you didn't want to see me until I obtained the lightning blade."

"Never mind that, come in here."

Cedric slowly walked into the room and saw Brock, Giselle, and Sheska waiting for him.

"What's this about?" he asked as he pulled the brim of his hat closer to his face.

Mathis stood up. "There will be a change of plans. Not all of you will be going to retrieve the lightning blade."

Cedric looked up. "Am I not to go?"

"You will be going, don't worry. Come closer to me. Take off the hat."

Cedric took his hat off and walked toward his master with his head down.

Mathis lifted his chin up to look at the scars. "I apologize for what I did to you last night."

Cedric jerked his head away from Mathis's hand. "What are these changes you want to make?" he asked with impatience.

Mathis turned around and sat back down on his throne. "You will retrieve the lightning blade, and Giselle will go with you. Brock and Sheska will stay here. I have some training for them."

Cedric did not attempt to hide his anger, and Giselle couldn't hide her worry. Mathis held up his hand.

"Fear not. I am not angry with them. I will do them no harm. Today is the start of a new approach I want to try with you, my children."

"What do you mean?" Brock asked.

"I mean, if the four of you help me finish my plans, I will let you go free to live your lives when we are done."

"Is this but a jest, or are your words sincere?" Cedric asked.

Giselle reached out with her magic toward Mathis.

"Giselle! If you try to probe my mind one more time, you will not like the result."

"I...I'm sorry, Master." She bowed her head.

"This is no jest." He snapped his head toward Giselle. On occasion she would attempt to probe his mind to see if he was lying or not. This time she got caught. "You will all have to help retrieve the weapons I seek, and then ritual will begin to change the world. Once we are done, I will cut my strings from you."

Cedric put his hat back on and headed out of the room. "So be it. Giselle, let's go."

The elf nodded her head and caught up with him. They waved at the others as they left the room.

"Do you think he is telling the truth?" Giselle whispered when they were halfway up the stairs.

"He is lying through his teeth." Cedric glanced at her with a serious look. "He will use us for our power to get what he wants, then we will kill us."

"What makes you think that?"

"A feeling that I can't shake."

"Only time will tell." She put her hand on his shoulder for reassurance.

"I guess so." Cedric looked back at her. "Have you ever ridden on Mordecai's back?"

"Ride on his back? No, I haven't. Why?" Giselle was a little afraid of the dragon.

"How do you think we are getting to Zeledon?" Cedric asked with a sly smile.

Giselle stopped for a moment. "Are you sure...it would let us do that?"

"Yes, I'm sure. There is nothing to worry about. Watch and see. Morty will warm up to you in no time."

"If you say so." Her voice was shaky.

Both of them finally got to the roof where Mordecai the dragon was sleeping. Cedric took his hat off and handed it to Giselle.

"Morty!"

The dragon snapped its head up. Cedric had his arms out as if waiting to receive a hug. Morty started to wag his tail so hard it was making the roof shake, or at least it felt like it did. Giselle took a few steps back.

"Come here, Mordecai!" Cedric yelled out.

The dragon ran toward him on all four legs and jumped on him and knocking him to the ground. Giselle let out a yell, but she quickly noticed that Cedric was okay. The dragon was smothering him with affection and licking his face.

"Okay, okay, that's enough, boy," Cedric said with a smile. He got up and wiped the dragon saliva off his face. He looked over at his companion and reached his hand out to her. "It's okay. Come here."

She grabbed his hand, and he pulled her closer to the dragon. Mordecai was still wagging his tail.

"What do I do?"

"Reach your hand out toward him. Stay calm no matter what. He can get defensive."

She reluctantly put her hand out with her palm up. He sniffed her hand, then proceeded to sniff up her arm and her shoulder until he was face-to-face with her. He licked her face. She couldn't hide her smile. She proceeded to rub his neck. His blue scales were smooth but hard.

"See? He's not so bad."

Giselle smiled. "Yeah. He's sweet."

"Let us be off then. With Morty, we could get there in less than a week. Maybe five days."

"Really? That fast? Normally, it would take the better part of two weeks to get there on foot."

Cedric patted Mordecai's back. "My boy here is fast."

The dragon nodded his head with his younger sticking out. "We need to get past the guardian. What better way than above."

"Your right, I suppose, but do you think the legends of the guardian are true?"

Cedric sighed. "Honestly, I don't know, but we should play it safe and avoid him if we can."

Cedric hopped on the dragon's back and helped Giselle up. The dragon's back was surprisingly comfortable, she thought. She sat behind Cedric.

Just before they took off, Mathis made it to the roof.

"Time may be of the essence. Others may come for the lightning blade."

"What makes you think that?" Giselle asked.

"I have foreseen it. I will open a portal for you to fly through, far enough to not get noticed. You should reach your destination by nightfall."

"Thank you, Lord Mathis," Cedric said.

Mathis proceeded to open the portal by creating a circle and expanded it by stretching his arms out. Mordecai took off and flew right through.

VI

ARRIVAL AT ZELEDON

"WAKE UP, BOTH OF YOU!" Avalene the wizard yelled out when she walked in to Caedus's room. He and Alanna drifted to sleep a few hours earlier. "It is midday now. Let's have some lunch before we are off for Zeledon."

Alanna jolted awake. Caedus was still as dead as a rock.

"We will be out shortly, Ava."

The wizard smiled and walked out of the room.

Her hair was all over the place. She pushed it all back before waking Caedus up.

"Get up, sleepyhead," she whispered as she rubbed his arm.

He still wasn't moving.

She got on top of him and started to shake him.

He finally opened his eyes and looked up at her. "Wha-what are you doing, Alanna?"

She covered her face in embarrassment. "You wouldn't wake up, you silly oaf. You sleep like a troll!"

Caedus smiled. "Was that Ava's voice I heard?"

Alanna nodded her head. Caedus put his hands on Alanna's thighs. She still never got off him yet. Her face was as red as her hair. She quickly got off of him.

"I'm sorry, Caedus…if I made you uncomfortable."

Caedus got out of bed and offered to help her up as well. "Not at all, my lady."

She grabbed his hand as he pulled her out of the bed. "Falling asleep next to you has put me at ease."

She rubbed his cheek with the back of her hand. "The feeling is mutual. Let us not delay any longer. The food smells good." She led the way out of the room and down the hall to the dining room table by the fireplace.

Therion just finished setting the plates on the table for four. Avaline was already seated, her staff leaning on the wall next to the fire.

"Ah, the two of you are awake!" Therion yelled. "You got enough beauty sleep?" He smiled.

Caedus patted the older man's back.

"Look at Alanna. She surely doesn't need any beauty sleep. But you, my boy…you may need plenty."

Therion and Caedus liked throwing the occasional jest at each other every once in a while to lighten the mood. Caedus just smiled and sat down, but not before pulling out a chair for Alanna to sit first. Lastly, Therion sat. The food looked great. Slices of bread with butter, mashed potatoes with peas, and some sliced boar meat with glasses of milk and water.

"This looks great, old man, but where is Emilia?"

Therion answered while chewing on some of the meat. "Em ate already. Shortly before you woke up, a raven came here for her. She had something to take care of at the Grey Hawk's compound before you head off to Zeledon."

"I see. This was about what happened yesterday?"

Avaline nodded her head. "Yes. Truly unfortunate what happened to that young man. She wanted to be the one to tell his brother what had happened to him."

***

Hamoon stood ready right next to Emilia. Dominick was summoned to one of the common rooms of the compound. Blackshiv also was there. He sat on a stool, drinking some wine, with his cane leaning on the counter. Once you walked into the room, the bar was on the left side and on the right was a fireplace. There were a few wooden tables in the center. A luxurious red carpet covered most of the floor.

Emilia sat at one of the tables while Hamoon stood between her and the headmaster. Dom walked in the room, half covering his eyes, as the chandelier lights were bright. His head was pounding from the bender he was on yesterday.

Did I do something while I blacked out yesterday? he thought worriedly. *I must have done something to demand the presence of Hamoon and the headmaster. Who is that young lady?*

Hamoon stepped forward. "Dominick, we have some rather disturbing news to discuss."

"What did I do this time?" the bearded man asked. "Who's the lady?"

Emilia stood up. "You don't remember me from yesterday?"

Dom had a puzzled look. He started to scratch the top of his head. "Actually, I don't remember much of yesterday at all. What did I do to you?"

Blackshiv downed his drink and took a deep breath. "Have you noticed your nose? It's broken."

Dom wondered why he was having a hard time breathing. He gently touched his nose and winced. "Ow! I take it you did this to my face, miss? For what it's worth, I apologize for whatever I did."

"I appreciate your apology, but it sounds like this isn't the first time something like this happened to you. Don't you think that continuing the consumption of ale and wine is dangerous?"

"Don't forget brandy!" Dom spurted out. "Good stuff there, would be a shame to leave out."

Everyone looked at him with disgust, especially Blackshiv.

"I'm sorry, I know I shouldn't be drinking the way I have. It's hard. I have been trying to find a way to stop for a few years now. I don't have the willpower. I don't know what to do."

Dom felt very ashamed now. Yeah, he knew he wasn't the best guy, but he considered Hamoon and the headmaster men he looked up to, men he aspired to be in the future. He tried to lead as a role model for his younger brother Bastion, but sometimes he felt that he failed as a brother also. He spent most of his earnings on alcohol. What kind of example was he leading?

"Your alcoholism is not the reason we summoned you today, even though we are willing to help you break free of your addiction," Blackshiv said, now sitting on the wooden table next to Emilia.

"I am confused then. What was I summoned for?" Dom asked nervously.

Blackshiv and Hamoon looked toward Emilia. She immediately started sweating. She looked back at Hamoon. He nodded his head and gestured his hand toward Dom for her to speak. She stood up and walked a little closer to him.

"Your little brother, Bastion..."

Dom took a few steps back. "Bastion? Has something happened to him? I don't know what I would do if something..." He couldn't bring himself to finish.

Emilia's eyes were watering. "Yesterday, there was an escape from the dungeons. Bastion and I were in pursuit with others. I ran ahead to catch up with my father and brother, but before I got to them, a building exploded. Bastion grabbed me to shield me from the impact, at too high a cost." She wiped some of her tears away. "Your brother is dead. He is dead because of me."

Dom fell to his knees with his mouth wide open in disbelief. "Bastion, my little brother?" He whispered, "My little brother!" He covered his eyes and started to cry hysterically.

Emilia couldn't hold it in either, and she started to cry also.

Hamoon and Blackshiv had their heads down. Shiv covered his eyes to hold in his cry. Hamoon tried to console Dom, but there wasn't much he could do except pat his back and hold his shoulder.

"Your brothers are with you," he said.

Brothers, meaning the other Grey Hawks, the brotherhood they shared as they all bonded together over time.

Emilia hesitantly put her hand on Dom's other shoulder. "I'm so sorry, Dom."

Dom looked up at her. He looked like he was about to say something, but he couldn't bring himself to say any words.

"Can I come back later to talk?"

Dom barely managed to nod, then she turned around to walk out of the room.

"May I accompany you to the exit?" Blackshiv asked.

Emilia gestured for him to come along. As they both walked out, they still heard Dom's cries from down the hall. She almost couldn't take it. She could not imagine what it would be like if she were to lose Caedus like that. Blackshiv patted her back for reassurance.

"Do you deal with situations like this all the time?" she asked.

"Unfortunately, I do. One of the many duties of being headmaster."

"It must be difficult. You have attachments to these men. I can see that they look up to you."

"Yes, my dear, it is. Everyone in my organization is my family. We formed strong bonds over the various quests we took together. From the outside, we are perceived as simple sellswords or mercenaries. Most people think we only care about the reward and the next adventure, but this place is a sanctuary for anyone who needs it. Many of my people don't have homes or family to go to." He slammed his cane on the ground. "In here they matter!" His hands started to shake. "When Dominick was just a lad, he came here with nowhere to go and he carried a little baby with him, his brother Bastion. I have known that young man his entire life. Dom raised him, as well as I, and the others pitched in here and there. The way things were heading, Bastion was first in line to take my place as headmaster someday, when he was ready." He wiped a tear away.

"I had no idea, I'm so sorry, Shiv. I feel—"

Before she got to finish, Blackshiv put his hand up and raised his voice.

"Do *not* feel guilty over his death! He saved your life at the cost of his, this is true, but he never hesitated to do the right thing. He was selfless, and if he had another chance, he would have done the same thing without hesitation!"

"As…as you say. But I still feel terrible."

They arrived at the outer gates of the compound.

Blackshiv put his arm around Emilia's shoulders. "It is okay to mourn, but don't let Bastion's death consume you. From what I know, you start training in the magic arts today. Focus your mind there for the time being."

Em tilted her head to the side. "How did you know about that?"

"You should know by now that I know everything around here."

"I guess it was foolish to ask."

"To other matters, my dear, the path to magic is not for everybody. You seem strong and capable, but it is still a perilous journey for power."

"Do you have any advice for me?"

Shiv stroked his hair back. "I am not at liberty to say anything about it, but there is one thing you must know. It is the most difficult part of the journey."

Emilia couldn't contain her curiosity. "What is it?"

The headmaster sighed. "If you obtain the power of magic by going through the trial of the well, you will not be able to leave Zeledon until the guardian deems you worthy. If he finds you are not, you will be stripped of magic forever."

"Trial of the well? And the Guardian of Zeledon is real? How does he deem someone worthy?"

"I have already revealed too much. And oh yes, the guardian is real, and he is much more powerful than the stories made him out to be—and a lot meaner. You must be cautious."

"Thank you for the information. It is time I made my way to meet with the others. Can I come back later to see Dom?"

"It may take a while for him to come around, but when he does, I shall send for you." He reached out for a handshake.

Emilia obliged with a smile, and he kissed her hand before she turned around and left.

Emilia decided to walk through the marketplace, where the majority of the chaos happened the day before. A lot had been cleaned up; but it was, of course, closed until further notice. Most of the shopkeepers were repairing or putting together new stalls, and builders came to reconstruct the damaged and destroyed buildings.

One of the shopkeepers was a small goblin, no taller than two feet or so. He had an interesting stall of trinkets from his travels and many foods from different cultures. He was a good cook. A lot of people in

Cresthill didn't like him when he first arrived a few years before, for most goblins are thieves and he wasn't trusted by many.

Nevertheless, he wanted to prove that he was not like his kin, for he was kicked out of the goblin underground. Bit by bit he gained recognition by most common folk and the other shopkeepers. He put out fair prices for his goods and cooked for customers right in front of them. He gave the other shop owners discounted prices. The respect of the people around him was all he wanted.

As Emilia walked by, she saw the little goblin crying next to his damaged stall. "Lobul, what's wrong?"

He looked up at her. He sniffed and wiped his nose. "My shop. It's destroyed. I don't know what to do."

Emilia bent down and touched his shoulder. "It's okay. I have to leave town for a day or two. When I come back, Caedus and I will help you build a new shop."

Lobul's face lit up. "You would really do that for me?"

Emilia chuckled. "Of course, I will. You know Caedus, my father, and I are working with the king and the Grey Hawks to find the people who did this."

"Good! There must have been dozens of them with all of this damage!"

Emilia's facial expression changed to almost a grimace. "Three."

Lobul tilted his head to the side. "Three? Three people did all of this?"

"Unfortunately, yes. These people are very dangerous. That's why so many of us are working together to recapture them."

"I hope you catch them, Em."

"I hope so too, Lo." She pet the top of his head. "Keep your head up, okay?"

Lobul smiled and nodded. "When my shop is back up, I'll make you and Caedus some of your favorites!"

Emilia laughed. "I look forward to it. I'll see you soon." She stood back up and walked out of the marketplace. Just before she left, she took a moment to look at the spot where Bastion saved her. A chill ran down her spine, and she quickly walked toward the base of the mountain.

Cedric and Giselle had been flying on Mordecai's back for almost six hours. After they got through their master's portal, they were still a distance away, to not attract attention to whoever resided in Zeledon. The view was amazing, being so high up. They could see for miles in every direction. The wind felt nice, Cedric constantly had to hold his hat on top of his head, but he eventually stuffed it in his bag so it won't fly off.

Giselle wore tight brown leather pants and corset with matching bracers. She put on a dark- blue hooded cloak to keep warm from being so high up. She didn't like to carry weapons around much, but as long as she was outside, nature itself was her weapon. Just in case, she carried dual wielding daggers on her belt.

Cedric looked back at his elven companion. "Let's take a short rest. Mordy is getting a bit tired."

"Sounds good. I wouldn't mind stretching my legs for a bit."

Cedric patted Mordy's back. "Anywhere you'd like, buddy."

The dragon knew that meant it was his choice to pick where they were going to land. He turned his head back and roared in excitement.

They held on tightly as he quickly flew closer to the ground. He picked a spot right along the northern side of the Winding River.

"We are no more than a day's walk from where you got branded," Giselle said softly as she took in the view.

Cedric quickly grabbed his shoulder. How could he already forget the immense pain he felt yesterday? He grimaced. "Yeah, but with Mordy we could get there in no time."

"I don't think that is such a good idea."

"What do you mean?" Cedric saw that the elf kept her eyes fixed on something. He stood next to her to see what she was seeing.

"Breathe in deep, Cedric. Close your eyes."

He obliged. Sometimes he forgets that Giselle is much older than he and his other two companions, even though he comes off as the leader. Elves typically look young, but they are older than they seem in many cases. He actually doesn't know who is older, Giselle or Lord Mathis. She has many years of magical experience, and he takes her advice whenever she gives it.

"Feel around you. The border of Zeledon is not far off."

"I can...I can sense where the border is." Cedric then opened his eyes. He opened them wide, in fact.

Giselle smiled. "You can see it too, don't you?"

"Yes! The borders of Zeledon is protected by some form of dome? Can we not get in?"

"We can," Giselle sighed. "The dome is a barrier to alert this Guardian of intruders, by land or sky. So taking Mordecai would give us away just as much as simply walking in."

"I see," Cedric put his hat back on. "But this lightning blade we seek is deep into the lands, wouldn't it save us time to have Mordecai to drop us right on top of where we need to go?"

"That...actually sounds like a great idea. If we walk through the border, our presence will be known. Then we have to run and hide and possibly fight before we get to the blade, but if we are dropped right on top, all we have to do is escape once we get the blade."

"Yes! So it is settled then." Cedric put his hands on Giselle's shoulders. "You know, I think we make a pretty good team."

"As do I." She smiled and jestingly pulled the brim of his hat over his eyes.

"Lord Mathis always had it as you and Brock against Sheska and me, but if we all stick together, it will all work out."

"I agree. After last night, I don't think Lord Mathis will try to pit us against each other anymore. He knows we can't be controlled in his way for very long. Thanks to your efforts."

"We have all grown." He gave her a look because he genuinely can't tell what her age could be. "We have our own desires in life, and that includes not living under his thumb. He knows it's only a matter of time before he can't control all of us at the same time anymore. That's why he told us that we can live as we wished if we helped him finish his plans willingly."

"Do you think it is because we are all becoming stronger? Or that our lord is growing weaker?"

"He is plenty strong," Cedric said quietly.

Giselle put her hand on the small wounds Mathis gave him last night. He grimaced, but he didn't pull away.

"But I don't think he is as strong as I originally thought. I think that we should help him finish his plans so we could go free."

"But do you think he will simply just let us walk away? Just like that?"

"No, he is going to try to kill all of us when he gets what he wants." He was about to say something else, but he quickly stopped himself.

The look on his face told Giselle that he was hiding something. "I see. Let's sit and eat for a bit, then continue on. Sound good?"

"Yeah, let's eat." *She suspects something now. I can't let her figure out my plan, at least not yet!*

Mordecai breathed fire onto a pile of wood to huddle around and cook some food.

"Em! Everything go well at the compound?" Therion yelled out as he waved from the distance to catch her attention.

Emilia continued her fast pace toward the others. They are now at the base of the mountain outside of the city where Therion's house stood on the top.

"Things went as well as they could, I suppose."

Dominick's cries still rang in her ears. She didn't know what else to say. Nothing really *went well* at the compound, and she had expected Dom to lash out violently. Perhaps it was the only good thing about the whole situation, but seeing him break down like that put her at great unease. *What can I do to make things right?*

Therion gave her a bear hug and lifted her off her feet. This always seemed to make her smile, no matter her mood. He put her down, and Alanna gave her a hug.

"How are you holding up?" the elf asked.

"I'll be okay, thank you." Emilia looked over at Caedus, who winked at her.

He reached his hand out to her. She locked forearms with him as he pulled her closer to hug her. "You'll be all right, Em."

It didn't take much from Caedus to make Emilia smile. They were raised as brother and sister, and for the most part they always got along.

"Is everyone ready for the journey?" Avalene asked as she leaned on her staff. Everyone nodded. "With a good pace, we should reach our destination by nightfall."

Caedus couldn't hide his excitement. Alanna thought that was cute. She was rather excited as well. She was about to be one of the youngest elves in history to attain magic. Most elves wait a century or so before even considering it. She is a young thirty-six. To most elves that was no older than a child, but since she was raised by humans, she felt like she was well into adulthood.

The five of them were starting off on the road heading north when they heard someone yelling in the distance. Therion turned around first to see Victor Vog, the new Champion of the King and commander of the Cresthill army, chasing after them.

"Hey! Hey! Wait for me!"

The rest of them stopped as Victor caught up with them. He was out of breath, and he put his hands on his knees.

"What's wrong Victor?" Therion asked.

"Oh nothing." He was still panting. "I was wondering if you wouldn't mind my company on your journey."

"You want to come with us? Whatever for?" Caedus asked.

"Ah, Caedus, you still look like a lad with your clean-shaven face. Can you even grow a beard?" Victor teased.

Caedus folded his arms. "Yes, I can, moustache man!"

These days Victor sported such a bushy moustache. You couldn't see his upper lip anymore.

"And who are you calling a lad, look at those scrawny arms."

Compared to Caedus, Victor was a smaller man muscle-wise. Caedus would probably beat Victor in a contest of strength, but Victor could destroy Caedus in a sword fight any day.

"I came to apologize for yesterday. It was my priority to protect the king, and with all of the chaos, I mistook you for a threat."

Caedus laughed. "It is quite all right, Victor. It has all been settled."

"I know, but I was not there to apologize after everything calmed down."

Caedus put his hand on Victor's shoulder. "Really, it's nothing. Do not dwell on it."

Victor smiled. He patted Caedus on the back. "If I am not mistaken, you are going to Zeledon to learn magic?"

"Yes, that's right," Avalene said.

"My father. I have been meaning to visit my father for a while now, but I have not made the time."

"Who is your father?" Emilia asked.

"My father...is the Guardian of Zeledon."

After resting up for a while, Mordecai was ready to continue flying. He seemed more eager than the other two. Giselle was preoccupied by what Cedric was trying to hide from her, and Cedric was more fearful about the possibility of running into the Guardian of Zeledon. Even Lord Mathis steered clear of this man. How powerful could he be?

Cedric jumped on the dragon's back first, then offered to help his elven companion up.

"We should try to arrive around nightfall, it will be easier to transition into the darkness."

"Good idea. Let's be off then." She grabbed his hand as he pulled her up behind him on the dragon's back.

Mordy roared and flew off, creating a strong gust of wind that blew out the fire they had set. As they got closer to their destination, Giselle held on to Cedric's waist a little tighter. Not enough to hurt or anything, but enough for him to feel it. Cedric never had romantic feelings toward Giselle, but the way she was holding him, it felt right. No time for such matters now though, but maybe another time? They arrived at the top of the dome barrier.

Giselle pointed toward the north. "We should find the blade we seek in that general area."

Cedric pulled out the Windblade. The hilt pulsed in the same direction. "You're right. Let's get off here."

Giselle pulled his hat out of his bag and pressed it onto his head. He was now a wanted man after all. She didn't want to take any chances.

His blade in one hand and holding his hat on his head with the other, he jumped through the barrier and landed on his feet. He used a gust of wind to soften his fall, but going through the barrier, he felt an intense shock. Next, Giselle dropped and Cedric caught her. Their faces were closer; their hearts were beating. Giselle never felt this way toward Cedric before. They have known each other for years, but now he seemed so attractive. Both of them moved away. This was no time to discover their feelings for one another.

Mordecai flew off, roaring loudly, hoping the Guardian would follow him and draw him away from Cedric and Giselle. The Windblade was pulsing violently now; they were close.

"That cave! Over there!" Cedric pointed his blade toward it. "The lightning blade lies inside somewhere."

In the distance a man has been watching them since they landed. His steed began to move toward them.

Cedric heard galloping behind them, and it was getting closer. They quickly turned around, but saw nothing there. They turned back around, and the man was directly in front of them.

"How did you get in front of us? Who are you?" Giselle yelled out.

The man patted his chest. "Me? Who am I? You are on my land! Who are you?"

Cedric's attention was on the man's steed. It was no horse. It looked like a giant deer with silver fur and antlers with a rainbow glow. The man looked to be in his midthirties. He had light- brown hair down to his shoulders, blue eyes, and a thin mustache. He kept a sly smile on his face.

"Are you the guardian?" Cedric asked with a hint of fear.

The man jumped off his steed, which ran off after he whispered something in its ear. He had on an orange vest with ragged brown pants and worn-out boots, but surprisingly no weapons on him.

"It matters not who I am. I am not going to ask again. Who are you? Why are you here?"

Cedric pointed his blade at the man. "Our business is our own. I suggest you step aside."

The man laughed. "Oh, that's not the right answer." Then he vanished.

Cedric frantically looked around, but the man was gone.

"Behind you!" Giselle yelled out.

Before Cedric could turn around, he was tripped from behind. He fell on his back, and the man came in for a punch, which Cedric barely dodged. Good thing he did, because the man put a small crater in the ground where Cedric's face was just a moment ago. Right after he missed, he disappeared again.

The man reappeared in front of Cedric and punched him in the jaw. As Cedric fell back, the man appeared behind him and punched him in the cheek.

"Teleportation magic?" Giselle whispered to herself.

The man relentlessly attacked from every angle and without allowing Cedric time to react.

"Have you had enough?" the man said as he smiled.

Cedric put his hand up as a sign to hold off any more potential attacks. He was severely outclassed in this fight. He was beaten half to hell and not even a scratch on this strange man.

"Are...are you the guardian?"

The man laughed. "I see you are curious of the old legends. I am Regan! And, yes, I am the Guardian of Zeledon. One of the seven."

Giselle and Cedric were in disbelief. Not just one, but seven?

VII

THE OVERSEER

"THE GUARDIAN OF ZELEDON IS my father," Victor revealed to everyone.

Caedus was in disbelief. "Your father? I thought the Guardian of Zeledon was…a legend, a mythical creature to keep people away."

Victor laughed. "The legends are partially true! He is no creature or beast, but he does watch over Zeledon, and he is extremely powerful."

Emilia ran her hands through her blue hair. "Interesting…" She looked back at her father. "Do you know about this man, Papa?"

"Oh yes, I do. The old bastard is one of the most powerful fighters and magic users in the realm, if not the most powerful."

"Really?" Caedus asked. "Stronger than you?"

"Oh yeah," Therion said without hesitation.

It was hard to believe anyone was stronger than Therion. He was a prideful man, but to admit out loud this guardian was stronger than him is a feat in itself. Emilia and Caedus looked at each other with surprise.

"Very fascinating. I look forward to meeting him. Will he be the one to teach us magic?"

Avalene shook her head. "No, he will only guide us on where we will have to go, and I will teach you once we are at the well."

"Are you going to be training us as well?" Alanna asked Therion.

The older man laughed. "No, no, Avaline is the better teacher. The guardian bamboozled me out of some money a while back on a bet. I told him next time I came around, it would be double or nothing, so I'm coming to collect."

"Oh, I see."

"No worries though. He and I go way back. He's an old pal of mine."

"What is this well? You mentioned it last night," Caedus asked in a slightly impatient tone.

"The Well of Magic. It flows through all of the realms in existence. It is the universal supply of magic since the beginning of time."

"So we are going to travel to another realm, the Well of Magic, to train?"

"Yes, that's right. The only way to travel between realms is through the heart of Zeledon, which is why it must always be protected."

"I see. Very intriguing. This only boosts my excitement to start!"

Avalene smiled. "I admire your enthusiasm, young Caedus. Let us not linger and head north, if we are to make it there by nightfall."

Everyone nodded, and the six of them journeyed on the road to the north to Zeledon. The road usually took a week or so to get where they were going, but the king insisted on the faeds opening up a portal for them to go through to substantially shorten their trip. After all, the new Champion of the King, Victor Vog, can't spend too much time away from his city.

<hr>

Lord Mathis took Brock and Sheska to the far side of the city of Dulangar. Most of the ancient city was half destroyed buildings from the mage wars a thousand years ago. Before the mages tried to take over though, they trained together in an arena-like setting, to test out their magic abilities in open space, without the worry of collateral damage.

They left by foot. Mathis led the way while the others lingered behind. They were a bit more than intimidated. Where was their master leading them? Was he going to take them to the old training grounds and beat them senseless? Was he going to kill them? The tension was so thick it was hard to breath. Sheska was sweating profusely. Brock was surprisingly composed. His face was stone. He quickened his pace to meet the stride of his masters.

Mathis smiled to himself. *He must have exhausted all of his fear last night.*

"Are we going to the old training grounds?" Brock asked without even looking toward his master.

"Yes, we are. I have something different I want to try out today."

"How so?"

"When we get there." Mathis looked behind him to see Sheska trembling. He reached his hand out to her. "Come here, girl."

She gave him her hand. As soon as he grabbed her, her fear faded away. By making physical contact, Mathis was able to send his sincere thoughts of not wanting to hurt her and rushed it through her body. She was much more relaxed now.

It was another ten minutes or so of silence until they reached their destination. Once on the black sands, Mathis threw his hooded cloak off and let it fly through the wind. He tied his gray hair back behind his head. He almost never took his cloak off in front of his disciples, but since he did today, it told Brock they were going to do something different.

Beneath the cloak was battle armor. A silver glow with blue trim. It bore similarities to the armor of the Cresthill army, but different enough to know it wasn't from there. It had sleek curves, as if the elves designed it; but it looked very old, battle worn, and not exactly clean. But it showed at one time, before he took the mantle of "Lord Mathis," he must have been a renowned warrior from a faraway land. Even though his cloak was off, Mathis took no chances of anyone seeing what he really looked like. Even though his hood was off and his hair was out, his eyes glowed with such intensity that his entire face was a haze, barely something someone could recognize.

Mathis smiled. "Oh, it feels good to wear the old armor."

"It looks ancient! How old are you exactly?" Sheska asked. Since she was from Xemoor, she had a good idea of the different kinds of armor used around the world, and the one Lord Mathis was wearing was nothing she had ever seen before.

"It is not how old I am, but where I am from. I am not from Afelith."

"Where are you from, Lord Mathis?" she asked.

Brock was paying special attention because they still don't know any of their master's personal information. He never shared it to them.

"I come from a place called Witches Valley. It is very far from here."

"Witches Valley? I don't think I am familiar with the place. Where is it?" Brock asked.

Mathis gave him a look as if to silently say, "Who would dare to ask that?" "Far from here."

"As you say, Lord," the taller man said quietly.

"What's a witch?" Sheska asked.

Brock was curious as well.

"A witch is like a female wizard, but twisted by the dark arts. They are vile creatures."

"So you are like a male witch?" Sheska asked.

Brock nudged her violently. *Why would she ask such a thing?*

Lord Mathis's response was surprisingly calm. He simply nodded his head and pulled out his hand with his palm up.

"What is in your hand?" Sheska asked her master.

Mathis opened his palms to reveal two strange forms of root. "These are very rare. If ingested, they calm the body and mind, which can make you ready for anything with a clear head."

"Why do you have them?" Brock asked.

Mathis put his arms behind his back. "It is no secret the two of you show more fear toward me than Cedric and Giselle." He reached his arms out to hand his apprentices the roots. They took them without hesitation. "You will eat these, and when it comes into effect, you both will attack me with everything you have!"

"Why do you think we need such help?" Brock asked with a twinge of offense.

Mathis quickly grabbed his shoulder. Brock was caught off guard by it and proceeded to flinch. Mathis noticed.

"See! That is why. You both are too wound up around me! Afraid of what I might do or say." The older man sighed. "I know I wasn't forgiving, raising all of you, but enough time has passed. We have a few things left to do, and then we can part ways for good, if you so wish."

Both of them felt his words were genuine. It was one of the rare occasions when Mathis doesn't have an angry face on.

Sheska ate her root, and when she did, she closed her eyes and took a deep breath and sighed with relief.

Brock looked at his root and threw it on the ground. "I don't need help. I will come at you with everything!"

Mathis smiled. "Good, good!" He took a few steps back and put both of his arms out, purposely baiting his apprentices to attack him. "It is time for you to face your fears! Now come at me with everything you got! And nothing less!"

Brock ran toward his master with intensity, with Sheska close behind. He came toward the right and Sheska on the left. She covered her hands in ice for more powerful punches while Brock seemed to have more control over his power. Instead of having something explode, he had his hands steadily aflame. He never knew he could manipulate fire to this degree, but his pumping adrenaline helped him achieve a new level of control, similar to how Cedric gained new levels of control over the wind.

Both fire and ice punches headed toward Mathis at both sides. He crossed his arms and caught both fists in his hands, feeling the extreme sensations of cold and heat. If he felt pain, no one could tell because his facial expression was blank. He quickly smiled. "This is going to be more fun than I thought!" He laughed aloud, and it echoed through the abandoned city.

After coming through the other side of the portal, they were only a few miles away from the borders of Zeledon. Therion led the way as the sun was about to set. Victor was right behind him, followed by Caedus and Alanna, and Avaline and Emilia in the back. Therion was eager to try to win his money back from the guardian. He was tricked, or bamboozled, out of his money last time—or so he said. Victor knew how mad Therion was, because his father told him all about how he won his money from the wolf a while back. In all honesty Therion was fooled out of his money, but thinking about it couldn't stop the young man from smiling.

Everyone wondered what this bet was though. Therion would not speak a word of it until the Guardian was with them also.

"Have patience! I do not wish to speak of my bet at this time." He was starting to get on edge about it the closer they got to Zeledon. He turned around to Victor. "Wipe the smile off your face, Vog! I know why you're holding in your laugh. I'm sure he told you about it, didn't he?"

Victor couldn't help but to chuckle. "I'm sorry, Therion. It's just a bit silly how you—"

Before he uttered another syllable, Therion grabbed the younger man's mouth to stop him from continuing. His massive hand covered most of Victor's face. "When...we get there, Victor! Do you understand?"

All he could do was nod his head.

Avalene made a face of almost disbelief toward Therion. "What would make you want to resort to violence? Is it really so bad?"

Victor couldn't help but laugh. He even stopped walking and put his hands on his knees; he was laughing so hard. "You will see, we are almost there." He looked around before continuing. "Hey! Everyone, I know an alternate route to get to the cabin faster. We could reach it before the sun goes down."

"Very well! Lead the way, young Victor," Avalene said with a smile. She was exhausted. From coming back from a quest yesterday and now to another journey wears on a lady, especially someone as old as she is. But no one had ever lived to be her age before, except her wizard companion. He resided to the east far beyond the Lasgarothian forest.

She smiled at the thought of him. He went by the name of Malagan. Thinking back it must have been about twenty years since she has seen him last.

Therion laughed loudly. "We have made it! Now everyone stop pestering me with questions. All will be answered shortly!"

Ava was thinking about her past adventures with Malagan and lost track of time. They must have taken Victor's shortcut for about a half hour.

Therion led the way. He put his hand up in front of him and jerked it back. "Ow!"

"What's wrong?" Emilia asked.

Therion sighed. "This here is the border into Zeledon. We may enter, but not without a shock. We are going to feel it going in." He looked toward Victor and pointed at him. "Your father is a maiden."

The younger man laughed. "As I have been told. He must already know of what has transpired yesterday, is all."

"Yeah, I know. But still, unnecessary. Do you think a small shock would stop the villains from entering?"

"I suppose not, but let us not dwell on it. Let's get to the cabin."

Therion went through the barrier first with a grimace. Everyone else went one at a time with twinges of pain here and there. Once everyone got through, they followed a small dirt pathway leading to the house of the Guardian.

It was a beautiful cabin built with rock and wood, seeming to be very spacious. Nothing but nature as far as the eye can see. Therion stomped on the porch and kicked the front door open.

Everyone else thought it best to stay a few paces back, except for Victor, who was right behind Therion.

"Hey! Old man! You have some visitors. Get off your ass!"

Caedus crept inside slowly, followed by the three ladies behind him. The inside looked like a nice common room from a higher-end pub of some kind. The main thing Caedus took a liking to were the candles. They were being held on the center of the table by antlers. Not ordinary ones though, these had a rainbow glow to them.

A roaring fire kept the room well lit, but in the corner behind the bar, a man was sitting down with a mug of ale in his hand. His hood was up covering his face with shadow. He picked up his mug, finished the contents in one sip, and slammed it on the counter, causing everyone to snap their heads toward him.

The man stood up. His brown cloak was worn and tattered. His glasses were now visible since he wasn't in the dark anymore. He didn't look as old as led to believe, but also Avaline doesn't look her age by a longshot. Clearly, advanced use of magic could slow down or stop aging if used the right way. The legend of the Guardian is centuries old. This man looks no older than fifty or so.

"Who do you think you are to barge into my home like this?" He momentarily adjusted his glasses. "Wait." He smiled. "Only one maiden in the realms wears that vest! Therion, you came back to win your money, huh?" The man put his arms out for a hug.

Therion laughed. "James, you son of a whore, how are ya?"

Both men embraced as old friends would.

Caedus looked back at Avalene. "James?"

The wizard simply nodded. He turned to Emilia and Alanna. "A basic name for someone as renowned as him, no?"

Emilia tilted her head to the side. "Maybe?"

"From what I know, he goes by many names," Alanna interjected. "Maybe this is the name he goes by when with other humans?"

"Maybe. But who knows. I am just happy to be here," Emilia said.

"Are the Guardian and my father friends or enemies?" Emilia asked the wizard. "He didn't have anything nice to say about him the whole way here, and now they are hugging."

The older woman laughed. "You know, I don't even know what goes on between those two. They act like brothers, if you ask me."

The Guardian, also known as James, next went to hug Victor. "How are you doing, my boy? It has been a while since you visited. Getting tired of coming all this way to see your old man?"

"Not at all, Father! You know how it is, working closely for the king. I don't get a lot of free time."

The older man took off his hood. "I know, I know, my boy. It was but a jest! It is great to see you though." He put his hands on Victor's shoulders. "Every time I see you, you grow up a little more. Where does the time go?"

Victor just simply smiled.

Avaline went behind the counter and looked at the drink selection. James had the rarest collection of ales and wines from across the world. She poured herself some wine from Alexandria.

"We have these three here to begin magic training."

James folded his arms and inspected the three of them. "What do we have here?" He started to pace around them. "Princess Alanna, everyone knows you. You are an elf, so your connection to magic will be strong."

"Ward, actually. I have no claim to the throne."

"I know, I know. Ward, princess, similar." He focused on Emilia now. "The daughter of the wolf, interesting. Your mother is well-known as well. Kashisu, the former sellsword. You come from a strong bloodline. You may fare well with magic if you pass the trial of the well."

Emilia tilted her head to the side. "You know my mother?"

"Oh yes. I know everybody who has ever used magic in this realm."

"I see."

The Overseer faced Caedus. He got a little closer than the younger man was comfortable with. "The son of Savas, former Champion of the King. Your father wasn't too well adept in magic, but no one surpassed his willpower." The Overseer took his glasses off and closely eyed Caedus again. "The red lightning from last night. It struck you, didn't it?"

"Yes, it did. How did you know?"

"I sense your confusion. It seems you have been granted the power of magic without taking the trial first. Why? I do not know." He looked around the room at everyone. "No one has ever gained the power of magic like the way he has last night," he said as he pointed at Caedus.

"What does that mean?" Caedus asked.

"In all my years no one has ever gained magic in that way."

"The Guardian does not know?" Avalene said in a jesting tone. "He knows everything, does he not?"

The Overseer looked back slowly. "Had enough of my wine yet, Ava?"

"Oh, relax, only one glass, because we are old friends."

He waved his hand at her as a gesture to silently say, "Enough already." "The hour grows late. Are you tired?" the Overseer asked everyone.

"A little," Alanna said.

"Not too much," Emilia said after.

"Not really." Finally from Caedus.

The Overseer smiled. "Good, because your training will take place tonight. You are not going to sleep until it is decided if you are all worthy of magic." He eyed Caedus again. "I have something else planned for you, since you already possess magic."

"I see, what would you have me do?"

"First, we will escort the ladies to the trial of the well, and I will personally oversee what I have in store for you, young Caedus."

"As you say, I am ready!"

"I like the enthusiasm. You remind me of your father when he was your age."

Caedus smiled. He wished he had more time to get to know his father, have a conversation with him man to man. He owed it to Savas to make things right with Cedric, or at least try to. Who knows how far gone he had become.

Against one of the walls was a small bookshelf, Emilia gravitated toward it out of curiosity. The books were very old. Some were barely held together. Since the Overseer rarely leaves Zeledon, maybe he read books continuously over the years?

Maybe next time I come I'll bring some new books for him to read, she thought with a smile.

The most worn-out book appealed to her for some reason. She carefully picked it up from the bottom shelf. The leather binding was almost non-existent, but just enough to keep it together if you're careful. She blew some dust off and wiped off the rest to see the title.

"*The Overseer Chronicles.* What is this book about?"

The Overseer quickly turned around and snatched the book out of her hands.

"Be careful with that!" the older man spouted. "These are not in good condition. I don't want to have to piece it back together if you dropped it."

"I'm sorry. I meant no offense. I was just curious."

The Overseer smiled. "It is quite all right, my dear. These books are just old relics. I know them all by heart, but this one here"—he held the book up so the title was facing her—"this is the last book of its kind. I cannot get another one if I tried. It belonged to my predecessor. He passed on the title of Overseer to me."

"I see. I apologize for mishandling it. What is an overseer?"

The Overseer sighed and put the book down. "Essentially the same role as the Guardian here, except my duties exceed all of Afelith, not just Zeledon."

"Very interesting. Maybe I could be the next overseer," Emilia said in a jokingly manner.

The Overseer smiled. "That would be nice, young lady, but let's get started with magic first."

"Sounds good!"

Alanna put her hands on Em's shoulders and started to shake her in excitement. Caedus smiled at both of them. The Overseer lead the way through the back door to the open landscape, but about twenty paces beyond the door was a table with two chairs. Victor immediately started to laugh. Therion gave him a stare of death, and the Overseer threw his robe off and sat down.

"Before we start everyone, are you ready to try to win your money back, Therion?"

The wolf already started to sweat on his forehead. He flexed his arms and headed to the table.

"What is going on?" Alanna asked Victor.

Everyone else gave him their undivided attention because Therion refused to talk about how he lost his money last time.

Victor had to hold his stomach because he was laughing for a good ten seconds.

"You can all clearly notice the wolf is a much bigger man than my father?"

Everyone nodded.

"So a while back my father challenged Therion to an arm-wrestling match, but he didn't know how strong he really was, so he thought it was going to be an easy win. But my father is a lot stronger than he appears, and he took Therion by surprise and won his money. From what I have heard, that was roughly what happened, is it not?"

Avaline couldn't help but laugh. She leaned on her staff for dear life. Alanna chuckled, but Caedus and Emilia were in a state of confusion. Was Therion really bested by this man? I guess everyone was about to find out how true the story was.

Therion sat down as the wood from the chair creaked.

The Overseer took his glasses off and smiled. "It's time to get down to business."

Therion gave a small smile, but in all honesty he was nervous. "So are we on agreement of the terms from last time? If I win today, I'll get double the money?"

"But of course. And if I win again, you give me double what you paid me last time."

"It's a deal!"

They shook hands, then readied their poses for the match. They agreed to use their right arms for today's match.

"Wait!" Caedus yelled out. "Old man, your arms are broken, both of them. This contest should wait a few more days at least."

The Overseer tilted his head and put his glasses back on. "Oh, wow, the boy is right. I'm surprised I didn't notice earlier. There must be about six fractures at least. What happened?"

"How does he know all of that by just looking at his arms?" Alanna whispered.

"It's his glasses, infused with magic power to enhance his sight tremendously," Avalene whispered back.

"I could still hear you!" the Overseer snapped. "I may be old, but not as old as you, wizard! My sight isn't what it used to be, but my hearing is sharper than ever!"

Avalene just took another sip of her wine as if the Overseer didn't say anything at all. After all the centuries, the Overseer was one of the only people alive as long as her, so she must have heard all he had to say and it didn't faze her anymore.

The Overseer quickly stood up. Something was heading their way—and fast.

"What's wrong, Jim?" Therion asked worriedly.

"My baccus is coming this way."

"What's wrong with that?"

The Overseer quickly faced everyone. "My apprentice sent him to me. We have intruders in Zeledon."

Caedus moved next to Avaline. There was no point in whispering now since the Overseer could apparently hear them. "A baccus?"

"Yes, the last few baccus are protected in these lands."

"How does he know if there are intruders?"

"The baccus are telepathic, and this specific one is linked to the Overseer."

"I see." He rubbed his head and sat on the porch steps. "I never knew so many of the legends were based on fact and so close to home."

The baccus jumped over the table set for arm wrestling and stood next to the Overseer. It was as big as a horse, and it had the same rainbow glow to its antlers just like on the table inside. In the sun the silver fur had a blue glow to it if you stood in the right place.

The Overseer stroked its snout and pressed his forehead against it and smiled. "How many intruders?"

Two. Regan incapacitated one, and the other put up no resistance.

The voice was heard by everybody, but individually in their own heads. The baccus cannot physically speak, so it puts what it has to say in the heads of who it chooses, in this case, everyone here.

"Wow, did you really just speak inside of my head?" Caedus asked.

The baccus locked eyes with him. *Of course. This is the way of the baccus.*

"I see."

"Okay, here is what's going to happen," the Overseer yelled out. "Avaline, I will take you and the girls to the portal to the well, Caedus will come with me to check on who these intruders are and what they want, and Therion will stay with Victor and the baccus here until Caedus and I return."

"I'm not going to just sit here!" Therion protested.

"Yes, you are! Unless you want me to break your legs also, you maiden!" He couldn't help but smile. "Caedus and I will be back shortly."

"As you say," Therion said with a grimace. As everyone began to walk away, he yelled out, "Dick!"

The Overseer spun around in surprise. "What did you just say?"

Therion chuckled. "I thought you had good hearing? Get out of here. I'm going to help myself to some ale."

Victor couldn't help but laugh at the squabble.

The Overseer turned back around and whispered to Caedus. "Of course, a dog would go for the ale."

"My hearing is just as good as yours, Overseer! I heard that!"

Caedus and the Overseer laughed.

"What do you call yourselves, the two of you? What's the nature of your relationship? It seems to change every few minutes."

"I guess you can say we are old friends? I can't really put it into simpler terms."

The five of them walked toward the portal to the well as Therion stood next to the baccus.

"You know, I don't know how you put up with him all the time. It has been ten minutes, and I am exhausted from being around him."

The baccus let out a roar, which mimicked a laugher. *You know he is not always bad. He just likes to poke fun at you.*

"Yeah, your right, but still, what a dick," Therion said under his breath.

"He may be a dick, but he saved your hide more than a few times in the past," Victor chimed in.

Therion sighed. "Yeah, you're right. Let's drink his ale."

A few thousand paces behind the house was a circle made from stone in the middle of the open field. The Overseer stretched his arms out and created a circle with his arms, and as it materialized, he pressed it onto the ground to match the circle of stone. The portal's other side had a bright blue glow to it.

"Who's going in first?" the Overseer asked.

"Do we just…jump in?" Emilia hesitantly asked.

"It is quite safe. The three of us have to go in."

"As you say." Then she jumped in as if jumping into a river, followed by Alanna, who waved at Caedus before she jumped. Then Avaline, who threw her staff in first, then herself. After she got through, the portal closed up.

It was just Caedus and the Overseer.

"How will they get back?" the younger man asked.

"There are seven guardians. One of them is on the other side and will assist them on returning."

"Seven? There are seven guardians?"

"Yes. It's true, I am the original guardian from the legends, but I have taken on help over the years. For the past four hundred years or so, there has been five of us, and in the last hundred years, I have taken on two more."

"Interesting. Maybe after all of this training, I would be interested in hearing more stories of your past."

"Maybe, but for now let's see what these trespassers want in my lands."

VIII

TRIAL OF THE WELL

EMILIA FELT LIKE SHE WAS falling through the portal for miles it seemed. After a few minutes she finally fell into a body of water. It was dark all around her, but the water she was in was glowing blue. It gave off light to her surroundings. It seemed to be an entrance to a cave of some sort, and she was just outside of it. She looked up and narrowly escaped Alanna landing on top of her, followed by Avalene. The three of them walked out of the water together. This body of water was strange. It was like a beach where you can go in and out of the water without jumping or crawling out, but there was no sand, just smooth rock.

As they walked away from the water, they also walked away from the light so Avaline tapped her staff on the ground twice for the jewel on top to start glowing, almost like a lantern. Emilia grabbed as much of her hair as she could in her hands to squeeze together to drain some of the water out.

"So is this the Well of Magic?"

"This is one of the pathways that leads to it," the wizard said without turning around. She led the way while the two younger women lingered behind her. "After we go through this cave, your trial will begin, and I will meet you at the well on the other side."

"Do you have any advice for us before we go in?" Alanna asked.

"Keep your head level, and take deep breaths. That is all I can say."

"As you say," both girls said in unison unintentionally.

The wizard turned around and reached her arms out to hug both girls. "One more thing, time does not flow here like it does at home."

Both girls' eyes widened.

"What you see in your trial may be in the past, something in the present, or something that has not yet come to pass."

As soon as she let go of them, she smiled and gestured for them to move forward into the cave. Once they got in front of her and turned around, she vanished. The trial had begun.

"Do you suppose we are to take the trial together?" Alanna asked.

"Your guess is as good as mine."

They walked slowly together. It was so dark that they had to stand shoulder to shoulder.

"How are we supposed to know where to go if we can't even see?"

The words "We can't even see" echoed, and a pathway started to light up before them. It led deeper into the cave.

"That was convenient!" Alanna said with a smile.

They felt a little more relaxed now that they could see. The lighted path was almost like glowing glitter scattered around the ground but in a straightforward direction. It was glowing blue just like the water. The path was slithering like a snake, then it all of a sudden split in two. They noticed that the cave split into two paths, one for each of them to follow.

Emilia grabbed Alanna's hand and squeezed it gently. "Good luck!" She smiled and ran toward the left path.

Alanna yelled out after her, "You too, Em!" She ran toward the right path.

⌒⥤〜

After chasing her path for a few minutes Alanna started to see a light. After she reached it, she was blinded for a few seconds. When she came to, she was outside.

"Am I still in the realm of the well?" she said aloud, but something felt off. Her voice was much higher pitched than it normally was. She looked at her hands and noticed they were child's hands. "What's going on? Where am I? Is this part of my test?"

She was in the woods, much like the edge of the Lasgarothian forest where her clan lived years ago. She looked up to see the sun shining through the blue-and-purple leaves. It was a nice day. She ran over to the creek to look at her reflection, to see her younger self from thirty years ago stare back at her.

"Am I reliving a memory?"

Horror struck her as she noticed something she would never forget. She had a cut on her left cheek. The only time in her memory where she got a cut there was the day her clan was massacred, and she was about to relive it again.

She started to cry. "No, no, no, no, not again! I can't do this again!" She quickly wiped her tears and ran toward the camp. "I have to see my parents while I have the chance!" Her tears started to fade, and she smiled. She hasn't seen her parents in three decades. This felt so real, but this was her test, right? It had to be. But what if it wasn't? Was she really back in time? If she really was, would she have remembered her life as a woman in her midthirties? She still has all of her memory. This was all too overwhelming, and she felt dizzy. She was overthinking too much.

Test or not, she wanted to see her parents. Once in the village she ran past the tents she remembered in the same exact places all those years ago. She slowed down near the village center where the huge fire was. It wasn't lit yet, but it was being prepared. Every night at sundown the clan would eat together around the fire. The logs were taller than she was. They were all tilted on an angle and ties together at the top, and in the center was where the kindling went. She smiled and started to run again toward her family's tent.

She made her way and moved the pelt out of the way, which served as a door, more like a privacy screen that lead to the inside of her family's tent. She ran toward her mother with tears of joy streaming down her face. In reality she hasn't seen her mother in years.

"Mama, I'm so happy to see you!" she yelled out as she grabbed her mother fiercely.

"Why are you crying, my dear? Is everything all right?"

Alanna wiped her tears away but kept an enormous smile on her face. "Yes, I just missed you, is all."

Her mother smiled. "Silly girl, you saw me this morning before you left to play in the woods."

Alanna forgot that she was in the form of her younger self, so she played along.

"What happened to your cheek? You have a small cut."

Alanna lightly touched her cheek. "Just a scratch from a tree branch, that's all."

"Let's take care of that, shall we?" Her mother grabbed a bottle of healing ointment and rubbed it onto a small purple leaf and gently pressed the leaf onto Alanna's cheek. "How does that feel now?"

Alanna couldn't stop smiling at the fact that she was with her mother again. "Better!" She embraced her mother once more. *This didn't happen last time. Have I been given a chance to change the course of my personal history? Can I save my clan?*

Once the leaf was secure on Alanna's cheek, her mother kissed her forehead. It made her smile.

"Jacqueline? Alanna? Is anybody home?"

Alanna's face lit up with joy. It was her father!

"We are here, Papa!"

The tall elvish man walked into the room, not without Alanna tackling him with joy.

"I'm so happy to see you, Papa!"

He got down to one knee. "I haven't been gone that long my dear, only a few days." He brushed her cheek with his fingers. "What happened to you? Are you all right?"

"I'm okay, just a scratch."

"All that matters is that you are okay." He kissed Alanna on the cheek, then stood up to greet his wife.

"Vamire, how I missed you so!" Jacqueline spouted as she fell into his arms.

He grabbed her tightly and kissed her fiercely.

Alanna covered her eyes but couldn't help but smile to be reunited with her parents.

"Aren't you speaking at the clan supper tonight?" Jacqueline asked.

"Ah, yes. Since I lead the hunt, I shall speak about the journey we took for tonight's meal."

"Are you prepared?"

Vamire laughed. "Of course, my dear wife! I will only speak the truth. No need for fancy speeches."

"As you say, but I heard that Chieftain Miroku will be in attendance tonight."

"Worry not, my love." He grabbed her shoulders and smiled. "I will not embarrass the clan or this family." He kissed her forehead.

⚬

A huge fire was lit in the center of the village with everyone in the clan in attendance, about twenty-five elves or so, including Miroku, the chieftain, as Jacqui said earlier. Vamire didn't think his wife was being serious, but there he was sitting in the circle with everyone else. A twinge of nervousness hit him, but there was nothing to be afraid of, right?

"Everyone from Clan Narain! Welcome to tonight's special meal that my companions and I have hunted for all of us to feast on tonight."

"Did you find a baccus?" someone yelled out, followed by everyone laughing. No one has seen one of those in centuries.

"No, no, I'm afraid not. But I do have some surprises for all of you, because I could not be more proud to be part of this clan. May it live on for future generations to come!" He raised his wine glass, as did Miroku, followed by clapping and a few cheers.

Alanna sat cross-legged with her mother smiling.

Vamire put his glass down to continue. "First off, we collected—"

In midsentence a dagger struck him in the chest. Vamire groaned in pain and fell to one knee. Everyone panicked and started to scatter. Jacqui grabbed Alanna and stood up. Before anyone could get too far, men started to drop from the treetops and forced everyone back into the circle. The men had swords and bows to keep everyone from moving. Everyone in the circle were holding hands.

One man approached Vamire with an axe resting on his shoulder. "I see you found my dagger, elf!" the man yelled, followed by a laugh.

It was too painful to attempt to pull the dagger out. Vamire looked up at the man. "What is it that you want? Why attack us unprovoked? We are a peaceful people."

The man bent down to get closer to the elf. "You see, elf, we are bandits. We came here to take your valuables. So tell me, where are they?"

"What? Our valuables is what you see before you, the clan together as one!"

The bandit kicked Vamire in the chest, narrowly missing where he was just stabbed and forced him to fall on the ground. The bandit laughed. "That…was not the answer I was looking for." He looked around at the other fear-stricken elves with his men smiling behind them. "You have to have something, so speak up!" He lightly put pressure on the knife sticking out of Vamire's chest. If enough pressure is pressed, the blade will pierce his heart.

"I speak the truth!" the elf yelled out. "We do not possess the kind of riches you seek! Us dark elves value the bonds of friendship and family more than material possessions! Look around you!"

The bandit humored him and looked around. "I don't see much."

"Exactly! We live in tents. We eat by the fire. We do not need much to be happy as a community!"

Alanna felt sick. She knew this was the moment where her father was about to die. Tears streamed down her face. She held her mother tightly.

"You see now," the bandit almost whispered to Vamire, not knowing that elves have better hearing than humans. "I don't think I have a use for you then."

"Jacqui! Alanna! I love you both!" Vamire yelled out as the bandit stomped on the blade that pierced his heart. He died instantly.

Alanna cried out in despair, just as she did thirty years ago. Tears were shed among the whole clan. Most covered their eyes. The bandit looked straight at Alanna and smiled.

"So…you must be this elf's daughter? Come here."

Alanna shook her head. The man forced her away from her mother's arms. She stood over her father's body. She bent down and kissed his forehead. She didn't do that originally, but she felt it necessary. The bandit pulled her back up and stuck his axe by her neck while pulling her hair to keep her head up. "I will kill everyone here, one at a time, starting with this girl, if I don't see any valuables!"

Alanna felt calm. She knew that the prince was going to save her with the wolf and the champion any second now.

Jacqueline stood up. "Did you not hear what my husband said before you murdered him? We do not possess the valuables you seek. Now let my daughter go!"

Just then another bandit came from behind and stabbed her in the back with a longsword and pierced through her chest. As she fell, she reached her arms out for Alanna.

She started to panic, because the prince should have been here with his men by now. The bandit locked eyes with her.

"So your parents are rebellious. You're too dangerous to keep alive!"

It felt like her heart was going to burst out of her chest. This did not happen last time. Was this really her end? She failed Emilia, Avaline, Caedus, and, most of all, her parents.

The bandit let go of her so he can grab on to his axe with both hands. He began to swing for her neck. Before she could say a word, it was too late, his axe cut her head clean off.

⁓⤬⁓

Emilia woke up in her bed. She sprung up and headed toward the backyard's sandpit. For some reason, she felt that she had to go there. She saw a robed man in red and black, maybe a wizard, standing out there by himself. He turned around toward her.

"Em, I didn't know you were here."

Who is this man? she thought. *And why is he at my house?* Looking closely at his face, she realized it was Caedus! Not the Caedus she knew though. He was older, by a few decades at least, and he had two scars on his face. One from the bridge of his nose, crossing his left cheek all the way to his ear, and the other from his forehead, through his left eye and crossing his other scar down to his chin. His left eye wasn't open. He probably didn't have a left eye from that scarring. He also had a long braided beard and long hair tied behind his head, but that was the face of her brother.

"Caedus?"

He simply nodded his head. The pain on his face was unmistakable. Something terrible must have happened, in all her years she never seen him like this.

"I know I haven't been here in a long time. I didn't mean to intrude," he said quietly.

"You're always welcome here, Caedus, you know that!"

He gave a sad smile. "It has been some time since I heard you say that." He hesitantly reached his arm out for a handshake. The look on his face broke her heart. Instead of giving him a handshake, she gave him a hug like she hasn't in years and squeezed him tighter. It managed to give this older Caedus a smile. What happened between them to where he would be so hesitant around her?

She grabbed his face and laced the scars with her fingers. "What's wrong, Caedus? What happened?" She couldn't help but to ask.

He turned away from her to look at the sun rising. "Everyone's gone. The companions were disbanded, no more Phoenix squadron, a war is coming, and we are not prepared for it."

"War? What war? And who are the companions?"

Caedus gave her a curious look. "How old are you, Em?"

"What?"

"Just answer the question, please."

"Twenty. Why?"

"That is why you are acting strange. This is your trial of the well, isn't it?"

Emilia actually forgot about that. The last thing she remembered before waking up here was seeing a bright light in the Well of Magic. "Yes, it is. But I don't understand what I must do?"

Caedus sat down on the porch. "The trial is rather tricky. I don't think I can help you pass it, but I may give you some advice."

"Of course. Did I tell you how I passed it in the past? Well, your past?"

"You did, and I believe the well sent you to me in this time to help you."

"Really? How so?" Emilia felt a twinge of excitement.

Caedus stood up and clasped his hands behind his back. "Tell me, Em, what do you fear more than anything?"

"What?"

Caedus turned around to face her. "You have to escape the well by facing your fears."

"I...I don't really know really? I don't think I'm scared of anything."

"Are you scared to lose someone? Me perhaps? Therion?"

Emilia rubbed her chin. "Of course, I'm afraid to lose you both."

"In this time, we lost each other. I have done unforgivable things, and we parted ways years ago. It is good to see you again, even in this capacity." He looked in her eyes. "I know what it is. It's something you never admitted, but I knew what you were afraid of when we were younger."

"And what would that be?" she asked curiously.

"You'll see, Em."

"If I am in the body of my future self, then what is going to happen when I go back to the past?"

Caedus sighed. "I'm sure that you're going to attack me on sight."

"I would never..."

Caedus's look of despair was heartbreaking when he looked away from her again. "After what I have done, you certainly would."

"What did you do that was so horrible?"

He looked at her again. "I...I cannot tell you."

She grabbed his shoulders. "Why not?"

"Because if you know what I did, and in your time, what I am about to do, you would expect it. You would alienate yourself and try to prevent it. You have to live your life in the now and not concern yourself with what is to be. All I will tell you is that I chose to act upon the lesser of two evils. It had to be done."

"As you say, but—"

Caedus grabbed her chin with his thumb and forefinger. "You must not tell anyone about this meeting, no matter what."

"I...I don't know."

"You must swear it!"

Emilia pulled a dagger off Caedus's belt, and she cut her own palm. Blood started to rise out of the wound, then she cut Caedus's palm. They clasped hands with each other's, blood mixing into the others wound. "I swear, brother, I will not tell anyone."

Caedus smiled. He barely managed to open his left eye so he could look upon her more clearly. "Looking with both of my eyes helps focus my power."

"What do you need to use your power for now?"

Caedus pressed his thumb on her forehead and whispered something she couldn't understand. Maybe an ancient language?

"I am sending you back to the past."

Before she could say anything else, he pressed his thumb extremely hard on her head and pressed his palm into her chest. She fell onto the ground, but she continued to fall, like her spirit was falling beyond her body. She saw a white light and then nothing.

***

Alanna woke up screaming. She quickly stood up and grabbed her head and neck to see if they were still attached to her head. After everything was in place, she fell back down, breathing heavy and shaking in fear. *Did I just die? Where am I now?*

She quickly realized where she was. She was in the woods again where she was playing and where she cut the side of her cheek.

"Did time reset after I died?" She was very confused. "I have to do something different to pass the test or else time won't stop resetting."

She ran toward her village and waited for the clans' meal to start. She greeted her mama and papa like she did earlier, and her mama tended to her cut on her face just like she previously did.

Alanna was determined to change what was about to happen. She was going to save her parents and her clan. She was sitting next to her mother in the circle by the fire just before her father was about to address the clan. She looked up in the trees where she knew some of the bandits were hiding to see if she could spot any of them.

She couldn't specifically see them, but she saw movement. Just before her father was about to speak, she stood next to him in front of everyone.

"There are bandits in the trees!" She pointed up. "They mean to attack us!"

Vamire crouched down to meet her gaze.

Everyone started to look around.

"What are you talking about, Alanna? What bandits?"

As he spoke, they came out of hiding, from the trees like Alanna said. The leader stepped forward, the one who previously killed her father and killed her. As he stepped forward, she took steps back until she was leaning on her father.

"Clever girl!" the bandit yelled out so everyone could hear. "You saw what your whole clan could not." The bandit unsheathed his dagger and pointed it at her. He carved the healing leaf off her face and caused a new cut to bleed on her cheek.

"You stay away from her, you scoundrel!" Vamire yelled as he pushed Alanna behind him, but she refused and stayed put.

"You are not going to hurt my clan!" Alanna yelled to the man.

He laughed and grabbed her shirt. "You see, girl, that is where you are wrong!"

Vamire grabbed the man by the neck, which caused him to let go of Alanna. The man was off his feet, choking to death in the hands of the elf. Alanna couldn't believe what she was seeing.

"I don't care who you are!" Vamire yelled out. "Nobody hurts my daughter and gets away with it!"

The man couldn't speak. He was at the point of passing out when one of his men came behind Vamire and stabbed him in the back. He immediately let go of the bandit and fell to his knees. Jacqueline screamed in terror, and for doing so her throat was slit to silence her.

The man who killed her looked at the rest of the clan, who were afraid to move. "Does anyone else want to speak up? You will end up just like her!"

No one said a word, but many were tearing in silence.

"Mama!" Alanna screamed out. She tried to run to her, but Vamire held her back with his arm. He pressed her face against his shoulder. "Do not look, Alanna! We are too late."

He wouldn't dare look back. He couldn't bear the sight of his wife on the ground robbed of life with blood everywhere, and he tried to spare Alanna of that same sight. The knife was still in his back, and he was growing weaker by the second.

The leader of the bandits struggled to stand after being choked. He rubbed his neck and coughed. When he came to, he was furious. "You just made your last mistake, elf!" He picked up his axe and slowly walked toward Vamire.

Alanna stood in front of him. "Leave my father alone!"

"Look what we got here," the bandit said with a smile. "Brave little girl, but that's not going to save you now!"

He rose his axe up in the air to strike, but suddenly he stopped. He dropped his axe and fell on the ground. Alanna was stunned. *What's going on?* Then she noticed an arrow on his back. She then looked up to see three young men—a prince, a wolf, and a champion—here to save her and the clan.

They came to save me! Just like when I was a girl! As she thought that, she forgot that she was in the body of her younger self.

The three saviors had other men with them to help. And they started taking out the bandits one by one. A few people in her clan unfortunately didn't make it in all the chaos, but her father was still alive!

She turned around and grabbed his hand. He was very weak and couldn't stand. He managed to grab his daughter's face with both of his hands. "My baby girl! I fear…that my time is almost up."

Alanna started to tear up. "No, Papa, don't say things like that. These men came here to save us. They can help you!"

Vamire smiled. "There isn't enough time. I lost too much blood. I only have moments to spare."

Alanna didn't realize how much blood he lost. His entire back was covered along with a pool forming at his feet. "You must do something for me, my dear."

"Yes, Papa! Anything!"

"Live your life. Live a long and happy life. Be with people you love."

"But I love you, Papa! Stay with me!"

He wiped the tears off her face. He touched the clan tattoo she had on the left side of her face, and it started to glow. "Your mother and I will live with you forever. She loves you, and I love you." He smiled, then he fell to his side, never to wake up again.

Alanna cried loudly. She leaned on her father's dead body and buried her face to muffle her crying. After a minute someone touched her shoulder. It was the prince.

He bent down to one knee. "My name is Leandrol. Are you hurt?"

Alanna shook her head. "I'm okay, but not my parents."

Leandrol looked behind her to see her father slumped over as well as her mother another ten paces back, lifeless.

"Do you have any other family?"

Alanna shook her head.

He reached his hand out to her. "Would you like to stay with me then? I'll take care of you."

Recalling her memories as a child when this previously happened, she hesitated because she didn't know if she could trust him, but now knowing the wonderful father he is to become, she smiled and hugged him, which made him smile as well.

Everything suddenly froze as everything turned into a bright blue light and then nothing.

⌁

Emilia ended up in front of a castle, but not the one she was familiar with.

"Where did Caedus send me? Am I in the present?"

She approached the castle. It was unguarded. She went right through the front gate. The castle seemed to be one of the only buildings intact. The rest of this city was destroyed, wherever this was.

Once inside there was a tattered flag hanging. A green background with a white staff in the middle and yellow stars surrounding it. This was the symbol of the mages. They had their own city ages ago. If she recalled correctly, the city was called Dulangar.

She felt like her purpose was to get to the top of the tower. After many flights of stairs, she reached a throne room, where a lone man sat wearing a hood, but underneath she could see severely damaged battle armor.

"Excuse me?" Emilia said quietly but managed to echo across the room.

The man violently woke up. He must have dozed off. "Who goes there?" He stood up. "I can see you, girl, but I cannot sense your presence."

Emilia didn't know what to say. The man walked toward her slowly. Even though he was getting closer, she couldn't make out his face but she was able to see his eyes, glowing and yellow. Fear struck her heart as she realized who she was standing before.

"You…you are Lord Mathis!"

"Yes, but the question is, who are you, young lady? How did you get past my barrier around this city?"

"Honestly…I don't know."

Mathis reached for her, but his arm went through her. "You must be astral projecting."

"What does that mean?"

"That means your body is not here, but your spirit, or your astral form is here. Why are you here, girl?"

"Emilia. My name is Emilia. And I do not know why I am here. I am supposed to face my fears in a trial, and I was brought here."

Her voice was calm, but on the inside she was terrified. This was the man who killed the Champion of the King, Caedus's father. Just being in his presence is chilling.

Mathis let out a laugh, which made Emilia even more uncomfortable if that was even possible. "So, young Emilia." He looked straight at her. It felt like he was reading her thoughts. "You fear me? But why? I have never seen you before."

Why was I sent here to face him? Emilia was confused. Surely, she was afraid of him, but she didn't think that she could simply overcome her fear of him. If anything, seeing the man in person made her fear him more.

Suddenly she remembered something her father used to tell her ever since she was a girl.

"It's okay to be afraid. Every living being is afraid of something, but being able to stand up against what you fear defines who you are."

She smiled, but Mathis didn't take it kindly.

"What's so, funny girl?"

She pointed at Mathis, almost close enough to touch him if her real body was there.

"Mathis! I am the sister of Caedus and Cedric!"

Mathis actually took a step back. *Sister? Surely I would have known by now that Cedric had a sister.*

"And you killed their father, the Champion of the King!"

"Ah, I see, you are not of their bloodline." He turned his back to her. "So you were raised with young Caedus, I take it? While I raised Cedric?"

"You sound like as if you adopted him! You murderer! Kidnapper! Torturer!"

He faced her again. "It is most unwise to insult me, you arrogant girl. What are you going to do? You and Caedus are going to kill me? And take Cedric back? Open your eyes. I let Cedric do as he pleases. All of his actions are of his own accord."

"You're lying! Sheska told me when we were in the dungeons. She is terrified of you, and the rest who you have here against their will."

"You must have met Cedric however brief in Cresthill."

"Yes, what of it?" Emilia asked with impatience.

"Have you seen his eyes? They are yellow like mine."

"What is that supposed to mean?" Emilia's tone was getting bolder with each exchange.

"My other disciples have normal eyes, but Cedric does not. Why do you think that is?"

Emilia didn't have an answer.

"Because Cedric enjoys being evil, just like me."

Emilia couldn't hide her worry. What if Mathis was right? What if she and Caedus couldn't get Cedric back? What if he doesn't want to come back? The look on her face made Mathis laugh, which echoed throughout the castle.

"You must be lying!" she shouted.

"I am a lot of things, but a liar is not one of them."

"As you say," she said mockingly. Her confidence in the conversation grew because Mathis didn't know where she really was, so he couldn't hurt her. Now he knew who she was, their next meeting was inevitable, but now she felt more at ease to have had this exchange with her lifelong enemy up close.

No one was unstoppable. She has Caedus, her father, Alanna, Avaline, and Cresthill behind her. United they will not lose to one man, and she was going to lead them.

"This conversation has been...interesting, young Emilia. Our paths will cross again, and sooner than you think."

"Count on it!" She felt a weight lifted off her. Her fear turned into courage. Then she saw a bright blue light, and then nothing.

Alanna woke up floating in a warm pool of glowing blue water. She realized that she could stand with the water at chest height, so she began to try and figure out where she was.

"Is this part of the trial?"

After looking around she realized that the trial was over. She could feel...life all around her. Life in the water, life in the mist and rocks surrounding her, and she could feel three people are near. One had a significantly stronger presence than the other two. That must be Avaline.

Another one was a familiar feel, which must be Emilia. The third person, she never crossed paths with because she can't sense who it could be.

It was strange. She was just gifted magic senses, and it already felt right. She felt more whole than she ever had been. She guided herself toward where Emilia was. When she found her, Emilia was still unconscious, still floating in the water.

Suddenly she jerked awake, violently coughing.

"Emilia! It's okay! I'm here." Alanna rubbed her back and pushed Emilia's hair out of her eyes. She cupped her cheek and smiled. "Are you okay?"

Emilia breathed deeply a few times. She felt...Alanna's presence, soothing and friendly. Much deeper of a connection than when she last saw her. "Yes, I'm fine." She pulled Alanna in for a hug.

Their magic senses intertwined to create an unbreakable bond of friendship. Both sensed it together and smiled.

"We did it, Em. Let's go find Avaline."

They held hands as they looked for the wizard and whoever was keeping her company. The water started to slowly drain away, so they could walk again. After a few twists and turns, they found Avaline and a scary figure next to her.

Avaline gave her staff to the scary man and reached her arms out to hug both younger ladies. "You passed the trial, congratulations! I can already sense your power, both of you."

They all smiled. When they separated, the wizard retrieved her staff.

The tall figure came out into the light and greeted both of them. "Congratulations the both of you." He smiled. He reached out to give each of them a handshake.

"Thank you. And what is your name?" Alanna asked.

"I am Ezrian. I am one of the seven guardians. I am here to take you back to your realm."

"I see. Thank you." She slightly bowed.

Ezrian was a head taller than Emilia, who was the tallest of the ladies. He had red skin and long black hair with a long goatee with blue eyes, and his veins seemed to be glowing blue as well. He carried a spear and wore black pants and boots with a brown vest.

"If I am not mistaken," Emilia asked Ezrian, "you are a demon, are you not?"

He smiled. "Yes, I am. Most of my race are evil, but I turned my back to that life a long time ago."

"I see. I am interested to hear more about your life sometime, if you had the time."

"Of course, my young friend. All you have to do is come back here and I'll tell you all you need to know, but from what Avaline has told me, you have much to do back on Afelith."

"Yes, we do. I shall come whenever I can."

Ezrian smiled again. "And I will be here."

"How do we get back?" Alanna asked.

Ezrian slashed the air with his spear, tearing a hole in the air, and the other side was Zeledon. The ladies exchanged their good-byes to the demon and jumped through.

IX

BROTHERS' REUNION

CEDRIC LAY DOWN ON A small bedroll in a cell he was put in by Regan after putting a massive beating on him. During the fight, Giselle didn't engage, partly in fear in what might have happened to her and partly because the thought Cedric had some ulterior motive for her to come with him in the first place. To her it seemed that he was about to reveal his plan.

"I grow tired of asking," Regan said with his arms folded across his chest. "Why are the two of you trespassing on my land?"

Cedric finally stood up. Giselle didn't like to see pain on her companion's face, but she didn't show her concern. She was sipping a cup of tea on a wooden chair outside of the cell.

"I want to obtain one of the legendary weapons this land supposedly carries." He shot Giselle a look and winked. "I kidnapped this *elf* on the way. From what I have heard, elves have the magic to break barriers to get into lands like these."

Regan looked toward the elf without turning his head. "Is this true?"

She had no idea Cedric was going to pull something like this, but then again she wasn't a wanted fugitive like he was. In a way he was trying to protect her, which was sweet, so she went along with it. She nodded her head nervously to Regan, to play off that what Cedric was saying was true.

If for some reason he didn't believe her, she showed him her wrists, which had rope burns on them from her hands being bound.

It seems that he was telling the truth, Regan thought.

Cedric tried to hide the surprise on his face. If Regan looked at him, it might have given up the whole charade but he was looking at Giselle's wrists. He didn't really tie her up. Was she using illusion magic? She must have. There was no other way. She gave Cedric a quick wink without Regan noticing.

⚬⚬⚬

Caedus and the Overseer made it to the abandoned city in the heart of Zeledon. Well, it is mostly abandoned. Six of the seven guardians live here, with the exception of the Overseer who lives closer to the border in his cabin. These days Zelodon is mostly used just as a mutual meeting place of the guardians, and on occasion they used the jail for suspicious characters that trespassed, such as today.

"What do you intend to do to them?" Caedus asked.

"I'm not sure. It depends really."

"Depends on what?"

"Why they came here to start. Every once in a while traders come through here, which is of no concern to anyone, but these people were in open conflict with my apprentice. So I will question them, get both sides of the story, then come up with a verdict."

"I see. So since these lands are independent from the other kingdoms, you are free to do as you please to these people?"

"That is correct, but don't get me wrong. We are not tyrants, nor do we lust for blood. We are fair. We have a sense of honor."

"That's good. I would imagine that most people wouldn't take the same actions if they were in your place."

The Overseer smiled. "And that is why I have been chosen to oversee what goes on here."

"Chosen by who?"

"That is"—the Overseer looked at the younger man—"a story for another time."

They arrived at the town jail that looked worn on the outside with bars on the windows. Once they got inside, Caedus noticed how dusty it was. Before today it must not have been used in years. The Overseer led them downstairs where the cells were.

"I feel something…"

"What is it?" the Overseer asked with interest.

"I don't know, I feel a sense of familiarity…from someone down there."

"Huh, I guess we will find out why."

Regan saw his master coming toward him with someone else. *Who is that?*

"Regan, my boy!" the Overseer gestured for Caedus to move forward. "This young man is Caedus. I will oversee some of his training later."

They shake hands.

"Nice to meet you, Caedus."

"Likewise."

"Who do we have here?"

Caedus couldn't shake the connection he felt in here. He looked around the room. It was the person in the cell, but he was sitting in the corner covered in shadow. While the Overseer and Regan talked, Caedus walked up to the cell.

"Get up! Show yourself!"

He was louder than he intended, loud enough to stop the others from talking.

"What's wrong, Caedus?" the Overseer asked.

The man stood up to reveal who he was.

"Cedric?"

The Overseer patted his shoulder. "Do you know this man?"

"He is my brother."

The Overseer shot Cedric a look. "Come closer into the light, young man."

He took a few steps forward and took his hat off.

"I see now! You strongly resemble your father, son of Savas."

Cedric slightly bowed. "Thank you for the compliment."

Caedus turned around. "Can you leave us? I would like to speak to my brother alone for a while."

Regan shot the Overseer a curious look, but the older man nodded. "So be it, Caedus. We shall go upstairs."

The elven women, followed by the two guardians, left the room to leave the brothers alone. They were face-to-face now, separated by iron bars.

"Talk to me, brother."

"About what?" Cedric asked.

"Everything!" Caedus grabbed his collar and pulled him even closer to the bars. His face was now against them. "Why haven't you come back? What has he done to you?" he asked while staring into the yellow eyes of evil his brother possessed.

From looking at both of them, most people would guess that Caedus was physically stronger out of the two. He was muscular and built bigger, not to say that Cedric wasn't in good shape. He was leaner and probably faster. It didn't seem that Cedric would be able to release his brother's massive grip on him. He at the very least thought he deserved to be yelled at like that in his own mind.

"Too much story to tell," he said while looking down, ashamed.

"Well," Caedus said as he let go and sat down in the same chair the elven woman was in. "It seems right now that we have some time."

"It seems that you are right, brother." He sat down as well, cross-legged on the floor.

"Did he do that to your face?"

Cedric felt the marks Mathis left on him last night, the five puncture wounds through his cheek. "Yes," he said in a whisper.

"Tell me what this Lord Mathis of yours wants. What's the end game for him?"

Cedric looked up at Caedus. "He wants to use the legendary weapons together, at least the ones that control certain elements. Wind, fire, water and ice, lightning, and earth."

"What does he plan to do with all that power?" Caedus asked with alarming concern. "He is already powerful enough!"

"I don't know. He never told us," Cedric whispered. "I think he plans to kill all of us when we get the weapons for him anyway."

Caedus took a deep breath. "Why wouldn't he just get the weapons himself then, instead of using you?"

"The thing about these legendary weapons, not just anybody can use them."

"What do you mean?" Caedus asked.

"These weapons are not chosen by a wielder, the weapons themselves choose a wielder."

"I don't understand, Cedric. What do you mean they choose their own wielders?"

Cedric looked up at his brother. "The weapons are alive, Caedus. If they so choose, they will not obey someone who attempts to use their power by force."

"That's very…interesting. So what if the weapons you are after won't let you wield them? The whole plan just goes under."

"I thought that as well, but Lord Mathis has the gift of foresight. He looked into our futures to see where we had to go for our compatible weapons."

"I see, so the four apprentices of Mathis you are a part of? Was that elven woman one of them?"

"No, I kidnapped her on the way here." Cedric let his false sense of being ashamed overwhelm the fact that he was lying.

"What? Why?"

"These lands have barriers, do they not? I figured that it would be easier to bring a more attuned magical creature such as an elf to help me break in."

"As you probably figured out, that wasn't necessary. Now you probably scared that poor woman for life." Caedus was beginning to wonder by doing such an act if his brother is redeemable at all.

"You may be right, but I couldn't take any chances."

Caedus sat back down. "What do you mean? Why are you even here?"

"One of the weapons is located here. The lightning blade is somewhere in Zeledon."

"Do you know where exactly? And do the guardians know about it?" Caedus was curious. He was hanging on everything Cedric was saying.

"The king possesses the fire blade. That's why he was attacked the other day. My partner Brock should be able to wield it with his powers. The locations of most of the legendary weapons were in the king's study. Therion caught me though, as you already knew."

"Sheska was telling the truth then."

Cedric now stood up. "So you met her?"

"Yes. When me and Em stopped her, the guards thought that the three of us were in on an assassination attempt of the king. So the three of us were tied up together in the same room. We had nothing to do but talk, so we got to know her a little."

"Who is Em?"

Caedus smiled. "I was raised with her. She is like a sister to me. The two of you would get along well I would imagine."

Cedric scoffed. "In another life maybe."

Caedus shook his head. "No. This is the one life we have. Make the most of it and come back with us to Cresthill."

Cedric stood up. "I am a wanted man in Cresthill! I killed two men and escaped prison. I will not be welcome there, except in the gallows."

"That's not true!"

"Your naivety is astounding, Caedus! If I go back to Cresthill, I will be executed!"

Caedus looked down ashamed.

"Do you think just because our father was friends with the king that he would just look the other way? I didn't do a petty crime that could be overlooked, like rob a store. I took lives and destroyed a part of the city."

Caedus grabbed the bars between him and his brother and leaned on them. "I know! But you are my brother! We were born to protect each other, no matter what! I would go to the ends of the earth to keep you alive. There can always be another way." He put his head down and whispered, "I don't want you to leave again, Cedric. Don't leave me again. Let's work it all out, Mathis, all of it. Let's do it together, please." Caedus tried to hide the fact that his hands were shaking, so he put them behind his back.

Cedric also put his head down. "If only it were that easy. I can't explain how Mathis controls us. It would be hard to understand."

"Try me."

Cedric looked up at him. "Mathis can use us, like puppets, in a sense."

"What do you mean?"

"All of our bodies are…tied to him somehow. With simple hand motions, he can control the way we move. We are literally his puppets, but he also gives us free will. But of course, if we don't do something he doesn't like, he will use us as he sees fit."

"I see. Does he use this on you often?"

"No, almost never. He pulled all of us toward him when we escaped Cresthill, so we couldn't be followed by your faeds. He used a portal to pull us through and closed it just before the faeds got close enough."

"You know," Caedus said as he sat back down. "Therion and I were in pursuit after you just behind the faeds, but we were knocked back by the garment shop exploding. I assume the man who helped you escape can control fire?"

"I had no idea that you were also after us. And yes, my partner can control fire in a sense. He can make things explode by touching them. We think if he takes the king's fireblade it can help keep his powers under control."

"I see, so that's what he was doing. He created distractions by making different areas of the marketplace go up in flames."

Cedric nodded.

"Was he raised with you? And Sheska?"

"Yes, they were. Sheska and I are very close. Brock and I, we are like brothers, but we don't always see eye to eye. We train together all the time, mostly because we want to beat each other senseless sometimes."

"What of the other? There are four of you?"

"Yes, the fourth. She is the closest to Lord Mathis. Her name is Minerva. Human, black hair, yellow eyes like mine."

"Where is she now?"

"Back at our hideout with Mathis most likely. She is adept in potion making, so she is always in Mathis's lab, coming up with new things to make."

"Like what?"

"Temporary endurance enhancers, magic boosters, things like that."

"I see." Caedus looked into his brother's yellow eyes. "So you inherited our father's powers? Through his Windblade?"

Cedric gave a half smile and whispered, "Yes, yes, I have. I reached beyond a level he was able to obtain in his lifetime."

"So his Windblade deemed you worthy of being its new wielder?"

"I found out that Father made his blade accessible to the both of us."

"Before Mathis murdered him and took you away."

Cedric looked down and nodded.

"What do you think Father would think of you now? What you have become? To use his own weapon to kill people."

Cedric violently grabbed his brother through the bars. He couldn't contain his tears. "Do not...Do not ask me that!" he whispered in a shaky voice. "The only comfort I take in his death is that he hasn't seen what I have become."

Caedus grabbed his brother's arms and leaned his forehead against his. "There is always another way. We just have to figure it out. Don't you want to redeem yourself?"

"There is no redemption for me, brother," Cedric said in a serious cold tone.

Anger flared in Caedus from what he just heard. "Why would you think that?"

"Look at me!" His eyes glowed with fury and hate. "I am a murderer, a kidnapper, a wanted man. I'm the apprentice of the dark lord! I cannot go back to a normal life!" Cedric felt for the empty sheath that usually carried the Windblade on his back, only to feel nothing there.

Caedus was leaning on the bars. "What are you reaching for? Father's blade? Where is it?"

"When I was captured, I must have dropped it but I can call it back to me whenever I want." He smiled.

Caedus cupped his chin. "What do you mean?"

"Just watch." Cedric raised his arm as if reaching for something. After about twenty seconds or so nothing happened.

"Watch what?" Caedus was getting impatient.

Cedric rolled his eyes. "Just wait, it's almost here."

Cedric looked at the small window at the top corner of his cell. It had two bars on it so a person couldn't crawl out of it, but a weapon could fit through. The Windblade soared through the window and landed in Cedric's hand.

Caedus took a few steps back.

"No matter where I am, the Windblade could always find me."

Caedus heard of the legendary weapons doing things like that, but seeing it was a different matter entirely. "Impressive, brother. So what happens now? I can't just let you escape."

Cedric sheathed his sword onto his back. He hesitantly looked back at his sword as if it said something to him.

Caedus's eyes widened. "Did the Windblade just...whisper to you?"

"You heard that as well? I thought I was the only one who can hear him speak."

The blade vibrated on his back. *I can be heard of anyone in the Savas bloodline.*

"So Mathis cannot hear you?" Caedus asked.

That is correct, Master Caedus.

"You know I cannot just let you help my brother escape!"

We don't want to escape. We want you to come with us.

"The only reason I would go with you is to kill Mathis. Are you willing to help me do that?"

We both know that you are too weak to face Mathis. It would be a no contest.

"Then what do you want with me?"

"The lightning blade that we seek. We have reason to believe that it will answer to you, not me," Cedric interjected.

If for some reason it doesn't accept you as a master, the Windblade went on. *I could attempt to persuade it to answer to you.*

"I see," Caedus said.

I don't think it will come to that though.

Before Caedus could respond, the entire back wall of the cell Cedric was in burst into bricks flying in all directions, hitting the brothers, but most of the impact landing on Cedric.

When the dust cleared, Caedus saw a blue dragon crouched over Cedric. It bit his clothing to lift him up and flip him over its head onto its back because the break-in must have knocked him out.

The bars were still intact, so Caedus couldn't get to his brother.

Before the dragon flew off, Cedric woke up.

"Mordecai!" he yelled. "Not yet! Break these bars down!"

Mordecai, the dragon, used its tail to knock the bars away for Caedus could get closer. He barely just got out of the way as the bars flew in different directions around the room.

"Why do you have a dragon?" Caedus asked.

Cedric pet it on the head. "Mordecai here is my friend. I raised him since he was born. He followed the Windblade as I called it here, so he knew where to break me out."

"Loyal friend." Caedus folded his arms. "Tell me about your plans before the guardians come back down here."

"There is no time!" He hesitated for a moment and looked around. "Caedus…do you trust me?"

Caedus left his mouth open, deciding on how he should answer. There wasn't much time until the guardians came downstairs. He reached out with his newfound senses and attempted to read his brother's intention. The only thing he felt from Cedric was…sincerity. He wasn't lying!

"I do!"

Cedric smiled. "Then follow my lead. He won't hurt you."

"You mean the drago—" Before he could finish, Mordecai wrapped his tail around Caedus. His arms were stuck, so he couldn't resist.

Regan and the Overseer made it to the wreckage, but they were too late. To their eyes Cedric escaped while taking Caedus away. The Overseer snapped his head toward Regan.

"Can you teleport into the air to catch them?"

Regan shook his head. "No, not in the air. If only Therion were here, he would be strong enough to throw one of us up."

"It seems we are too late now."

"We can't just sit here though!"

"We should summon the baccus. We need Therion here to track the dragons scent. His nose is stronger than the baccus's, but we should have both of them here. Avalene as well. If this goes sideways, we need the three of them together. That's our best chance against a dragon."

"I see. Should I summon the baccus?" Regan asked.

"There may be no need. Therion would have heard this wall break and the dragon roar from the cabin."

"Are you serious? I know he has superhuman senses, but he is miles away."

The Overseer smiled. "I'm sure he will be here soon enough. I sense the baccus on the move already."

"What of the elven woman?"

"As I see it, she may do as she pleases. Also the ladies should be back anytime now from the Well of Magic."

"Who do you mean?" Giselle asked as she came down the stairs. She looked at the damaged wall and gasped. "By the goddess! What could have done this?"

"A dragon by the looks of it. The prisoner must have had it waiting to break him out," the Overseer said while looking into the sky.

"That is just…dreadful. I hope you catch that horrible man!"

"As do we, my lady. He took his brother with him," Regan said.

"Is there anything I can do to help?"

The Overseer looked at the elf. "Some of his companions are making their way to my cabin. We will come up with a plan when they get there."

Giselle smiled. "I would very much like to meet them."

X

AN ANCIENT PROPHECY

SHESKA FELT RELIEVED. SHE AND Brock gave it their all against Lord Mathis, and in her opinion they really took it to him. His armor was severely damaged, and for the first time they drew blood against their master. It certainly was a confidence booster for sure, but at the same time she couldn't help but think, was Mathis holding back on them?

When she took the root Mathis gave her, she has never been in a more relaxed state. That's why she fought so well against him, with no worry or fear. She never liked to admit it, but she was more so on the cowardly side; but earlier has proven to her that to grow as a magic user, a fighter, and a person, she must overcome her fears and face them.

After her bath she went to see how Brock was doing. He has taken a lot more damage than she has in the fight, mostly because she thought Mathis targeted him specifically more than her. Not to say he couldn't take it. He was big and strong, but there was no other like Mathis. They have reason to believe that he was still hiding some of his abilities from them.

When she got to Brock's room, she noticed his hands were shaking. "Are you okay?"

He looked at her and smiled. "Yeah, it's just adrenaline."

She stroked the cuts and bruises all over his face. "How about these?"

"They will be fine. Nothing major, surprisingly."

"Yeah, your right. Hey, do you think Lord Mathis is changing?"

"What do you mean?"

She stood next to Brock, who towered above her, next to the window. "I mean, he went easy on us. At least, I think he did."

Brock squinted and grabbed his chin. "Maybe."

"The other night he almost killed you, if it weren't for Cedric intervening. He is too powerful when he is angry."

"Yes, but…when we fought him, he wasn't angry, he was…enjoying himself." His eyes widened a bit. "Actually, that was the first time I think I ever seen Mathis happy, at least in the small extent it was."

"I see that you do not speak ill of me as you did the other day." Lord Mathis said behind them.

Sheska grabbed her chest and lost her footing for a second. "Lord Mathis, I had no idea you were behind us."

Brock was just as surprised. "Were you there the whole time?"

"No, I just got here." He grabbed their shoulders. "I have a job for the two of you."

"What do you need, my lord?" Sheska asked.

"As you know, Cedric and his Windblade are bonded. They make each other stronger."

"Yes, what of it?" Sheska asked.

"Each of you can be bonded with such a weapon. It is only a matter of finding where yours may be located."

"I see," Brock said. "So the king's fireblade, that was meant for me?"

Mathis smiled. "Exactly, but we shall acquire that one another time." He looked at Sheska. "I may have found where we could find yours, girl."

She looked at her master curiously. "So you mean to say…that all of us have an enchanted weapon to create a psychic link with?"

"Yes. I have foreseen it."

"What about Giselle?" Brock asked.

"She already has hers."

"Those two daggers of hers?" Brock asked.

Mathis nodded.

"I never would have guessed. So only Sheska and I are left?"

Mathis nodded again.

"What of this lightning blade you need? None of our powers involve lightning."

"That is what I need personally."

"I see. So where are you going to send us today?" she asked.

"I am sending the two of you to the Ice Mountains in Alexandria."

"The Ice Mountains?" Brock asked concerningly. "Do you know how far that is, and dangerous?"

"Yes, I do." Mathis eyed both of them. "I wouldn't send you there unless I thought you two could handle it together."

Brock folded his arms. "You know that no one has ever come back from the Ice Mountains."

"There's a first time for everything." His laugh echoed inside the castle walls as he left the room.

Avaline lead the way from the well back to Zeledon, followed by Ezrian, who had Emilia and Alanna holding on to his staff to prevent them from falling between the realms. When travelling between the realms, you cross through a vortex that moves impossibly fast. If someone were to fall through while between realms, you may end up anywhere and never seen again.

The thought of falling terrified Emilia and Alanna. They held on so hard to Ezrian's staff that it may have started to crack. Since they were hanging from both sides, they noticed the middle of the staff was starting to bend from their weight on each side. They looked at each other concerningly, and without a word they instinctively hugged each other and held on to the middle of the staff to stop it from a potential break.

After moving so fast, they arrived back on Afelith. Avaline and Ezrian landed on their feet perfectly while the younger ladies fell on the ground. Avaline looked at them and smiled.

"Soon enough you both will learn how to travel through the realms with ease and without fear. It takes time."

Alanna sprung to her feet first and held her hand out for Emilia. She looked up and grabbed her hand with a smile. Just as she was being pulled up, she grimaced and pulled her hand away.

"I'm sorry, Em. Did I hurt you?" Alanna asked.

Emilia looked down at her hand. The blood pact she made with Caedus from the future was still there, a large gash across the palm of her hand. "No, it wasn't you. I thought this would go away after the trial. I guess what happened was permanent?"

Alanna grabbed her hand. "This looks terrible. What happened?"

Before Emilia was able to say a word, Avaline interrupted her. "What happened in your trials is only meant for you to know, no one else."

Em brushed some of her blue hair out of her face. "As you say."

The wizard nodded. "Let us go back to the Overseer's cabin to bandage that up for you."

"Yes, and drink some wine. I am exhausted," Alanna said with a smile.

"Congratulations the two of you," Ezrian said while leaning on his partially bent staff. "I sense that you intend to use your magic for the greater good."

"Yes!" Alanna shouted a little louder than she expected. "We want to protect the people of Cresthill and whoever so needs our help."

"That is good to hear."

Emilia and Alanna noticed how bent his staff was.

"I'm sorry on behalf of both of us for what we did to your staff," the elf said.

"Oh, this old thing? Don't worry about it." He tapped it on the ground, and as he did, it became as good as new. Strait as an arrow. "See? Good as new!"

"That's a neat trick," Emilia said quietly. "Are you coming to the cabin with us?"

As the sun rose, the contact on his red skin started to burn. He put his hood up. "No, I must get back. Someone has to guard the well at all times."

"I see. Thank you for helping us get back." She shook his massive hand.

He proceeded to shake all of their hands before departing into the portal they came from.

"Shall we go back to the cabin?" Avalene asked.

Both of the younger ladies smiled and nodded.

"If Caedus and the Overseer are not back yet, we can pick Therion up and head toward Zeladon."

"That's the abandoned city in the heart of these lands?" Alanna asked.

"Very good, Alanna!" the wizard said with a smile. "Not many people are even aware of its existence."

"I like to read about history on my spare time."

"A very good subject to know. Those who don't learn from the past are doomed to repeat it." Her staff seemed to disappear in midair when she put her arms around both younger ladies. "Emilia, Alanna, you have taken your first steps into a larger world. Are you ready for this?"

"We will do whatever it takes!" Emilia shouted.

"That's good to hear. At first having magic senses can be overwhelming and you may be disoriented at times, but I am here to help you control it."

"In what way do you mean?" Alanna asked.

Avalene looked at the elf and moved some of her scarlet hair that was blocking a portion of her face. "Since you came out of your trial, couldn't you…feel Emilia's presence when she was nearby? Followed by Ezrian and myself?"

"Come to think of it, yes."

"When you have magic, when anyone has magic, they can sense others. Mostly only other magic users. Sometimes strong emotions from a person or animal. You can literally feel anger or hate someone may have toward someone or you can feel the love and joy family members share together. It is everywhere, and at first it will be overwhelming. Going back to the city would not be wise for a while."

"How can you sense magic users from normal people?" Emilia asked.

The wizard moved her lips in a strange motion, side to side as if she had so etching in her mouth. Sometimes she did that while she was thinking. "It's hard to explain. It would be easier to show by example. I guess you could say…a person who wields magic has a more intense presence compared to a normal person."

"I see. Interesting." She grabbed her hand again. She almost forgot that she was still bleeding.

"Let's get inside, shall we?" Alanna asked. "Let's fix that hand up."

"Yeah, don't you notice that—"

"That your father is not here despite the Overseer's instructions," Avalene interrupted.

"Exactly," Emilia said quietly. "Do you think everything is okay?"

"We shall find out soon enough." Avalene pointed to the cabin and put her hand on Alanna's shoulder. "Fix her up inside. I shall look around."

"As you say. Be careful," the elf said.

The wizard nodded and walked away. Her staff materialized in her hand again, mostly to pose as her walking stick it seemed, but a wizard's magic is amplified tenfold with their staff. Even though she may not need it, she used it as a warning in a way. If any sort of troublemakers such as a petty thief or vandals sees a wizard with a staff, they may think twice before trying anything around her.

They have been up all night, and the sun has just risen. She was too tired to get into a conflict with anyone. Even though Zeledon were among the safest places in the world, the recent activities of Lord Mathis has put her on edge, more than she would like to admit.

She pressed the jewel on the top of her staff onto the side of her head and pulled out a transparent flowing thread out of her mind, which made the jewel glow. The glow was bright enough to blind anyone in front of her. She raised the staff, then slammed it on the ground, creating a massive shockwave. It didn't create any damage, just intense winds around her. Once the dust settled, her senses were able to reach a much wider range. She was feeling for Therion's presence. His aura was stronger than most people. He had a very strong presence, and since she couldn't sense him, he must have been far away.

Come to think of it, the last time she used the jewel to amplify her magic must have been decades ago. Her staff harnessed power, but the jewel she always liked to use as a last resort, but something in the air felt foul. Something was out of place; she could feel it. Was that why Therion left the cabin? What did he and the baccus go after?

She stood still and reached out with her senses, but Therion was nowhere to be found. She sensed the baccus with Victor running toward the city. Therion wasn't with them though, but something else was. A darker presence, a wild presence. It was Therion's werewolf alter ego.

The wolf was running alongside the baccus, both of them at incredible speeds, faster than any horse can run. But what are they running toward?

⟷

Caedus couldn't move. The dragon had him bound with its tail. It was hard to breathe, but before he was taken, he sensed that Cedric's intentions were genuine. He wasn't in any danger, or at least he would like to hope so. They were hundreds of feet up in the air, if the dragon were to loosen his tail, he would fall to his death.

Cedric must have put up the charade that Caedus was being taken against his will so it wouldn't seem like he was colluding with a wanted man. Caedus appreciated Cedric trying to protect him like that, but it never should have come to a situation like this. Why did Mathis have to destroy the lives they had as kids? They were robbed of growing up together, and now they are estranged young men.

Caedus was getting himself too angry by thinking about Mathis. He took a few deep breaths, well, not really deep because the dragon was almost squeezing the life out of him. He tried to speak out over the intense sound of the wind.

"Where are you taking me?"

"To the location of the lightning blade," Cedric yelled without looking back at his brother dangling in the sky.

"Let me on the dragon's back."

"No!" he shouted. "We have to keep up the appearance of you being taken against your will. That way they won't charge you with aiding a wanted man."

"I appreciate what you are doing, but no one can see us up here."

"You never know." He turned around this time and adjusted his hat. "I don't want to take that chance with all of these guardians around. We only met two so far. There are five more."

"Seven?" Caedus asked.

"Yeah, I said the same thing after Regan took me in." Cedric patted the dragon's back and pointed to the north. "That's where we have to go, boy."

Mordecai roared and straightened like an arrow to increase his speed. Cedric loved when he did that; but Caedus, on the other hand, didn't feel comfortable swaying back and forth and bound by the tail. The dragon landed hard on the ground while making sure to keep his tail up so Caedus didn't violently land on the ground. Cedric gestured for his brother to be released. The dragon hissed at Caedus reluctantly, then let him go.

Once he landed on the ground, Cedric held one arm against his brother's back to keep up the illusion that Caedus was there against his will. A small opening to a cave were next to them, and according to Cedric's information, the lightning blade should be inside.

"This way, Caedus. Let's get inside and with haste!"

"All right, all right. Take it easy."

Once they got inside, the dragon blocked the pathway so no others may enter.

When Caedus turned around due to lack of light, it seemed like that dragon blended in with the cave wall. "How did he…?"

"Mordecai can camouflage into his environment. So now if anyone goes to look for us, all they see is big rocks on a small hilltop because he blocked the way. To them he will just look like one of the rocks."

"I see, very useful." He turned to look at Cedric. "Where did you even find a dragon? Let alone an obedient one."

"Brock and I found an egg in Alexandria a few years ago. When it hatched, I was the first thing he saw and I have taken on the role of his parent ever since."

"That's nice." Caedus patted Cedric's shoulder. "I'm glad you found some form of happiness over the years."

Cedric didn't turn around, but he smiled. "Yeah…Mordecai, my growing boy. You know he is only grown into one third of his size?"

"Really? He is already massive!"

"Yes, he is! Let us talk of Morty another time. Let's us focus on the task at hand."

"As you say, brother." He was partially leaning against the cave wall because it was so dark, but Cedric seemed unaffected.

"Can you see in here?" Caedus asked.

"Yes. With my yellow eyes, I can see in the dark just fine." He looked back at Caedus. "It's the only upside of having them, I suppose."

"What do you mean?"

"You have no idea what I had to do to obtain these eyes," Cedric said in a faint whisper.

Caedus felt a huge weight of guilt his brother now felt. As fast as it came, it was now gone.

He can control his emotions very well, Caedus thought.

The pathway was very linear, no room for exploration really. Cedric lead the way with Caedus close behind. As they continued along the path, they also went deeper and deeper underground. Naturally, as they went deeper, it got much colder. Cedric had more layers of clothing on, so he felt fine. Caedus lived on the top of a mountain. Yes, it was cold up there, but not like this. It's almost to the point where both of them could see their breath.

After about another hour of treading along, they were finally getting somewhere. It became less dark, but there was no fire. It was easier for Caedus to see without his brother's aid.

Where was the source of light coming from? they both wondered as they made their way and realized the source was in the walls. Ancient markings were all over the walls illuminated with yellow light.

It was mostly writing in a forgotten tongue as well as drawings. As they walked along, it seemed to tell a story.

"Can you read this?" Cedric asked.

"A little. I studied ancient languages with Avalene."

"What language is this?"

Caedus felt some of the markings on the wall. He pointed to a drawn figure holding a staff. "You see this?" He looked toward Cedric, who nodded. "This is a mage. This seems to be one of the languages they used before they were wiped out."

Cedric folded his arms. "So you're saying that these markings are over a thousand years old?"

"At least."

"What does it say?"

Both of them followed the drawings carved into the walls. Some were surprisingly detailed, and each drawing had text underneath. The first one was a mother holding two babies, one in each arm.

"The twins will rise." Caedus started to walk to the next one.

"Is that all it said?" Cedric asked.

"Yes, let's move on."

The next drawing showed the twins grown-up in hooded cloaks holding their hands out in unison seeming to try to close a portal. Behind them was the same woman, their mother it seemed to be, holding her hands out too, to help them close the rift.

"The twins will vanquish evil and bring everlasting peace to the realm."

"What do you suppose that means?" Cedric's interest had peaked.

"Rather vague, don't you think?" Caedus faced his brother. "Do you think that could be us?"

"I cannot say. The thing I am more interested in is the woman. If this is us, then that means she must be our mother. We don't know a single thing about her, not even her name. Maybe she will find her way back to us?"

"There is one man who might know about her," Caedus said quietly. He almost hesitated to say anything at all. Twenty years and no mention of their mother. Does he even want to make an attempt to get to know her? To contact her in any way? Why did she abandon them when they were born? A part of him didn't want to see her, and another part of him always wanted to. Both of them felt that way actually.

"Who do you mean?" Cedric asked.

He tried to hide his excitement. You couldn't see it, but Caedus sensed it.

"The Overseer. He was the one who accompanied me to your cell. He knows every person in the world who has magic powers—or at least it seems that way. He knew our father. He must know who our mother is."

Cedric wiped his forehead. "We can figure that out later. Let's get what we came here for."

Caedus nodded as they moved on.

They didn't have to walk that far, another fifty paces or so before the cave was at an end, and on the back was a world map, even bigger than the one in the Cresthill study.

"It seems that the lightning blade is not here, but the mark of the real location is."

Cedric then turned his back to the map.

"What are you doing?" Caedus asked.

"You must be the one to find the lightning blade so Mathis can't have it. He can sense if I'm lying. So If I don't know where it is, I wouldn't be lying to him about it."

"I see, clever approach." Caedus continued to look for the real location of the blade while Cedric went back to look at the ancient drawings on the wall. "Wait, Cedric."

"What is it?" he said without turning around.

"You need to take me to where the lightning blade is anyway. The Windblade has to communicate with it to convince it to let me be its master."

"Shit, you're right." He turned around slowly. "No going back now. I'll do what I can to convince Lord Mathis that I couldn't retrieve the blade."

"But he will know you're making it up!" Caedus yelled. Looking at the scars on his brother's cheek, he thinks Mathis would do a lot worse if he goes back to him empty-handed.

"I'll figure it out, Caedus. I'll think of something."

"Like what?" His voice echoed through the cave with intensity.

Cedric pointed at his brother as he got closer to him. "I have an idea! I can teach you to call the Windblade as I do, so no matter how far you are, it will come to you. When we part ways, I'll take the Windblade back with me, then when you arrive at the lightning blade's real location, summon the Windblade to aid you if you need it."

"That could work! We thought it was here, so you can tell Mathis that it was supposed to be here, but it wasn't!"

"Yessss," Cedric said with a sly smile. "There is one thing I don't understand though."

"What is that, brother?"

"Where did this all come from?" Cedric said. "This ancient prophecy? Does this mean I should leave Mathis now, or wait for his plan to unfold before cutting ties with him?"

XI

WANTED

I N THE FAR NORTH ON the border of Afelith and Alexandria lies the Dwarven Mountains of Thundering Heights. A black-haired, long-bearded dwarf looked into the sky.

"Eagles? Something serious must be going on."

The other dwarf, older and almost completely white haired, yelled out from inside a cave.

"You must be seeing things! The eagles haven't been used since..." He stepped out and looked up. His eyes widened. "You speak the truth!"

Eagles are used around the world to spread news fast. They are only ever used for emergencies. They have not been seen flying the skies in decades.

"What must have happened?" the younger dwarf asked.

"We shall find out, my son," the older dwarf said.

The eagle dropped some rolled-up parchment bound by a leather cord next to where the two of them were standing. The younger dwarf reached down to pick it up and began to unwrap the cord. It was not one piece of parchment but three, three wanted posters. The first one was a young man with yellow eyes and a skinny face with long blond hair, the second person was a Xemoorian woman, and the third looked to be an Alexandrian. Wanted for murder, attempted assassination of the king of Cresthill, destruction of the city, and escaped imprisonment.

The reward was ten thousand gold pieces per person. The older dwarf's eyes widened. "Ten thousand? Each? I can finally retire with this loot. We can both retire with this! We have work to do, Dhosar."

"The offer is tempting, Father, but these people are incredibly dangerous. We need a plan, and we may need help."

"Not if we only catch one of them, at least, one at a time." The older dwarf studied the posters carefully and pointed to the girl. "You see that?"

Dhosar looked closely. "Fear in her eyes. She may be the easiest to catch. That doesn't mean it would be easy."

"Yeah, they seem to be magic users, which puts us at a disadvantage."

Dhosar was curious. "How would you know if they are magic users?"

"This one here, with the yellow eyes, at least he is a magic user. I can tell you for sure. We should steer clear of him. He may be too dangerous to capture, alive at least. He is the most dangerous of this lot," the older dwarf explained.

"Is it because of his eyes?" Dhosar asked.

"Yes, eyes like that means he has been exposed to dark magic for too long. He may look young, but he must be powerful. Those eyes I have only ever heard of before today. I never actually seen them until now."

"A bit scary, don't you think?"

The older dwarf grabbed his son's shoulders. "A little. But I am Dalog, and you are Dhosar, the greatest bounty hunter duo in these lands!"

"Yes, sir! Where should we begin?"

Dalog started to play around with some of the braids in his beard. "They recently escaped from Cresthill. They could have gone in any direction. We should head over there and stop at a few towns on the way to ask around."

"As you say, but since we are powerless against magic, wouldn't it be wise to get out of our chain mail and put on our leather armor? For better movement."

Dalog bellowed so loudly it echoed across the mountains. "Not a bad idea, my son. Let us head back home and change. We should travel in the wagon as well, keep a low profile. We don't want anyone to think we are bounty hunters. It could scare our targets into hiding."

"Let us depart, we should get on the road before midday." Dhosar patted his father on the back as they prepared to start their new hunt.

The Grey Hawks were not the only sellsword faction in Afelith. In the southern country of Xemoor was the home of the Desert Serpents led by Kashisu, Emilia's mother. Most of the Xemoorians have a similar look, all with purple hair and eyes with bronze skin due to the intense heat. Some made an effort to stand out to tell them apart from the rest of their race.

In Kashisu's case, she had a few strands of her daughter's blue hair infused into her own for a different look. Everyone knew who she was from her status as headmaster and probably the most recognizable face in all of Xemoor. She stood as the unofficial ruler of the city since there was no royalty there. Her faction was the most powerful in the city. She kept things under her control to an extent. She wasn't in charge of everything that went on. It was a place where a lot of under-the-table deals went down. It was a place where people went to disappear if they so wanted. She was more or less the face of the city.

The Desert Serpents' base was a fortress. Even the criminals in the city knew better than to try to break in. On the top of the spire was the highest point in the city. It was Kashisu's favorite place to think.

The blocking of the sun made her look up. It was an eagle dropping something off. At the sight of the eagle, Kashisu's second-in-command came running over.

"Is that an eagle?" she asked.

"Yes, Kara." Kashisu didn't bother to turn around when she answered.

Kara didn't understand how calm Kashisu always managed to be. Someone in her position undergoes a lot of stress on a regular basis, and seeing an eagle isn't an everyday affair. Something terrible must have happened, and Kashisu barely paid it any mind, like it was normal.

Kara grabbed her mentor's shoulder. "How can you be so calm when eagles are in the sky? Something must be going on."

Kashisu turned around and put her hands on Kara's shoulders. "We don't know what's going on until the eagle gives us the information. Calm down."

"Yes, mistress," she whispered.

Sometimes Kashisu couldn't believe how much Kara has grown. She was like a second daughter to her. Her hair was very short. It was also very light. Sometimes it even looked like dark pink. She liked it though. It gave her, her own look. She was of average height; and of course, whenever Caedus and Emilia were around, they bragged about how much taller they were than her. She let them have their fun because when it came to sparring, she had the upper hand on them most of the time. She lived for being the best fighter she can be. Maybe even one of the best in unarmed combat in all of Xemoor.

The eagle dropped its parchment toward the ladies. Kara caught it and handed it to her mentor.

"Let's see what we have here, shall we?" Kashisu muttered mostly to herself. She unraveled the leather chord to see the three wanted posters. "One of our own, Sheska? I don't think I know her." She handed Kara the poster of her. "Next, no known name, Alexandrian by the looks of it. He looks dangerous." She handed that poster to Kara as well. "And lastly….Cedric? My Caedus's Cedric?"

Kara snatched the poster from Kashisu's hand. "The brother that Caedus always talked about?"

"Impossible!" She looked at his face once again. "But the resemblance is there. This man looks almost exactly like Savas, Caedus's father. It must be him."

"What are we going to do about it, mistress?" Kara asked with a bit of a worry. Mostly for Caedus. Did he know of his brother's return? Kara partially grew up with Emilia and Caedus when they came to Xemoor over the years. They felt like siblings to her.

"Get some of our men ready for travel by nightfall. We are going to Cresthill."

Victor led the way toward Zeledon while riding the baccus and the wolf running beside him. About ten minutes he was about to drift off to sleep because Therion and the baccus were talking nonsense to each other for hours while drinking. He drank as well, but he had his fill. A few pints and he was satisfied, but the other two were pounding it down, almost a barrel of ale each. Humans couldn't take that much at once, but then again, neither of them were human.

Before he knew it, Therion stood up and while doing so knocked over the wooden chair. That snapped Victor out of drifting off to sleep.

"Therion? What's wrong?" the younger man asked.

"Something is wrong." He ran outside.

Victor and the baccus followed. Therion held out his hand by his ear to attempt to hear something better off in the distance.

"What is it you hear?" the baccus asked.

"Caedus has been taken captive by a dragon," he muttered.

"A dragon?" Victor yelled. "In this part of the world? Are you sure?"

"I thought I caught a whiff of dragon stench, but I thought the alcohol was playing tricks with me," the baccus said quietly.

Therion unwrapped the cloth around his arm to glance at his enchanted tattoo of the full moon, jumpstarting a transformation. His fangs grew as well as his claws, and his voice got deeper.

"I sensed it too. The dragon stench mixed with Caedus's as well as his brother Cedric's. I believe that Caedus was taken by this dragon under his brother's command. We must get to the city!"

Claws started to emerge from his boots, tearing them to shreds. His muscles grew with hair and mass, covering his skin. He screamed in pain as his body grew. The last part of the transformation was his face. His nose grew into a snout as he roared with fury.

Victor never witnessed one of Therion's transformations before. In all honesty, it was scary to him to finally see it now. He watched the man he knew disappear into a terrifying beast. He already thought Therion was tall, but this beast was at least two feet taller. The baccus had no reaction. It must have seen this transformation before.

"Are you ready to go now?" the baccus asked in a sarcastic tone.

The beast quickly turned around with focused anger toward the baccus. "Don't make me eat your flesh! Pest!"

Once again the baccus barely reacted.

The beast then turned its attention toward Victor. He tried not to flinch when it made eye contact with him. "Are you ready to go, Victor?"

He barely nodded his head. It seemed that a part of Therion was in there, but a very small part. This beast was something else entirely. It roared again and began to run toward Zeledon. It was so fast that it was almost out of sight already.

"Do you want to hop on my back?" the baccus asked.

Victor was still watching the wolf in the distance. "Yeah, let's go. Can you catch up to him?"

The baccus roared in laughter. "I am the fastest being alive!"

"As you say." Victor jumped on its back and held on to its blue-and-silver tinted fur. As the baccus began to run, Victor didn't feel any discomfort in the slightest and it felt strange. He had a lot of experience riding horses over the years on various assignments. After a while being on the saddle can get uncomfortable, but sitting on the baccus's back felt as if he were just sitting on a luxurious chair. Before he knew it they were right next to the wolf.

"Man, you weren't kidding!"

"You thought it was but a jest when I said I was the fastest alive?"

The wolf looked at them with disgust. "Don't make me laugh, you foolish rainbow!"

The baccus laughed. "Relax, you big oaf. I was just—"

"I have no time for foolishness!" the wolf snapped. "My boy could be in danger! Now get out of my way!" He then sped passed them and was gaining speed.

"We should leave him be and just follow for now," the baccus said quietly.

"You don't have to tell me twice," Victor whispered. "Do you think something really happened to Caedus?"

"I'm afraid so. I was able to sense what happened just as Therion did, but we need a clearer picture by going to where it happened in the city."

"I see. I hope he is all right."

"He should be," the baccus said with confidence.

"What makes you so sure?"

"The intruder I captured was Caedus's brother, Cedric. I believe that the wanted posters for Cedric and his companions are spreading as we speak. He will be the most recognizable face in Afelith by the end of the day."

Victor wasn't convinced. "But what does that have to do with Caedus being unharmed? We have no idea what Cedric is capable of."

"That may be true, but if Cedric has a shred of care for his brother as Caedus does for him, then I don't think he would bring any harm to him."

Victor stroked his mustache. "So you think Cedric escaped and posed a kidnapping to protect his brother from ending up on a wanted poster also?"

"Yes, I think it's a high possibility."

"The question is now, what are they trying to accomplish together?"

"The goddess only knows," the baccus said softly. "We will arrive once we get over this last hill."

"Really? That was fast!"

From his father's cabin all the way to Zeledon usually took hours, but with the baccus and the wolf racing, it only took a matter of minutes. If he didn't just ride the baccus here, he wouldn't have believed it possible.

"Up ahead I see Regan and the Overseer as well as our aggressive friend."

Victor squinted his eyes. "Who is that with them? Is that an elf?"

"Yes, she was in Cedric's custody when we caught him."

"Really? What for?"

"You can ask her now."

Victor has only been here a few times in his lifetime, and yet every time he is wowed by the beauty of what this city once was. He wished he could have seen it in its heyday. Most of the buildings still stood. Some are rubble. Some are still kept up. Most of the guardians still lived here.

The wolf ran off into one of the older buildings while Victor and the baccus stopped in the town square where the Overseer was heading to meet them. Regan and the elven woman followed.

The center of the town square stood a massive water fountain that no longer runs. It had a beautiful and intricate design that seemed to catch the elf's attention. She sat down on the stone ledge that surrounded the whole thing that kept the water inside.

Victor hopped off the baccus and reached out to shake Reagan's hand. "Where did Therion go?"

The Overseer chimed in, "It would be most unwise to call him Therion while in that form. He goes by Zakkon."

"I see," Victor said.

"He went to investigate where Caedus was taken." The Overseer put his head down. "Taken from right under our noses."

The elven woman stood up. "There was no way to know that a dragon was going to break through the wall and take them away."

"That is true, but still, for such an act to occur in the lands I sworn to protect…"

"Don't beat yourself up about it," Regan said while patting his mentor's back. "We will find them."

"And bring this Cedric to justice hopefully," the elf added.

"I'm afraid we have not been introduced." Victor shook the elven woman's hand. "I am Victor Vog, son of the Overseer and Champion of the King of Cresthill."

"A pleasure, Victor. I am Giselle, the wisdom of a small village to the north."

"I see, so you must be well adept in plants and nature, medicine making, and such."

"Yes, I am adept in nature magic. It makes my job much easier."

"That must be very useful." Victor kept a close eye on her. Under her blue robe he noticed leather armor. "Tell me, Giselle, do all wisdoms wear armor on a daily basis?"

Giselle wasn't one to panic when being called out. She had an answer for everything. "Oh this?" She loosened her robe for Victor and Regan to get a better look. The Overseer left to join Zakkon back where the breakout happened. "I am a veteran in weapon's training. From time to time I like to train in the fields beyond my village, and that's where that man, Cedric, took me." She didn't hide her anger when she spoke of Cedric.

"As you say, ma'am. I assure you that my people will bring Cedric to justice. We were in pursuit of him before he even took you."

She sighed heavily and placed her hand on her chest. "Oh, what a relief. With you and that wolf, I'm sure you will find him in no time."

"Especially since the man he just took away with this dragon is the wolf's son. It just got personal. Therion—I mean, Zakkon—will not stop until he reaches his target, in this case, Cedric. Also our team currently consists of three others—a wizard, an elf, and a human."

"You seem to have things well in hand. A wizard, you say? There are only two wizards in the world, one of them is your companion?"

"Yes, yes. Have you heard of Avaline?" Victor asked.

"Have I? Avaline is a hero of the ages! How do you know her?" Even though she was putting on an act, her excitement for the wizards was genuine. Even in an elf's long life, there still may not be a chance to run into a wizard.

"These days she resides in Cresthill. She serves as an advisor to the king. Being the Champion, we have worked together on many occasions."

"Wonderful! Simply wonderful I would love to meet her!" Cedric mentioned from time to time a woman named Avaline who watched him and his brother when they were kids when their father was away, but she had no idea that it was Avaline, the wizard.

"She is on her way here now, along with Emilia and Alanna," the baccus said from the edge of the courtyard overlooking the hills.

"Maybe you should pick them up then," Regan spat out.

"Three people on my back? You must be mad! I am no chariot. I am a living—"

"Spare us the theatrics, baccus! I know you are strong enough to hold the three of them, and anyway, it would take them hours to reach where we are. You can rest when you bring them here, you big baby."

Victor laughed. "He's right, you know."

The baccus blew through his nostrils in annoyance. "To think that the species of the baccus were once known to be godlike creatures to humans, now reduced to doing petty chores for them." He spoke to himself, but he made sure he was loud enough for the others to hear before he galloped away.

"Is he going to be okay?" Giselle asked.

Regan swiped his hand in the direction the baccus took off in. "He'll be fine. He's just dramatic. He was thinking of picking them up anyway before I even suggested it. He just wanted to give me a hard time."

"Time is of the essence. He knows what's at stake here," Victor added in.

"I see," Giselle said while she nodded. "So is that a telepathic horse?" Victor was visibly confused.

Before he could say anything, Regan answered, "Yes, ma'am, he is." He patted Victor on the back. Now he understood. The baccus is so rare these days if the wrong people found out about it they would try to hunt it and kill it for its valuable meat and bones. The baccus used his illusion magic to make this woman Giselle to see a simple horse while Victor and Regan, who know the baccus, can see it for what it really is.

"While we wait for the others, we should join my father and Zakkon."

※

In the destroyed room what was once a small jail, Zakkon, the wolf, inspected every square inch to find anything and everything he can to find a lead. The Overseer stood where the wall used to be where the dragon broke in.

"It has been some time since I have seen you in this form, Zakkon."

The wolf looked down at the man. "At least you have acknowledged me rightfully this time." His massive right claw wrapped around the Overseer's face. He didn't even react. He didn't want to give Zakkon a reason to get violent. He simply made eye contact with the beast.

"You don't want an...accident like last time, do you?"

The Overseer felt his left side and rubbed the massive scar Zakkon left him for calling him Therion by accident years ago. "Not this time." He slapped the beast's claw away.

Zakkon was furious at the gesture, but before it could react, the Overseer didn't give it the chance. "Focus at the task at hand, and stop letting your bloodlust take over! Or are you so weak that you have to give in to it? Think about Caedus! Your son! His life is all that matters now."

The beasts eyes widened, and it looked down, disappointed in itself. "I...I'm sorry, James. You're right. I must focus." Zakkon then reduced in size, turning back into Therion. He went back to normal height. The hair started to fade around his body, but all four of his claws remained and his fangs. He stayed in a half-transformed state. The Overseer knew Therion was in control now. All that remained of his clothes were tattered sections of his pants. His vest and boots were destroyed in the transformation. "I'm sorry, old friend, you know how it gets this close to the full moon. The bloodlust is almost out of control."

"It's quite all right, Therion. He only taunted me this time. He didn't resort to violence, as much as he wanted to," the Overseer stated while leaning on his scythe.

"I see. You must have said something to calm him down enough for me to come back."

"I only stated the fact that Caedus may be in danger. I know Zakkon has watched Emilia and Caedus grow up, and he would do anything for them, just like you."

"As we are one in the same," Therion said in a quiet tone.

"Don't be ashamed of Zakkon. You have the most control over yourself more than any of the other werewolves I met in my time."

"You really think so?" Therion asked with genuine curiosity.

The Overseer patted his old friend's back. "Absolutely. As you know there are not many of you left, and the few that are have no control over their bloodlust. They go on killing sprees you know that, but you don't. You have control."

Therion nodded and gave a half smile to the Overseer. He got on all fours and sniffed around the wall break. "Yeah, the stench of a dragon is unmistakable."

"We saw it with Cedric on its back and Caedus being held wrapped around its tail, but it was too far away to pursue without the baccus."

"Don't worry, dragons give off such a strong scent that I could follow it from great distances. I don't think they went too far."

"What makes you say that?"

"The stench is too strong for it to have gotten far. The strange thing is, I can't pick up the scent of the boys, as if they disappeared."

"But you can find the dragon?"

Therion smiled. "Without a doubt."

"If we get to the dragon, I'm sure the boys will not be far off."

"There is only one way to find out."

Before Therion got the chance to move, the Overseer grabbed his shoulder hard. "It would be most unwise to leave now without the baccus to help."

Therion sighed. "Are you serious? You know he's just going to complain the whole time. I don't have time for his games."

The Overseer struggled to maintain eye contact with the taller man. "I'll talk to him, and whether you like it or not, you know that we need him if we are about to face off against a dragon."

Therion shook his head.

The Overseer gripped his shoulder even harder and shook him. "A *dragon*! We will not fight one alone. We need the powers of the baccus."

Therion roared with fury and punched through some remnants of the brick wall. "So be it. Where is he?"

"He should be picking up Avaline and the girls."

"We could take Ava, but I don't want the girls to take part in this. It will be too dangerous."

"We shall discuss it when they get here."

Brock and Sheska decided the best way to cross the border into Alexandria without getting caught was to go under some of the dwarven passageways under the mountains in the borderlands. Since they were both wanted criminals, they had to figure out different looks for each other. Brock decided to let his beard grow out on this mission since it may take them weeks to get back. He stuck with a simple hooded cloak that rangers usually use. Most of them were green; some were brown. His was green. Most people left rangers alone. He thought it was the perfect cover. He slung a bow on his back to keep the ranger look, even though he never intended to use it.

Sheska cut her hair to shoulder length. Before it was down to her waist. She also dyed her hair blond and used her powers with water and ice to keep the appearance of her eyes being blue. She looked nothing like the wanted poster that was handed out across the country. They haven't stumbled upon their own wanted posters yet, but she was confident she didn't look like her normal self. Brock agreed.

Before reaching the underground of the mountains, they head to the small town of Chillpeak for supplies for the dangerous journey ahead. The town is a hidden gem really, in Sheska's opinion. The streets are filled with beautiful cobblestones of red and gray, and the townspeople are very friendly. Brock always enjoyed the food there as well as the ale. Well, Brock liked the ale everywhere, but he frequently came to Chillpeak for their own brand.

When they reached the south entrance, they crossed the small bridge above the river to enter the city. Once inside Brock nodded at the guards while making sure to keep his face in shadow with his ranger's hood. Most towns have a quest board, or job board. Chillpeak was no different. It was a way to keep up with current events in some ways.

Sheska stopped in her tracks when she looked at the center of the quest board. She violently pushed Brock to get his attention.

"What's wrong?"

She pointed at the three wanted posters of her, Brock, and Cedric.

"Oh, we must be cautious. Worry not, Sheska." He put his arm around her to lead her away from the quest board to anywhere else in the city where someone would notice who they really were. "Let's go to the pub, get some food, maybe a drink to calm down."

"Sure, let's go."

At the northern entrance to Chillpeak were two travellers approaching. The bounty hunter dwarven duo, Dalog and Dhosar.

"Ah, here we are. Let us wet our whistles with some ale. We could gather information at the pub," the older dwarf, Dalog, suggested.

"Not a bad idea," Dhosar said. "Let's go."

XII

DARKNESS RETURNS

"I T'S TOO DANGEROUS FOR THE two of you, and that's final!" Therion yelled out.

"We have every right to help you find Caedus! He's my brother!" Emilia yelled back.

Alanna thought it scary to yell at Therion like that, especially in a half-transformed state. His fangs were long and sticking out of his mouth, and his hands and feet were dangerous claws, but if anyone were to yell at him and get away with it, it would be his daughter.

"What about going up against a dragon do you not understand?" Therion spat back. "A dragon is a suicide run for me. What do you think it will be for you?"

"I'm not going to sit back while you risk your life for Caedus while I can do something to help!"

Avaline grabbed Emilia's shoulder from behind. "I agree with your father, Emilia. Going up against a dragon is too dangerous for you." She then looked toward Alanna. "For the both of you. I'm not even comfortable with your father coming, but we need him for his tracking. I will go, as well as the baccus, the Overseer and your father."

"What are we supposed to do then?" Emilia asked with anger.

"Regan will supervise your training to attune your newfound senses."

Regan simply bowed toward the younger ladies.

"I assure you he is a good teacher. Trust what he says and relax. We will take care of things, I promise."

"As you say," Emilia said with clear irritation.

"Don't worry, ladies. Caedus is in good hands with these three powerhouses on the chase," Regan said to reassure them.

"Wait!" Therion yelled out. "There is one other who should join us."

"You don't mean—" Aveline began to say before Therion cut her off.

"Oh yes. With him I wouldn't be worried about facing the dragon."

"How do you know if he would even consider joining us? He doesn't like to be disturbed," Avalene asked.

"I can order him to join us," the Overseer suggested.

"No, no…" Therion began to say while waving his pointer back and forth. "You do not need to give it as an order. Tell him that one of the sons of Savas is in danger. He will drop whatever he is doing to help Caedus."

"How can you be so sure?" the Overseer asked.

"He feels partially responsible for Savas's death."

"That's preposterous!" Avaline yelled out. "Mathis is the sole being responsible for Savas's murder!"

"That may be true, but he felt that if he didn't beat Savas senseless in the arena a few days prior, that Savas could have survived the encounter with Mathis."

The Overseer had a curious look on his face. "Did he tell you all of this?"

Therion nodded. "Yes, he did. It's a heavy burden for him to carry. I tried to convince him that he was not to blame, but he is a stubborn one."

"Who are they talking about?" Alanna whispered in Reagan's ear.

"His name is Turog," Regan whispered back. "A golrig, the last to fight Savas in the arena and the only one to ever defeat him. Savas was beaten badly. Turog feels he was to blame for Savas being in a weakened state when Mathis killed him."

"I see, but no one could have known that Savas was going to be attacked."

"Therion tried to sway his mind on a few occasions, as did I, but he still feels incredibly guilty."

Emilia leaned her chin on Alanna's shoulder and entered the conversation. "I heard James say before, or the Overseer, or whatever, that he can order Turog? Does that mean he is one of the guardians?"

"Yes, he is the newest guardian of Zeledon."

"You have to admit, Turog could turn the tide if he comes with us," Therion said to the Overseer.

"You're right. I think you should find him while the baccus and I follow the dragon's scent. Take Ava with you." He slammed his walking stick on the ground. As it hit, the stick turned into a quarterstaff and his raggety robes turned into silver-plated armor and his hair tied back with a leather chord and no glasses. He looked about ten years younger as well. He jumped on the baccus.

"When we get close enough, we will stop and wait for you to catch up."

Therion and Ava nodded and headed to one of the places Turog could be. Ava reached out with her senses to attempt to pinpoint where he could be. She got a general direction, and they headed toward it. Therion then used his sense of smell to track where he was.

"Let us hope he is in a good mood today," Ava whispered.

"Only one way to find out. Let us go with haste!" Therion led the way with Ava not far behind.

"How can Avaline keep up with Therion like that?" Alanna asked for anyone who might have the answer.

"The old woman is full of tricks," the Overseer said. "She has an incantation for everything, in this case, a stamina booster."

"That's useful," Emilia muttered. "Do you think we can learn things like that?"

"In time perhaps." Regan put his hands on his hips. "For now you must learn how to master your new senses, and we will go from there."

"As you say," Emilia said.

"It is time for me to be off. We don't know how far away this dragon could have gotten," the Overseer said.

"Be careful the both of you." Regan reached his arm out toward his mentor.

The Overseer grabbed the younger man's arm tightly.

"Make sure you stay out of range of its attacks."

The Overseer smiled. "Look at you! You sound like the teacher now." He gestured a good-bye toward the ladies and sped off on the baccus. "Are you coming, son?" the Overseer asked Victor.

He slowly got up. It seemed that he was half asleep during the previous conversation. "I might as well. Maybe my perks of being Champion can come in handy."

"What are you referring to?" Alanna asked.

"Ever since what happened to Savas, the king has been trying to find a way to keep that from happening again, so as of recently I have the ability to summon a faed to come to my aid at a moment's notice."

"That's rather useful," the Overseer whispered. "That will come in handy. Hop on, my boy. We should hurry."

The Overseer and the Champion of the King were off.

Throughout the conversation, Giselle kept quiet because she didn't want to get involved in an argument. She didn't know any of them well enough to weigh in on either side.

"Excuse me, Regan?"

He turned around. He almost forgot she was there. "Yes, my lady?" Before she said anything else, he smacked his own forehead. "How impolite. I'm sorry I haven't introduced you, Giselle."

"It's quite all right, really."

Alanna came forward with her hand out and a smile. "Hello, my name is Alanna. I am King Leandrol's ward from Cresthill."

"The pleasure is all mine, Alanna. I am a wisdom from the north." Giselle approached Emilia next. "How do you do, ma'am? I am Giselle."

Emilia shook her hand. "Emilia, I'm sorry I'm still worked up from arguing with my dad."

"It's all right, my dear." She turned her attention back to Regan. "Regan, I'd like to offer my assistance in helping them cope with their magic senses. I have experience."

"That would be great, actually. Okay then, the three of you follow me. We shall go back to the cabin, rest up and eat, then we will begin in a few hours."

Alanna and Emilia were excited. Giselle had a look of worry on her face. Alanna lightly rubbed her back as they walked.

"Is everything all right, Giselle?"

"Oh yes, don't mind me. This day has just taken a toll on me, that's all." In reality she was worried about this golrig, Turog. They usually don't reside in Afelith. They are scary creatures. It could be trouble if that beast decides to help them hunt for her ally, Cedric. She feared for his life now.

⁓

Lurking high above the ground, hidden in the tree branches not too far away, was a black- armored figure. This being has been tracking Caedus and Emilia for days now. No one has seen or heard this being, for it was trained well in the art of stealth, so well that none of the powerful beings such as the Overseer, the wolf of the mountain, and one of the legendary wizards could sense its presence, despite it being so close.

When the Overseer took off with the baccus, the black-armored figure started to follow them while staying above ground, jumping from branch to branch to stay above ground. What does it want with the Overseer?

After the path turned into open fields, the armored figure waited for the Overseer to get out of sight, so it can follow them with the baccus's tracks. The tracks lead on for miles in a singular direction until it ventured off toward the next forest. Just before entering the shade of the trees, the armored figure was blindsided by a quarterstaff. It was running too fast and didn't see the weapon set at eye level in its way. It fell right into the Overseer's trap.

As it was disoriented, the Overseer pointed the quarterstaff at the figure's neck. "Who are you? Why are you following me?"

"Let me stand up, and I shall explain," the figure said in a very deep voice.

The Overseer guessed that this person was using some form of enchantment to disguise his voice.

He removed the end of the staff from the figure's neck. "Don't think about running, you hear?"

The figure nodded.

The Overseer noticed a bow slung over the figure's back. "Take that off, will you? Put it on the ground slowly."

The figure did what he was told without resisting.

"Now take that helmet off."

"I have done what you asked, but I must not take my helmet off. I cannot afford to show anyone my identity, even you, Overseer."

The Overseer inspected the figure carefully. The armor was not of Afelith, that's for sure, but it looks elvish. The slimness of the person in the armor suggests that it's a woman underneath. The right shoulder bore an unfamiliar mark, a bow being drawn out to form a circular shape with a lightning bolt in the center, all engraved in red.

"So tell me, why were you following me and how come I can't sense your presence? It's almost like you don't exist in the eyes of the Well of Magic."

"I don't have time to explain all of that now. I'm here to prevent you from reaching the sons of Savas."

"And why would you do that?"

The figure leaned against the closest tree and folded her arms. "While you allowed the brothers to talk to each other while Cedric was in a cell, I eavesdropped on their conversation. Are you familiar with the legendary enchanted weapons?"

"Of course, I am. Keeping the weapons safe from the wrong hands is a big part of being a guardian. What of it?"

"This Lord Mathis means to collect them with his followers, for what purpose I do not know. Cedric was tasked with retrieving the lightning blade, but he staged the kidnapping of his brother to take him to where the blade is. He wants Caedus to wield it so Mathis never could."

"If someone else is deemed worthy of the lightning blade before Mathis gets his hands on it, then it would become useless to him, but how would they know if the blade would even accept a novice like Caedus?"

"Cedric seems to have been influenced by his father's Windblade."

The Overseer stroked his chin. "Interesting. The weapons are the ones to choose their master, but I never thought of a weapon suggesting to another one to accept a specific master. This could work."

"I couldn't hear anything the Windblade said, apparently only members of the Savas bloodline can understand it."

"That is not uncommon. I have seen cases like that in the past. If what you say is true, then we must find the others. We are set to meet up before we were to attack the dragon anyway, so we are safe for the time being."

"That is good to hear."

"What is your name?" the Overseer asked.

"You can call me…Reyna."

"As you wish, Reyna, but that is not your real name, is it?" He noticed her hesitation that she must have come up with a fake name on the spot.

"No, it is not. No one must know who I am."

"I respect that, as long as what you say is the truth."

"We have a common enemy in Mathis. I will do anything to stop his plans from going forward."

"I guess I'll just have to take your word for it. Anyway, we should wait here. The dragon stench is very strong according to my companion." He gestured toward the baccus. "The boys shouldn't be far off if the dragon is near. They could be in one of these caves nearby."

Therion and Avaline didn't have to go too far to find Turog. These days he frequently spent his free time sitting on the side of the river, soaking in the beautiful sights and the nature around him. Just as Therion was getting close, Turog's scent started to fade away. He quickly found out why, because he saw a massive figure standing underneath the waterfall. His scent faded slightly because he went underwater.

Turog turned around to see Therion and Avaline standing twenty paces or so away.

"My friends! I thought I sensed someone coming this way. What can I do for you, my friends?"

"We need your help, Turog." The golrig saw the seriousness in Therion's face.

"It must be important for someone with your ego to ask for help."

"Please, my old friend…" Therion motioned his hand to a stop. "We have little time to waste. My Caedus, Savas's boy, he is in danger. And we need your help."

Avaline decided not to butt into the conversation. If Therion couldn't convince him, then she wouldn't do any better. It was amazing to see the size difference between them. Therion made everyone look small next to him standing at almost seven feet, but Turog was almost two feet taller. Therion was looking up to just make eye contact with the golrig.

"The son of Savas, huh? Tell me what has happened."

"Savas's other son, Cedric, the one who was taken, he has returned. But as a follower if this dark lord, he murdered two guards and escaped prison. He then captured his brother, and he has a dragon under his control. That's what I am afraid of."

"Troubling news indeed." Turog scratched the back of his neck while leaning his other hand on his dagger hilt. "So you need me as backup against the dragon, is that it?"

"Only as worst case. We are going to try to reason with Cedric to let his brother go. What do you say, old friend?"

Turog didn't hesitate. His mind was already made up. "I shall join you. Lead the way."

Avaline was able to see a weight lifted off Therion's shoulders.

"Thank you, Turog."

The golrig patted Therion on the back.

The three of them headed toward the stench of the dragon. It was getting stronger. They weren't too far now. The Overseer should be around waiting for them somewhere.

Inside the cave Caedus reached out with his left arm, closed his eyes, and concentrated. He felt the gist of wind flowing toward him, and before he knew it, the Windblade was in his hand.

"Good!" Cedric yelled from hundreds of paces away on the other side of the cave. "Try it one more time." He then called the blade back to his own hands.

The Windblade will answer the call to anyone in the Savas bloodline, the only two left are the brothers. Cedric grew up using it to increase his own power. He formed a powerful bond with it. He has now forged the bond between his beloved blade and his long-lost brother, Caedus.

"Okay," Caedus yelled. Sweat poured down the sides of his face. This was his first form of training he had in magic, and it was fairly advanced to already create a bond with an enchanted weapon. It was a lot tougher than he thought it would be. Over the years he has built up his physical body for combat, but this training was something else entirely. He felt a constant headache brewing because he couldn't control how he felt other people's emotions. It was overwhelming at times. That's the first thing he was supposed to learn. Maybe after retrieving this lightning blade, he could go back to the basics. Stopping Mathis's plans is all that mattered to him now.

The blade was in Cedric's open palm. "Okay, now!"

Caedus once again reached his arm out, but this time he was able to call the blade much faster.

"Good! Now you'll be ready to call the blade from far away as I can."

Caedus put his hands on his knees as he tried to catch his breath. "Is it more difficult from a longer distance?"

"It shouldn't be. If you call the blade as you did now with less effort than before, you should be okay."

A wave of confidence flew through Caedus's entire body. He felt so powerful, ready for anything. But in the back of his mind, he knew that if it ever came to a serious fight with his brother, he would lose. He was already exhausted from just calling the Windblade to him a handful of times. Cedric was much more attuned to magic, and his senses were much sharper. Caedus tried to hide the disorientation he felt from learning too much in such a short amount of time and without being able to control it.

Cedric was able to tell though. His brother was sweating too much for such a simple exercise, but at the same time, he remembered how long it took him to get used to his senses. He suggested sharing the Windblade, which now seemed like something Caedus isn't ready for yet. "Are you sure you're up for this, brother?"

Caedus took a minute to catch his breath. "I have to be. We need to stop Mathis from getting the lightning blade. I have to be worthy of receiving it, no matter the cost."

"Just don't push yourself too hard. Creating a bond with the Windblade should be the hardest thing you have to do for a while.

Breath slow and deep. Try to relax. It is a race to the lightning blade, but we have the advantage. Mathis doesn't know where it is, and now you do."

"But what about his powers? Sheska said the Mathis constantly watches you guys. He could be listening to us right now. How do you know that he isn't listening to us right now?"

"It is true that he could do that, but he is a busy man. He could be watching us, but he doesn't do it all the time. He can sense of I am lying about something. That's why I didn't allow myself to see where the true hiding place of the lightning blade was. He can't extract that information out of me."

Caedus felt a strange sensation in his head. Something was…calling to him. A presence he wasn't familiar with. It was in the cave with him and his brother. He felt a strange jolt in his arm.

"Cedric!"

"What is it?"

"The lightning blade is here. It won't reveal itself until you leave the cave."

"How can you be sure?" he asked with interest.

"It's calling to me. I can feel it, but I must acquire it alone."

"As you say. I shall wait outside with Mordecai." Cedric turned around and began to walk away. After a few steps he stopped but didn't turn around. "Do you want the Windblade with you?"

"No, I have to do this on my own." His face was determined.

"Even after all the hard work you put in to wield the Windblade?"

"I'll be okay. Trust me, Cedric."

"As you wish." Cedric turned around to make eye contact. "Good luck, brother."

Caedus made his way back toward the prophecy carvings. Just before he got in view of the giant map, the floor collapsed under him. He couldn't catch his footing, and he fell down a downward slope with dust and dirt and rubble falling with him. He somersaulted a few times on this lower ground before being able to stop. When he finally stood up and wiped himself off, he saw it. The lightning blade on the other side of this massive empty room. It was pitch black except for the opening he fell through, now impossible to reach from being so high up, and the color blue illuminating from the blade itself, half stuck in a giant stone, meant for someone to pull out.

"You!" A deep voice echoed throughout the cave. It was hard to tell where the voice originated, but Caedus knew it was the spirit of the lightning blade. "Why do you seek my power?"

"I need your power combined with my own to stop a madman," Caedus said as he walked closer to the blade.

"Your own power? You have no power! I can see your mind, boy. You're arrogant, unbalanced, and weak! I have no reason to join you."

"I may be unbalanced and at times arrogant, but I am *not* weak!" His voice got louder with every word, and anger swelled in him. His clenched fists started to manifest red lightning, just like when he was struck the other night, but he created it himself through emotion. "What does a dusty relic know about power?"

The lightning blade laughed. "I sense your anger, boy. It fuels your power as I now see. You may be something...with hard work, that is."

"I spent years of training to get to where I am before you. I am no stranger to hard work."

"And yet you cannot control your power. Why is that?"

The lightning disappeared from his hands as they began to lightly shake. "I have only been exposed to magic the day before yesterday."

"And yet you can wield this amount of raw magic? How?"

"I'm not sure myself. But what I do know is that I need help controlling my senses and abilities."

"What makes you think that I can help you with such things?" the blade asked with curiosity.

"Because I know what you really are. You were one of the mages who survived the purge, only to live an everlasting life imprisoned in this weapon until the end of time. You have knowledge and wisdom, and you have nothing better to do unless you want to gather dust for another thousand years." Caedus felt a difference in the air in the room now. Instead of the overbearing feeling of intimidation, it now felt much lighter.

"Did you say a thousand years? I lost track of time long ago. I didn't realize it had been so long."

"Now you know. Are you willing to help me? Help me control my powers and take revenge on the madman who killed my father."

"Oh, so it is blood that you are after, hm?" The lightning blade laughed. "So your goal is to become a murderer? What then?"

"The man I am after is an enemy of Cresthill. He would be brought to justice."

"I see, so your quest is noble and personal. Very interesting." The blade was then silent for a few minutes. Caedus figured it was deciding on what to do next. "What is your name, boy?"

"My name is Caedus, son of Savas."

"Okay, Caedus, if you can pull me out of the stone, then I shall join you on your quest. I will teach you how to control your senses and powers."

Caedus kept a face of stone to hide his excitement. "Very well." He approached the stone. After the five steps to reach it, he grabbed the hilt with both hands and put everything he had into pulling it out. It barely budged.

"Come on, Caedus, you can do better than that!" the lightning blade teased.

Veins started to bulge in his arms and neck. He yelled as he pulled as hard as he could. Red lightning manifested in his hands again. It began to chip away at the rock the blade was stuck in. As chunks of rock were being destroyed, it became looser and easier to pull out. He yelled out once more and pulled so hard, and it finally released. The force he used to pull made him fly to the ground with the blade in his hands.

"How's that for power?" Caedus asked to mock the lightning blade.

"Clever approach, I must say! You lacked the strength to pull me out on your own, so you resorted to your magic to assist you to destroy the rock. Very clever indeed."

"I didn't plan it. It just sort of happened."

"I see, no less impressive though. Let us get out of here."

"Do you know of another way out?" Caedus asked.

It was too high to jump to reach where the cave floor was, which was their ceiling.

"Go behind where to rock was. There is a pressure pad there. Step on it."

Caedus stood on the pad. As it opened, a hidden doorway appeared in the wall. There were stone steps that led upward. He jumped off the pedestal and onto the steps. It went in a spiral motion until they reached a door at the top. He pushed the heavy door open with effort. Once through, he realized this door was the map of the world he was looking at earlier. He saw the hole he fell through about ten paces up, so he made a running start to jump over it and get out of the cave.

A few hundred paces after the jump stood Cedric. "So you wield the lightning blade at last."

"Were you here the whole time?" Caedus asked.

"I heard something like a cave-in, so I ran back to see if you were okay. I saw that you fell through the floor to a hidden chamber. I thought it best to not interfere, but I have remained here since you fell."

"I see. We got what we came for, so let us be off."

"Good idea. There is nothing else for us to do here."

Both of them made their way toward the front of the cave. Once they got to the entrance, it wasn't blocked by Mordecai anymore.

"Something must be wrong, let's go!" Cedric yelled.

Caedus was able to sense a few people, some familiar but two of them he didn't know. They came outside to see the Overseer, Therion, Victor, Avaline, a golrig, and a stranger in black armor standing ready to fight against the dragon, who was snarling ready to attack. The brothers ran in between them. Cedric more toward the dragon to try to calm it down, while Caedus confronted everyone else.

"Caedus! Are you all right?" Therion asked.

"Everything is okay, Therion. There is much to be explained."

Therion walked toward the boy. "Come here." The man squeezed Caedus in a giant hug. "I was worried about you there."

"It's okay. I wasn't harmed."

Cedric looked at his brother receiving care and love, and all he felt was emptiness. No one has shown affection toward him like that since his father was still alive. The Overseer sensed how the boy felt.

"Young Cedric! We can't just let you walk away from your crimes."

The boy didn't react. He just stood there with his hand on the dragon's snout, staring at the old man with his piercing yellow eyes. The golrig stepped forward. The dragon growled, but Cedric motioned for it to stay back.

"You look just like him, you know."

"What?"

"Your father, you're the spitting image of him."

"How did you know him?" Cedric asked.

Caedus was curious as well.

"I was the last to fight him in the arena." He held up his left hand to show that his thumb has been cut off as a result of facing Savas.

"You're the one he spoke of."

"Did he now? I considered him a friend, despite knowing him to be brief." He held out his massive hand. "I am Turog."

Cedric sensed no deception from him. His intention was not to capture him, only to meet him. Cedric shook his hand. It was more like Turog grabbing the young man's entire forearm; his hands were so big. The golrig simply smiled at Cedric, then walked toward Caedus. "Young Caedus, it is a pleasure to meet you as well."

They both smiled and shook hands as well.

"I always wanted to meet you, but I never had a name to go off," Caedus said.

"I'm here now, my boy."

All of a sudden the air became very thin. It became harder to breathe.

"Oh no," Cedric whispered.

"What is it?" Caedus asked.

Cedric looked back at his brother. "He's coming."

A portal appeared before them, as big as a doorway. No one was able to see what was on the other side; it was covered in red mist. They all heard a menacing laugh, then glowing eyes through the way. Then the dark figure walked through. It was Lord Mathis.

"So darkness returns," the Overseer said.

Therion stepped in front of Caedus, as did Turog, but Mathis quickly moved the both of them with simple hand movement. They went flying in opposite directions. Now it was just Caedus standing there. He was finally face-to-face with the man who murdered his father, the man who took his brother away, the man he was going to kill! He finally got a decent look at the lightning blade he was holding. In the cave he basically only saw the hilt from grabbing it, but it was so dark. It was tough to see what it actually looked like until now. It wasn't a curved blade like the Windblade but thick and zigzagged like a lightning bolt.

"You look so angry, boy! What's wrong?" Mathis asked just to mock Caedus.

Caedus's face was red with fury, so mad that red lightning was manifesting all over his body. Most of the lighting surrounded itself around his new blade. Justice would be served today.

The appearance of the red lightning actually made Lord Mathis stop laughing. He looked on with curiosity. He also noticed that Cedric failed to retrieve the lightning blade.

"So you learned a new trick, and you're holding my weapon. That won't be enough to defeat me, boy!" The dark lord lifted his left hand up and summoned purple lightning and cast it toward Caedus. It moved so fast that Caedus couldn't react. It was all over for him, he thought. Just as it was going to impact, a strong gust of wind swayed the lightning path just enough to miss Caedus. The only person who could have summoned wind like that was Cedric. Mathis looked over at his pupil with surprise.

"What is the meaning of this?" he yelled.

Cedric began to summon an intense amount of wind toward him and concentrated the energy into his palm, essentially creating the power of a tornado in his hand. His yellow eyes were almost as intense as his master's. It even struck a small amount of fear into Mathis.

"You are not to harm him," he whispered. "It's over for you, my master."

Mathis smiled. "You think you can take me on? It seems that you are a slow learner, or have you forgotten about the left side of your face?"

Therion then noticed that the boy had punctures all over the left side of his cheek. He began to move forward, but the stranger in black armor stood between everyone and the brothers with Mathis.

"You must not interfere!"

Therion was angry. "I will not stand idly by while my boy is in danger!" He moved forward again, but after a few steps he was frozen. He couldn't move. This stranger was using some kind of power to keep him in place. Turog couldn't move either. The Overseer didn't attempt to move, neither did Victor or Avaline.

"Now might be a good time to summon a faed," the Overseer whispered to Victor.

The young man nodded and held his hands together. "It may take a minute."

Cedric's attack was ready, and he charged for his master for a killing blow.

If I get hit with that, it really could be the end of me, Mathis thought. As much as he didn't want to admit it, Cedric possessed enough power to kill him, but he would never give him the opportunity to find out.

He had to think on his toes. How could he repel such an attack? Just as Cedric was close enough for impact, Mathis underhanded his palm on top of his pupil's, scooping up the sphere of wind to simultaneously take it from him and control it. It was now in his hands, and he aimed straight for Cedric's face. He was too close to dodge; all he could do was look in terror as he got struck with his own attack. As it impacted, it created an enormous cloud mixed with dirt and grass. Everyone was blinded by it.

Once cleared all Caedus saw was his brother on the ground in a small crater, lifeless with Mathis standing over him. He even tried to use his magic to sense his brother's presence, but he felt nothing.

"You bastard! I'm going to make you pay!" Caedus charged for Mathis. Red lightning was crackling all over his body. He lifted the lightning blade to strike.

Mathis didn't show that he was worried about the unpredictability of this boy's powers.

Caedus jumped over his brother's body to reach Mathis, but before he hit the ground, he was grabbed by the throat with one hand. The lightning disappeared around his body, and his blade flew in the opposite direction. The stranger caught it. He tried to pry Mathis's hand off his neck as he struggled to breathe. Mathis pulled the boy close.

"You have a fire inside you, kid, but don't think for a second that you can defeat me."

Caedus struggled to breathe, but he insisted on answering back. "I am going to make you pay for what you have done! Mark my words! You will pay!"

Mathis was so close that he could feel him breathing. "I'm going to let you live. You're not even worth killing. Come find me when you're strong enough to be a challenge." He loosened his grip on Caedus's neck and placed him back on the ground, but he still had a hold on him. "Take this as a souvenir, to have survived yet another encounter with me." Purple lightning manifested in Mathis's fingertips. He grabbed Caedus tight and burned the top left side of his forehead and dragged his finger down across his left eye down to the side of his mouth, creating a massive scar down Caedus's face. He screamed in agony, but he was helpless. Mathis was too overwhelming to stop.

Everyone else looked on in terror. Therion was shaking in anger.

Victor then slammed his hand on the ground and yelled, "I summon a faed from Cresthill!" Just as soon as his hand struck the ground a faed appeared before him.

Mathis quickly threw Caedus down and opened a portal, dragging Cedric's body through as he escaped. Therion and Turog ran toward Caedus as fast as they could. They lifted him up to sit. They supported his back to keep him up. Smoke still came from his left eye, and tears ran down his right eye. "Mathis killed him. He killed my brother!"

XIII

ESCAPE TO SMUGGLER'S WAY

D ESPITE HIS BEST EFFORTS, BROCK couldn't shake how worried he was. Chillpeak was a town where he and Sheska frequently went to. Many of the shop owners and people could recognize them. If they were found out, it was all over. His face was barely visible with his ranger's hood, but no one was as big as he was. Someone would put two and two together. Sheska was a bit safer. She drastically changed her appearance.

The Dancing Dragon was a small establishment. Through the doors were about five or six tables with the bar on the back wall. Brock ordered some of the local brew and some wine for when Sheska came back. She was buying supplies for the journey ahead at one of the vendors. Brock sat at the table at the left side. He sat against the wall so he could keep an eye on everything around him.

For once he drank his ale slowly, instead of inhaling it like he usually did. After a few minutes, two dwarves walked in. They looked like they could be father and son because there was a clear age difference. The older one had light chain mail with leather armor over it; the younger one just had leather. Both carried double-headed axes on their backs. Travelers or mercenaries, they must be looking for work.

Of course, they ordered ale. It was rare for a dwarf to drink anything else. The younger one pulled out a few papers to show the barkeep. Brock noticed it was the wanted posters of him and his companions. He kept his head down but listened to the conversation.

"Excuse me, young man." The older man waved his hand to get the barkeep's attention. He was a young skinny fellow with long blond hair tied behind his head and his sleeves rolled up to his elbows.

"Would you like another ale, sir?" the barkeep asked with a smile.

"Maybe, but we seek a little information first." The dwarf gestured for the barkeep to listen closer so no one else can hear. "Ya see, we are bounty hunters. Have ya seen any of these criminals?"

The barkeep's eyes widened. "Yes! These two right here"—he pointed at Brock's and Sheska's pictures—"these two make frequent visits here. They haven't been around in a while though."

"Really now?" the older one said. "How often do they come around?"

"About once a month, I'd say. It should be time for them to come around again any day now."

"Thank you very much, my good man," the older one said while flicking a gold coin at the man behind the bar.

"By the goddess! That's very generous of you kind, sir. Take two more ales on the house!"

Both of the dwarves laughed. The older one sunk his face in the ale mug while the younger one patted the old man's back.

"We oughta do more business here."

The old man nodded his head while still inhaling the ale without taking a breath.

"We could really score big with this one." He reached into his coin pouch and threw a few silvers on the counter. "A round for everyone!"

There were a few hurrahs where a couple of the regulars sat, a couple of old fellows in one corner. In the opposite corner seemed to be a ranger drinking by himself. The dwarves brought an extra ale and walked toward the ranger.

Brocks face was stone, but inside he was terrified. Was he found out? He was sure he could take both of these dwarves on in he needed to, but he didn't even ask around for the location of Smuggler's Way, one of the tunnels that leads to Alexandria. He took a deep breath and relaxed. He couldn't have been made, at least not yet.

"Gentlemen, quite generous to buy everyone a round."

Both dwarves sat opposite of him. The younger one slid the ale to him.

He picked it up and raised the glass. "Cheers to my new friends."
The three of them clinked glasses and took long sips.

"I am Dhosar," the younger one said. "And this is me father, Dalog."
The old man simply smiled and took another sip.

"I didn't mean to eavesdrop, small place and all, but you're bounty hunters?"

"Right ya are, ranger," Dhosar said. "You have us at a disadvantage. What's your name ranger?"

Brock wasn't good at thinking on his toes. He couldn't tell them his real name. He had to think of something fast. He took another sip of ale and made himself cough to stall for a few seconds. "Sorry about that, I go by drifter around here."

"I see, so ya must have a family then I take it?" Dalog asked.

"Yes. As you know being a ranger isn't the…safest profession. I just go by drifter so me and my family are left alone when need be."

"Wise choice," Dhosar said quietly.

Brock's eyes narrowed. "Yeah, so the two of you are after high-profile bounties. If I am mistaken, you want to ask for my help?"

"Sharp, this lad is," Dalog said with a laugh. "These bounties are magic users, and as you know dwarves have no affinity for magic, that includes having no way to defend against any potential magical attacks. If you help us capture just one of them, we will give ya a cut. Capturing both would be a bonus for us."

"Interesting…," Brock whispered while stroking his chin. He was playing along the best he could until Sheska got there. She was better at talking her way out of situations like these. He grabbed the wanted posters and inspected them. "So ten thousand a piece, huh? How much of a cut are you willing to give to me?"

"Name yer price, drifter," Dhosar said while squinting his eyes. Was this ranger trying to take more than he should?

"How about ten percent, and some information, if you should so have it."

"And what kind of information are ya after, ranger?" Dhosar asked.

Brock crossed his arms and leaned against the wall. "As you know, it's a ranger's job to do border security. There has been talk about a secret pathway people have been taking to go to and from Afelith and Alexandria. Do you know of what I speak of?"

Dhosar looked around to make sure no one else was listening. "You speak of Smuggler's Way. We may know where it is. So you want to know where it is, don't ya?"

Brock nodded. "It sure would make things easier for me. I could even get a promotion out of it. I want that over the reward money."

Dhosar looked at his father. The old man nodded.

"It looks like we could do business!"

Both dwarves stood up.

Brock stayed seated because they were now at eye level. He shook hands with both of them.

"We have a few more errands to run around town. Meet us back here at sundown."

Brock saluted them. "See you then!" When they walked out of the pub, he sighed in relief. He was frozen. He didn't know what to do next. If they really know where Smuggler's Way was, he needed to play along long enough to find it and fight his way through. Should he fight the dwarves? Should he kill them when they find the passage?

"Excuse me, m'lady," Dalog said quietly as he walked out of the pub.

The lady that happened to step in his path was Sheska. She spotted Brock in the corner and walked toward him at a fast pace. "We have a problem."

"You can say that again," Brock said as he continued to watch the dwarves walk out.

"Did something happen with those dwarves?" she asked with worry in her voice.

He nodded. "I'll get to them soon. What were you going to tell me?"

She looked around before she began. The only other people in the pub were the two old men in the far corner and the barkeep. She took a sip of the wine Brock got for her and took a breath. "People around town are talking. After seeing the wanted posters, they recognized us as regulars around some of the shops. Everyone is looking for us. We have to leave."

"Finish your wine first. Relax and listen. You're barely recognizable the way you look now. You'll be fine, and two, those two dwarves know where Smuggler's Way is. They will take us there at sundown."

"Dwarves don't help people out of the kindness of their hearts. What did they want in exchange? They never do anything for free."

"They are bounty hunters."

"What?" Sheska yelled as she slammed her fist on the table.

The two old men looked over, but they didn't really care.

"Listen!" Brock growled. "They think I'm a ranger. I promised them both of the 'wanted criminals' heads in exchange for the location of Smuggler's Way."

"And how are you going to help them bring *us* in?" she spat out sarcastically.

"All we need is for them to take us where we need to go, then we could escape. We can take them together."

"That's not the point. Were you able to get a read on them?"

Brock took the last sip of the ale the dwarves bought him. "I tried a few times. They were hard to read. I couldn't sense what they were feeling, or if they were lying to me or not. My guess is they know who I am, and they are going to set a trap for us."

"What are we going to do?"

"Honestly, I think we should go along with it and see what happens. Worse case, we fight them and flee. Smuggler's Way is the fastest route out of here, but if we can't go that way because of the dwarves, then we'll go over the mountains by the Forbidden Forest. It's longer, but no one would follow us that way, not even bounty hunters."

She sighed again and devoured the rest of her wine. "I suppose you are right. I just don't want to take any unnecessary risks."

"We'll be okay." He smiled. His smile made her smile as well.

She stood up. "I think it would be wise if we get out of the heart of the town until the sun sets. I don't want to get spotted by anyone."

"Lead the way." He then stood up, and they left the Dancing Dragon.

"We have to take him somewhere for medical attention immediately!" Therion growled.

Caedus was in agonizing pain. Lord Mathis burned a horrific scar down his left eye, and it seemed that his eye was welded shut. He couldn't open it. He couldn't even touch it, it was so hot. No matter how much pain he felt it didn't compare to just witnessing his brother getting killed by Mathis, the same man who killed his father.

He was angry, sad, and disoriented. Therion looked back at Avaline and shook his head, meaning that his boy's eye may not be able to be fixed. The look on his face was pure heartbreak. His boy was suffering in more ways than one, and he didn't know what to do to help him.

"Let me take him," Turog said. As he began to approach Caedus, Mordecai, the dragon, growled. The golrig put his hands up and took a few steps back. Therion didn't back away from Caedus.

Throughout the day Mordecai listened to his "parent" Cedric's conversations with Caedus. Dragons were not known to have much intelligence, but he knew that they were brothers, and if Cedric was really gone, he would take it upon himself to protect his only brother.

"It's okay, boy," Caedus whispered without looking back, even though the dragon was inches away. He gently bit onto one of Caedus's pauldrons to lift him up and place him on his back. Therion reluctantly jumped on the dragon's back to support Caedus, not without another growl, but Caedus assured that Therion was okay to be with them. Before he flew off, he grabbed the lightning blade from the stranger Reyna's hand so Caedus would have it when he recovered.

"We should head to my cabin!" the Overseer yelled for everyone to hear. He made eye contact with the dragon. "Can you understand me?"

Mordecai nodded with his tongue flopped out to one side.

"Follow him to my cabin," he said as he pointed to Victor on the baccus.

"Go back to the city. Ask Ezio if he can provide any of his healing ointments, then come back here," Victor said to the faed he summoned just a few minutes prior.

"As you wish," it whispered in a deep voice and vanished.

The baccus took off toward the cabin with Victor. The dragon followed with Therion and Caedus. Turog followed as well. That just left the Overseer; Alanna, the wizard; and the mysterious stranger Reyna.

"You made sure Mathis didn't see the emblem on your arm, why is that? Do you know each other?" the Overseer asked.

"Yes, at one time I knew who Mathis was, before he descended into madness." Reyna put her hand on the emblem on her shoulder. "If he saw this, he would figure out who I am. I wear this armor to protect my identity. I cannot risk anyone knowing who I am. Mathis has eyes and ears everywhere."

"I shall ask no more of you, but sooner or later you will have to give us more information if you are going to be around here," the Overseer stated.

Reyna nodded. She walked to the crater that was caused by Cedric's attack.

"I don't think the boy Cedric is dead," the stranger said in her deep metallic voice.

"What makes you think that? We all stopped sensing his life force the second he got hit with his own attack," Avaline shot back.

"It wouldn't make sense for Mathis to kill his followers. He intends to retrieve a certain set of enchanted weapons, and he needs Cedric to make that a reality. He is already the master of the Windblade."

"I understand that, but we saw what we saw," the Overseer stated.

"Then why did he take Cedric's body with him?" Reyna asked.

"You have a point there," Avaline said.

"Cedric could be inches from death but not actually dead. You two should know more than anybody that looks can be deceiving."

"Well, he does possess illusion magic," Avaline said. "He uses it to hide his face. Could this have been illusion magic as well?"

"That is what I believe. The question is, should we tell Caedus?" Reyna whispered.

"No, at least not yet," the Overseer said with a grim look. "He is already disoriented. Let him hone his senses and heal his eye first. I don't want too much on his plate."

Avaline looked at the decayed part of the ground, which Mathis stood on. "Evil oozes out of this man. He's too dangerous to come and go as he pleases."

"I agree." The Overseer tapped his staff, which changed his clothes from his battle armor back to his simple robes. "We must come up with a strategy. He's smart and powerful, not a good combination for an adversary."

"Now is the time to resurrect the Phoenix," Avaline whispered.

"You're right. I think it's a no brainer on who to select. You should go back to Cresthill, inform the king that Caedus, Alanna, and Emilia will become the new Phoenix squadron. I will prepare them here."

Avaline nodded. "I shall make my way to the cabin. Once the faed returns with medicine for Caedus, I will go back with it to the city."

"Good idea."

"What is this Phoenix squadron?" Reyna asked.

The Overseer leaned on his staff. "I shall tell you on the way to my cabin."

The sun started to set. Brock was a bit nervous, but the plan he and Sheska came up with was sure to work. The dwarves were already waiting at the Dancing Dragon for him to arrive. He pushed the swing door slowly and came inside. No one could have snuck in there if they tried. The hinges were so creaky, it turned everyone's heads toward the door every time someone came through. Being almost seven feet tall turned a lot of heads on top of that.

"Ah, ha, ha! There ya are, ranger! Are ya ready to depart?" Dalog shouted.

"Yes, sir! I'll buy us a round after you show me what I'm looking for," Brock said, playing along. He didn't want to talk about Smuggler's Way out in the open.

The pub was packed this time of day. Everyone was getting off work and having a drink or two on the way home by the looks of it.

It was dangerous being there. Too many people were eyeing him up.

"That's me, boy!" Dalog finished the ale he was drinking with a massive sip and slammed it on the counter. "Away we go!"

"Lead the way." Brock held the creaky door open to let both of them out.

The three of them followed the main road toward the northern exit of the village toward the mountains. Dhosar, the younger dwarf, lead the way with Brock and Dalog not far behind.

"So these fugitives," Brock reluctantly brought up. "Have any leads on them?"

"Unfortunately not." The old dwarf stroked his graying beard. "This is a particularly tough job. I don't like recruiting outside help meself, but we need it for this one. Great risk comes great reward."

"I see. I will do what I can to help," Brock lied. "Which one do you want to go after first?"

"The girl," Dhosar said, turning his head back. "She may not be a pushover, but she could be the easier of the two to capture."

"I see, good thinking."

From a distance Sheska was following the tree of them from the rooftops, waiting for them to get outside of the village. She couldn't make out what the three of them were saying, but it seemed like they were coming up with a plan to capture her. Earlier in the day Brock told her that the dwarves saw her as the weakest link, which could be true, but still she could take out a couple of arrogant dwarves in her sleep.

They crossed the northern bridge out of the village to the dirt pathways alongside the mountains. She waited until they were almost out of sight before following them further. They continued on the path a few hundred paces or so, just far enough to not be seen from the village. She noticed that they stopped.

"How much farther?" Brock asked.

"The Smuggler's Way is hidden behind those large bushes." Dhosar pointed, which looked to be about twenty paces away.

Brock moved one of the bushes over enough just enough to see past it. He wanted to make sure these dwarves were telling the truth. To his surprise they were. There was a hole in the mountain big enough for two people to walk side by side, like a small cave. It lead to Alexandria, where they needed to go to find Sheska's enchanted weapon. The dwarves moved close to him, a little two close. Both of their axes were out.

"I'm surprised you showed me. So tell me, how long have you two known who I really was?" Brock asked as he turned away from the hidden path. He crossed his arms, as if the dwarves posed no threat to him.

"From the start, lad," Dhosar said while leaning on his axe. He seemed to be using like a walking stick. "The second we sat down with ya we knew ya were trying to hide yer face."

"So you were leading me on from the start, aye?" Brock shot back. He put his hood down since he had no reason to hide anymore.

"Ten thousand gold pieces is a lot of money," Dalog spouted. "We would have preferred to capture the girl first, but you'll just have to do."

Fire began to manifest in both of Brock's hands. "If you think you can capture me, there is only one way to find out!"

He was clearly trying to bait them. Dwarves are more clever than people give them credit for. Since they keep to themselves for the exception of trading goods, not too much is known of their intelligence. Dalog and Dhosar are seasoned combat veterans, but they rarely faced magic users in their time.

Brock clapped his hands together to create a fireball the size of someone's head and hurled it at them. They somersaulted in opposite directions to become harder targets to hit. After getting back on his feet, Dhosar charged for Brock, swinging his axe wildly. He was a lot faster than Brock thought. He only narrowly dodged the first two swings. For the third strike, he swung his axe in a downward motion aiming for Brock's head. Brock caught the blade by catching it between his palms. It took a tremendous amount of effort to not get sliced. This dwarf was incredibly strong, and he was inching closer and closer to stabbing him.

Little did the dwarf know that Brock only needed to hold on to it for five seconds to turn the axe combustible. Brock used all of his might to kick Dhosar a few feet back. The dwarf fell into his father's arms, and before they knew it, the axe exploded into a thousand pieces. Sharp edges of the axe flew in all directions. Brock ducked and faced the opposite direction while the dwarves suffered most of the impact.

The old man Dalog was mostly blown back a few feet, but Dhosar suffered a massive cut from the right side of his nose, diagonally falling down his cheek toward his jaw. The cut was so deep it cut through his massive beard. All he could do was hold his face in pain. After seeing the pain on his son's face, Dalog was furious.

"Ya won't get away with hurting me son!" The old man ran toward Brock, throwing daggers at the larger man.

Smarter than charging with an axe, Brock thought. *These dwarves are no pushovers.* He dodged the first dagger, but the second one stuck him in the shoulder. It was a sharp pain, yes, but not as bad as he thought it would be. Before he had time to pull the blade out, the old man was already in front of him and grabbed his legs to attempt to take him down.

Brock almost laughed at the attempt, but Dalog squeezed the larger man's legs together and screamed as he lifted Brock in the air and slammed him on his back. Brock couldn't believe it. Before he had the chance to get up, the old man mounted him and reigned down punches. Brock blocked a few of them, but some got through. These dwarves were heavy-handed. They were a lot stronger than he thought they would be.

"That's enough!" a female voice yelled.

Brock and Dalog stopped fighting and looked over. It was Sheska. She was holding a blade made of ice against Dhosar's throat while holding his left arm out. As they looked closer, they could see that his arm was frozen solid. He couldn't move it. Dalog was able to tell that the ice was created by the lady's hand placed on his son's arm.

"Here is what's going to happen," Sheska said in a commanding voice. "You get off my companion, and you let us be on our way, or I'll kill this one." Her eyes momentarily gestured toward the younger dwarf she had dead rights to.

Dalog got off Brock and gestured for her to stop.

"We are not fools. Capturing ya isn't worth dying over. Please let me boy go."

Sheska loosened her blade off his neck, but she still held his frozen arm. "I figured you would have put up more of a fight. Maybe you aren't a fool after all. May we all live to fight another day."

"Ya can count on that, ya wench!" Dhosar spat out.

"You forget, *dwarf,* that you are in no position to badmouth me!" She chopped the base of his shoulder, which caused his frozen arm to shatter into a thousand pieces. The dwarf fell to his knees, looking at his own arm all over the floor. "Now you can't follow us," she said without even looking at him. She helped Brock up.

Dalog ran toward his son and wrapped his one arm around his shoulders to help him up. "Ya haven't seen the last of us I promise ya that, magic users!"

Sheska didn't care to react. They were beaten, and they were free to take the path to Alexandria.

"You okay, big guy?" She cupped her hand onto Brock's cheek. He had a black eye from the older dwarf.

"Yeah, I'm okay. Did you get the supplies?"

She pointed at one of the nearby trees where she hid her travel pack. It contained food and blankets for their journey. Brock went to get it to strap on his back, then led her to the cave of Smuggler's Way. He held one of the bushes to the side for her to enter first, then he followed.

"You were brave out there," Brock said quietly. "You have come a long way. I'm proud of you."

She blushed, but it was too dark for him to notice. "Thank you, Brock. That means a lot."

The farther inside they went, the darker it became.

"Can't you make a light?"

Brock manifested fire into his hand. "This should do for now." He looked down at his companion. "I heard rumors that the people who use this pathway set up a few camps throughout these caves. If we end up finding one, we should rest."

"Do you think we would be safe resting here? These caves are supposed to be filled with goblins and who else knows what." She wrapped her arms around his to keep warm.

"We should be fine. I'm more worried about what lies in the Ice Mountains."

"Tell me about it." Sheska was interested.

Brock wasn't really scared of anything, with the exception of Mathis, but the Ice Mountains have him worried.

"Legend says there are creatures up there. I think some called them Yeti. It was a story to scare kids in Alexandria, but some people believe them to be real because all who have ventured into the Ice Mountains never returned."

"I could see why you're worried. But if we work together, we can pull through. I think we make a good team." She now leaned her head against his shoulder.

"Yeah, we do." He smiled. "It should only take us two days to get through the pass, then we'll be in Alexandria."

"Are you excited to visit your homeland after all these years?"

"I'm not sure what to think. But we will find out in time."

XIV

THE KING'S SPEECH

I T WAS A NICE AND cool morning with the sun out. The sun rose about two hours ago, and the majority of Cresthill's population was gathered outside of the palace. With all the chaos that has been happening the past few days, the king has been rather quiet but he was ready to address the people of what has been going on.

The castle doors have been opened by the king's right-hand man, Gustaf, who raised both of his hands in the air as a sign for everyone to quiet down. "Citizens of Cresthill! King Leandrol will be out in a few moments! Please be patient."

"Are we in danger?" one of the ladies asked.

"What could have caused all that destruction in the marketplace?" a man yelled out.

"Why has the king been hiding for two days?" someone in the back of the crowd asked.

"We want answers!" a few people said yelled in unison.

"People, people, please stay calm," Gustaf reassured the crowd. "Once the king is here, he will not leave until all of your questions have been answered."

"Well, that's good news," one of the ladies in the front said with a smile.

"I assure you the king and queen will be here in mere moments."

King Leandrol sat on his throne, mentally preparing for what he was going to tell the people. Queen Amaya grabbed his hand, which was tapping on the side of his chair.

"Everything will be all right, me love. Our people will accept what you have to say."

He looked at his wife. She was just as beautiful as the day he met her. Her beautiful light- brown eyes were always his favorite. Her hair was tied up in a ponytail, and she wore a blue dress, signifying Cresthill's signature color of blue. Her necklace had a blue crescent moon with a star piercing the center of it, the same symbol of Cresthill's flag.

"I know, but it still doesn't make it any easier, my dear."

He wore his Cresthill armor, but instead of it being made of iron, his was made of gold. He also wore his red cape with his fire blade hanging from the left side of his waist. Only two people in Cresthill wear the color red in the castle—the king and his servant Gustav. He stood up and held his hand out for his queen to grab. The both of them made their way outside to ease the crowd. Two faeds accompanied the royal couple, as did the king's advisor, Avaline, the wizard. The night before she was brought back to the city by a faed with urgent news, news the king was going to tell the people of his city.

Some of the Grey Hawks were in between the people and the king as hired security, as well as a few royal guards and faeds.

Blackshiv raised his cane to his mouth. "Silence! The king has arrived." His cane had an enchantment to enhance his voice in volume if he so wished.

The crowd went silent on his command. A lot of elves and dwarves were in attendance as well for the upcoming feast day and baccus hunt a few days from now.

"Citizens of Cresthill!" the king shouted.

Blackshiv handed his cane over for Leandrol to use so all can hear.

"Can everyone hear me?"

Most of the people in the back put their thumbs up.

"Good! I have a lot of news to tell all of you. I'm sure most of you have been wondering what happened to the marketplace."

"Yeah, what could have caused such damage to the stone?" someone asked.

More people started to mutter, and the crowd once again grew restless.

The king raised his hand for silence and got it almost immediately. "The wanted posters we send around the land yesterday, those three criminals were here." The royal guards opened the wanted posters for everyone to see. "The young lady made an attempt on my life, some of you may have witnessed the other day. I was saved by the Wolf of the mountain's children, Emilia and Caedus."

"That's just horrible. Who would want to kill our king?" someone whispered.

"She was apprehended. Her name is Sheska. Later we found out the attack toward me was only a distraction for her accomplice to steal important information inside the castle. While attempting to steal this information"—he now pointed at Cedric's picture—"he murdered two guards in cold blood."

"Oh no!" a man gasped.

"Who would do such a thing!" a woman yelled.

"We apprehended him as well." He glanced at Avaline, then the queen. He hesitated before he continued, "His name is Cedric. It pains me to tell you that h e is the son of our beloved former champion Savas."

"The son of the Champion? The one who was taken away? If he was raised by a murderer, would he have turned out any different?" one of the men muttered.

"Why wait until now to return after all this time?" someone else asked.

"We don't have all of the details yet, but some of the pieces are coming together," the king assured the crowd. "After we had Cedric and Sheska in custody, this man I do not know by name"—he pointed at Brock's poster—"broke them out. He climbed to the outside of the holding cells under the castle, which is right above the marketplace. They jumped down and destroyed things as distractions to ease their escape. They barely slipped through the faeds' fingers before they were saved by their master, the man who killed my friend Savas. Apparently, he goes by the name of Lord Mathis."

"Lord Mathis? Sounds menacing. What does he want?" the barkeep of Luna's tavern asked.

"That is still a mystery, my friend," the king shot back. "From what we could gather so far is that this Lord Mathis is after some of the weapons that are enchanted with magic. His purpose for wanting them is unknown, but from the lengths he will go to get them tells me that his plans are dangerous and unsafe for all of us."

A few people gasped. Many faces were full of fear, and everyone was hanging on what the king was going to say next.

"About the feast day and baccus hunt that is supposed to take place in a few days, on October the thirty-first, it will be cancelled."

The people started to talk among themselves. Some of the dwarves and elves looked angry.

"Did we come all this way just for nothing?" one of the dwarves asked.

"Mind your tongue," Blackshiv spat at the dwarf.

He bowed his head for forgiveness. "I meant no disrespect, King Leandrol. We came such a long way. I may have a solution." This dwarf had blond hair, not as common in dwarves, with a beard but half as long as to what is standard for his kind. He looked on the young side, but since dwarves aged differently than humans, he could very well be older than the king. He wore chain mail armor with big shoulder plates and sword on his back instead of an axe.

"Oh? I would love to hear it," the king said.

"Since we brought carts of ale, and the elves brought their wine, and we have plenty of food and cooks, why don't we just have a feast tonight?"

There were a few yays in the background, and people continued to talk to each other.

"I know what ya want is for yer people to be safe, so we don't have to do the hunt, with dark wizards about and such. What do ya say?"

Gustav nodded his head in agreement, as did Queen Amaya and Avaline.

"That is a fine idea, master dwarf. I fear that dark times may be upon us, but tonight let us celebrate unity together. Elves and dwarves and men."

The crowd roared in applause.

"Might I ask of your name, master dwarf?"

"My name is Gaiman," the dwarf said.

"It's a pleasure, Gaiman. You lifted up the spirits of the whole city better than I thought I could!" Leandrol said with a laugh.

"Is something to be done to counteract this Lord Mathis?" one of the townsfolk asked.

"Yes, we have taken steps to counteract whatever Mathis is planning. For those of you who remember, years ago, Therion, the wolf of the mountain; myself; and the former champion, Savas, were known as the Phoenix Squadron. For those of you who do not know what that is, every generation three individuals are selected to work directly under the king, and not just me, the four kings of Afelith. They are peacekeepers who are bound by the Phoenix to repel evil. The night Savas died ten years ago, the Phoenix died with him and the squad was disbanded."

"Who will be in the new Phoenix Squadron now?" more than a few people asked.

"The Overseer of Zeledon has chosen the other son of Savas, Caedus; Therion's daughter, Emilia; and my wonderful daughter, Alanna. The three of them are training far away as we speak. The next time we see them, they will be this generation's Phoenix Squadron."

The crowd applauded. "The sons of Savas, on opposite sides of the conflict, is it wise to pit them against each other?" one of the elves asked.

"What would their father think of what has transpired if he were still alive?" one of the townsfolk said in a loud voice.

"I wonder that myself," the king replied. "As much as I would love to turn to my old friend for guidance, I cannot. We cannot linger on what is beyond our control. As for Caedus being sent as one of the three to counteract the plans of Mathis, at first I was against it. He is too emotionally involved, and I thought that he would do more harm than good." He looked over at Avaline and smiled. "But from what my advisor has told me, he has been focusing on the task at hand, despite what his personal feelings may be. His allegiance is with Cresthill, and if anyone is going to stop Cedric and Mathis, it will be him."

The crowd roared in applause.

"I believe that under the guidance of the Overseer, Caedus, Emilia, and Alanna, they will bring great honor to our kingdom and am confident that they will bring peace to the lands of Afelith!"

The crowd started to chant. "To the Phoenix Squadron! To the Phoenix Squadron! To the Phoenix Squadron!"

Blackshiv, Hamoon, and Dominick raised their right arms in the air, making fists. "To the Phoenix Squadron!"

The rest of the Grey Hawks in the area began to chant as well.

Gustav eyed the king and raised his eyebrows. The king nodded.

"To the Phoenix Squadron!" the man yelled with both of his hands in the air.

The royal guards then began to chant.

Queen Amaya stood up next to the king. She pulled Avaline toward them. The three of them yelled into Blackshiv's cane, "To the Phoenix Squadron!"

The king was happy the city was in high spirits, but he was afraid of what could potentially happen next. Mathis was extremely dangerous, and the fourth disciple has not made an appearance. He could be anyone. The thought went away as soon as it came though. He raised his hand for silence. "Let us prepare for the feast tonight!"

The crowd once again applauded. The dwarves already made their way to the kitchens and the elves in the great dining hall to prepare. The rest of the crowd dispersed to go about their day.

⚶

Dominick approached Avaline before she went back to the castle. "Excuse me, Lady Avaline?"

"Yes, what can I do for you, young man?"

What she said threw him off a bit because she looked so young, even though she was far older than anyone else.

"My name is Dominic of the Grey Hawks, and I have a message I would like for you to give to Emilia, if you should find your way to her again before she comes back, that is." He kept his hands clasped behind his back and stood straight to keep a presentable posture.

"I don't know If I am going back to help them with their training or not, but if I do, I can surely tell her what you want her to know."

"Thank you, m'lady. I want her to know that I am doing better than when we last spoke, and I am proud of her for being selected for the Phoenix Squadron."

"I shall tell her as soon as I am able." She squinted for a second. "Dominic? Your brother was Bastion?" He nodded. "I'm terribly sorry for your loss, from what I heard he was very bright."

"He was, m'lady. Even though I am his older brother, he was a better man than me." He put his head down.

Hamoon put his hands on Dom's shoulders. "You have made mistakes in the past, but may you live on to make Bastion proud."

He put his head back up. "I will, my brother Hamoon!" He turned his attention back to Avaline. "I don't want my request to be an obligation to you, m'lady, I just wanted to tell you in case you were to see her before I do."

"It's quite all right, Dominic. For the Phoenix to be reborn could take months. As soon as I am able, I shall relay your message."

"You are very kind, Lady Avaline." He bowed his head.

She bowed her head as well, then made her way to the castle.

⟨⟨⟩⟩

"Resurrecting the Phoenix Squadron is a bold move," Blackshiv muttered. "But if the Overseer suggested it, then we may be facing some dark times ahead."

"Do you really think so?" Hamoon asked.

"I do, but I also think Caedus and Emilia are perfect candidates. I hear Alanna is a skilled fighter as well, though I never had the chance to see firsthand."

"What do you think is going to happen now? Do you think Mathis will make another attempt on the king's blade?" Dom asked.

"I do, but since his first attempt failed, I think he will gather the others he needs, then he will come to the kingdom with full force. He will stop at nothing to get the weapon."

"If your hypothesis is correct, shouldn't we tell the king?" Hamoon asked.

"Yes, I will tell him now, and besides, he still has my cane," Blackshiv said with a smile. "For the time being, Hamoon, don't let the men take any more quests unless it's local. We need everyone here ready to defend the city if the occasion arises." The headmaster began to limp toward the castle on his own.

"Headmaster Blackshiv, let me accompany you to the castle. You're having a bit of trouble walking," Dom shouted.

He gestured for Dom to accompany him with his hand. "You see? You were a good man all along, the bottle just didn't let you know that."

"You may be right, Headmaster."

XV

THE LAST CHAPTER

THE SUN ROSE BEAUTIFULLY ON the outskirts of Zeledon where the Overseer's cabin was hidden. Alanna stood over the hill where she could see the city in the distance, with the cabin behind her. She didn't sleep at all the night before. Shortly after she arrived with Emilia, Giselle, and Regan to rest, Therion and Victor burst through the door dragging an almost lifeless Caedus with him. It was a horrific sight to say the least.

He had a massive scar on his left eye, leaving him unable to open it. He seemed to still be in shock from what happened. Therion did his best to try to calm him down, but he couldn't until Avaline appeared with one of the faeds with a concoction one of the mashkiki in Cresthill came up with to put him to sleep.

Emilia was pretty shaken from seeing the scar on Caedus's face. She wouldn't say why, for most of the night she kept to herself. She went pretty hard on the drink. Sometimes Alanna didn't understand why humans turned to alcohol when they face certain problems. She never had the desire to drink, except for the occasional fest or dinner party. She felt it best to leave Emilia alone for now. She'll come around; she just needs time.

"You know after all these years, I never get tired of seeing the sun rise here," Turog said with a smile. He sat cross-legged on the top of the hill. It amazed her that they were just about the same height when he was sitting down.

"Yes, it is beautiful," she replied with a smile.

She looked over to the bottom of the hill where a blue dragon was lying down. She saw the dragon bring Caedus here, but she had no idea where it came from. She saw a sword in its mouth.

"I wouldn't get close if I were you," Turog said. "This dragon is protecting the lightning blade. He won't let anyone near him but Caedus."

"Where did this dragon come from?"

"It was Cedric's, before his unfortunate end. The dragon saw the bond the brothers shared and decided to continue on with Caedus."

"Cedric's unfortunate end? What happened to him?" Alanna asked in an alarming tone. Now it made more sense seeing how Caedus was when he got there. It took more out of him seeing his brother die than the physical injuries he received. He couldn't even walk on his own when he got here.

"Sit down, and I will tell you what happened."

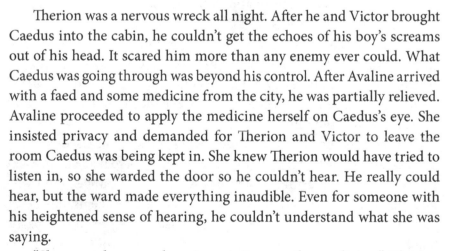

Therion was a nervous wreck all night. After he and Victor brought Caedus into the cabin, he couldn't get the echoes of his boy's screams out of his head. It scared him more than any enemy ever could. What Caedus was going through was beyond his control. After Avaline arrived with a faed and some medicine from the city, he was partially relieved. Avaline proceeded to apply the medicine herself on Caedus's eye. She insisted privacy and demanded for Therion and Victor to leave the room Caedus was being kept in. She knew Therion would have tried to listen in, so she warded the door so he couldn't hear. He really could hear, but the ward made everything inaudible. Even for someone with his heightened sense of hearing, he couldn't understand what she was saying.

"She must have used an incantation on the medicine," Therion muttered to Victor.

"Rare for the mashkiki to not have medicine strong enough for a gash," the younger man replied.

"True, but we have no idea how powerful that lightning was that Mathis used to cut Caedus so deep." He pressed his arms against the wall and began to lean downward as if tired. His arms were still fractured. They constantly ached, but with everything going on, he hadn't had the time to feel the pain until now.

Victor patted the old man's back. "He'll be all right. Just give a little time."

"The time is what worries me," Therion whispered.

"Go see how your daughters doing. That will pass the time. I'll check on Alanna."

Therion smiled and let Victor lead the way out of the hallway. He then grabbed the younger man's shoulders while walking behind him and playfully shook him. "You are a wise man, Victor. Savas would have been proud to see you succeed him."

"It's an honor so be Champion of the King. I try to live up to his legacy every day."

"Don't get caught up in his legacy when you have your own to make. I could see you becoming the best of all of us someday."

"That means a lot coming from you, Therion."

Both men parted ways after they got through the hallway. Therion went to the round table where Emilia was drinking, and Victor went to talk to Regan before he went outside to see Alanna.

"What's wrong, Em?" Therion asked as he took a big sip of ale.

"I saw...a vision of the future in my trial," she whispered without looking up.

"Yeah, what of it? You know what you saw is only one of many potential futures. It may not come to pass. Why did seeing Caedus freak you out so much? What does it have to do with your vision?"

She finally looked up. "He had that same scar in my vision, and many others. The look he had on his face in my vision, he was...defeated. He had given up on everything. He even said he wasn't welcome in our home anymore, and he was surprised that I was even talking to him. What could have happened to make things between us so bad? I could never picture us being in such a bad state. It was horrible."

Therion stood up and gestured for Emilia to stand up as well. After she slowly stood he embraced her. "I'm sorry, Em. We can only hope that the two of you remain as strong as you always have."

She nodded and smiled. "I want to see him."

"Wait until Avaline is done first."

"Yes, Papa." She hugged him again.

Regan gestured for Victor to follow him to the far side of the house where the baccus resides.

"We have something we would like to discuss with you, Vic."

"Is everything all right?"

"If we are careful, we should be. I may be paranoid, but I sense something is off."

Victor was confused. "What do you mean?"

The baccus interjected, "This elven woman Giselle, we suspect that all is not as it seems with her."

"She could just be an innocent woman who got caught up in all of this. We just want to be careful," Regan added. "But it seems strange that Cedric kidnapped an elf on his way here who to this very moment suppressing her immense power to not get noticed by us. I don't think she was taken against her will to come here. She could be working with this Lord Mathis."

"That is a bold claim," Victor replied. "But I sensed it too. She is much more powerful than she seems. It could be that her connection with nature is what makes her strong…"

"That is why we have a task for you, young Vic," Regan said.

"I would like for you to come with me to investigate this small town by the mountains, where she said she was an herbalist," the baccus said. "Ask around. See if her story is straight. And if it's not, we can confront her about her lying to us."

"Not a bad idea. If it's okay, I think we should wait to leave until Caedus wakes up."

"Of course," Regan said with a smile.

While Alanna stood on the top of the hill, Giselle wandered into the woods. She saw the Overseer approaching with an armored stranger. She could tell the stranger was a female with her body shape, but not much else. She recognized the bow on her back, and she was paralyzed with fear.

"No, it can't be her. She died a long time ago," Giselle reassured herself. As they got closer she saw the red emblem on the stranger's shoulder. Her face turned pale. She leaned on a tree because she lost feeling in her legs. "It is her!"

"Giselle! You don't look well. Do you need help?" the Overseer asked.

Just as the Overseer said that name, Reyna froze.

Giselle? Is that really her? It's been so long, she said in her head.

"I'm okay. I just came out here for some air. I am rather tired as well."

"Well, my dear, you are welcome to rest in one of the extra rooms I have," the Overseer said.

"I may take you up on that. Thank you."

"Go on ahead, Overseer. I will keep her company," Reyna said quietly.

"Very well, see you both inside." The Overseer proceeded to his cabin.

They waited until he was out of sight before talking.

"Is it really you?"

Reyna nodded her head.

"It can't be..."

"Yes, it's me." Reyna hit a hidden switch on her helmet to reveal her eyes. She took off her gloves and cupped Giselle's face into her hands. "My little flower."

Giselle burst into tears and almost fainted. Seeing her eyes was all the proof she needed. Reyna had to catch her. "He told me you were dead!"

"As far as he knows I still am. Why did you come here with him? You have been here all this time?"

Giselle took a few deep breaths to gather herself together. "Yes, I have. After we thought you died, there was nothing left except for him. So I joined him."

"You know how he was, how he is! He is still obsessed with power. And now he is using you, his own daughter, to obtain it."

"After you were gone, he stopped caring about everything. Losing you devastated him, devastated both of us, Mother!"

It's been so long since Reyna heard that word, *mother*. She wanted to take her helmet off and kiss her little flower, but she had more than one reason to keep it on. She couldn't take it off, not here. "I missed you so much, Zelle. I'm here now." She paused for a few moments. "Why are you here if you are working with your father? He sent you to infiltrate the people of Cresthill, didn't he?"

She didn't have the heart to answer. Her eyes watered, and that's all Reyna needed to confirm her suspicion. "It wasn't his idea! It was Cedric's. We trespassed here for the lightning blade, and Regan caught us. Cedric did his job by keeping me safe and implied I was his captive, so I had the freedom to complete my quest."

"I see…" Reyna sighed. "That has your father's teachings all over it. He taught you to adapt to situations on the fly. What do you plan to do now? Are you going to take the blade from under Caedus's nose now?"

"I will do what I must," Giselle said sternly.

"You can come with me, Zelle."

"Look closer, Mother."

Reyna reached out with her senses and concentrated on her daughter. She then began to see threads tied to her, the same threads that Lord Mathis uses to control his disciples. "Oh no, he wouldn't dare!"

"But he did, Mother, to me and my three companions. He has only used it on me once, but it was used to save my life. He helped me escape the faeds."

"That is still no excuse to use that incantation on you, or anyone else!"

Giselle could feel the anger swelling out of her mother now. She quickly collected herself and calmed down.

"If I find a way to free you of this, will you come with me?"

Giselle saw her mother told back tears. "Yes, Mother."

They embraced.

The Overseer greeted everyone on his way in and went straight toward the ward Avaline put up. He walked straight through as if it was an open doorway.

"That old man has a lot of tricks," Therion said as he sighed.

"How is he?" the old man asked, referring to the unconscious Caedus.

"You know I put that ward up for a reason," Avaline shot back without looking at him. Her concentration was on Caedus's left eye, which was welded shut.

"Do you think he could use that eye again?"

"The scar will be there for the rest of his life, the same as the burned handprint of the faed, but if he were to open his left eye again, it will take time, and even if he could open his eye, there is a strong possibility of him being blind on that side."

"Is there a way to fix it?" Caedus said as he slowly tried to get up.

"Did you just hear our whole conversation?" Avaline asked.

"Yes." Caedus gestured for the wizard to help him stand. She wrapped his arm around her shoulders to lift him up. She wrapped her other arm around his waist to support him.

"I shall gather everyone around," the Overseer said as he left the room. He had everyone gather to the back porch.

Everyone gathered around the back. Therion and Emilia came outside, Turog and Alanna came down from the hill, and Victor with Regan along with the baccus coming from the far side of the house.

"Young Caedus is awake. He shall be out here in moments."

After a minute Avaline and Caedus came through the back door. The wizard helped Caedus sit on the wooden rocking chair. Emilia came up to him first and put her hand on his left cheek. It was still hot where his scar was. She kissed his forehead. He barely even acknowledged her presence. He was suffering on the inside. The past ten years of his life felt wasted. He found his brother after all this time to see him die. He was upset, he was angry, but he was still in shock. He is incapable of showing emotion. It terrified Emilia because she saw the same look on his face in her trial from the future.

"Tell me, son, can you open your eye?" the Overseer asked.

Caedus shook his head.

"Your sight has become severely limited. You won't be much good in a fight in your condition."

"What do you propose?" Caedus asked.

"There is a rare form of magic. It heightens your senses in a fight so greatly that you would have the upper hand even if you were blind."

"What is this form of magic called?"

"The Incantation of Clairvoyance."

"Absolutely not!" Therion screamed in anger.

"What's wrong?" Emilia asked.

"Therion has hatred to the only man that could teach you this form of magic. I don't like the guy myself." The Overseer started to stare at Therion and raised his voice. "But this is not the time for personal grudges. You know this is the only way to get Caedus back into form, unless you have a better idea?"

Therion sighed. "No, I don't. You're right."

"Who are you talking about?" Alanna asked.

The Overseer gave Therion a look as if he should be the one to tell everyone.

He shook his head and whispered, "Spartacus."

Victor now gave Therion his undivided attention. "Did you just say Spartacus? As in the gladiator Spartacus?"

"Yes," Therion said with obvious annoyance.

"But I thought he died decades ago, did he not?" Victor asked as he tilted his head.

"That is what history tells you," the Overseer said. "But events always find a way to bend itself when it benefits the public."

"Why do you hate him then?" Caedus asked.

Therion paused and took a few deep breaths, then looked at the Overseer, who gestured for Therion to begin by nodding his head.

"Tell me what you know of Spartacus, Caedus."

"Not much, I must say," Caedus admitted while rubbing his head. "He was the only man to stay undefeated in the arena. He led a rebellion with the other gladiators and was eventually killed."

"Most of that was true. He was undefeated, the only one to this day in fact. He led the rebellion of slaves. Even though he was presumed dead in the last battle, his body was never found."

Therion sat on the creaky wooden step of the porch near Caedus. Everyone else was hanging on every word that came out of his mouth.

"When he knew the final battle was lost, he fled the battlefield and never looked back. He eventually got married and had a son." He paused again as the color left his face, then looked at Caedus. "The son of Spartacus was your father, Savas."

Everyone was in shock. The lineage of Savas was always kept secret. No one thought anything of it, but only a select few knew that Spartacus was his father. It's something the public didn't need to know, not that anyone was to believe it since the mass rumors of Spartacus being dead.

"If he is my grandfather, how come I never met him? Where has he been all this time?"

Therion stood up, but before he could continue, the Overseer gestured for him to stop.

"Therion is just going to get too worked up if he continues, so I'll tell the rest of the story."

Therion sat down in relief and let the Overseer continue.

"Your father was a very talented fighter, just like Spartacus, but his connection to the Well of Magic was particularly weak compared to someone like me or Avaline or Therion. He had to work a lot harder than the rest of us to keep his connection to the well. It's more common than you think, not everyone could sustain having magic abilities or senses, especially in humans."

"He managed to keep his senses pretty well, but he struggled to obtain any extra abilities," Therion cut in. He grimaced. "But *Spartacus* was ashamed to have a son with a weak connection to magic. He didn't care that Savas was a great fighter, all he wanted was for his son to master the Incantation of Clairvoyance so he could pass on his knowledge, but he considered Savas a failure for not being adept enough in magic to use his power, so he abandoned him."

"Spartacus abandoned my father? For something that he had no control over?" Caedus asked, with visible anger on his face.

"Savas lived for trying to make his father proud. He followed his footsteps and became a gladiator, but nothing Savas did impressed Spartacus." Therion sighed. "Savas was a far greater man than Spartacus ever was. He was just too arrogant and foolish to see that. Now he will never get the chance to make amends. Your father died knowing he had a father that didn't love him."

"But he died knowing he had two sons that loved him and many friends. That's all the family he needed."

That made Therion smile.

"So how did Spartacus react to my father's death?"

"As far as we know, he doesn't know that Savas is dead. In fact, he doesn't even know that you and Cedric even exist," the Overseer said.

"So I guess I have to become the bearer of bad news? Better yet, do any of you even know where he is?" Caedus asked.

"I know the region he is in, but I know someone who should know more," Avaline said. "Malagan the wizard knows where Spartacus is."

"Another wizard? Where is he then?" Caedus asked.

"Past the Lasgarothian forest is a place called the Wildlands, largely undiscovered and dangerous, but once you are past the elves' defenses of the forest, Malagan would most likely seek you out, since no one has gone to the Wildlands in ages."

"So after we find Malagan, you think Spartacus is just going to train us out of the goodness in his heart?"

"Men like him don't change," the Overseer stated. "All he cared about was passing on his knowledge to someone worthy before he died. He just didn't think that person was your father."

"What makes you think he would pass it on to me?"

"Because you have an extremely strong connection to the Well of Magic. Whatever that red lightning was, it obviously improved your life for the better. You were able to skip the trial of the well, which I have never seen before. The only explanation I could think of at the moment is you were struck by the well itself, hence your strong connection to it."

"I see," Caedus said, but obviously confused.

"Spartacus is going to be able to sense how strong you are. I have no doubt he would want to train you," Therion said. He turned around to Alanna and Emilia. "Same goes for you two. Alanna, your connection to the well is more natural since you are elven, and my little girl!" Emilia blushed. "You have grown more powerful than I could have hoped, and this is only the beginning."

"That being said, I have an announcement," the Overseer said loudly. "Once Caedus, Alanna, and Emilia learn the Incantation of Clairvoyance, I have chosen for them to become this generation's Phoenix Squadron."

"The Phoenix Squadron is the highest honor to obtain!" Alanna said with excitement. "Will the king go along with this?"

"My orders are above all of the kings," the Overseer said with a straight face.

Therion nodded to reassure what he was saying was true.

"Avaline is going to deliver the news to King Leandrol when she goes back to Cresthill."

"The faed will take me back before the king makes his speech this afternoon."

"I assume to let the public in on what's been happening the past few days?" Alanna asked.

"Yes, my dear, they have been growing restless being left in the dark on the recent events. A lot of fear over what has happened with the destruction of the marketplace."

"When do we leave to find Spartacus?" Emilia asked.

"As soon as Caedus is up for it," the Overseer stated.

"How about now?" Caedus asked as he stood up.

Alanna rushed to support him. He was a little wobbly, but he was okay. He was more than happy to have Alanna support him though. He couldn't get over how beautiful she was, how good she smelled, how soft her touch was.

"Are you sure you're ready to travel?" Victor asked.

"If we take it easy today and a little tomorrow, yeah. We have a long journey ahead."

"I am going with you," Regan announced. "I know Malagan pretty well, and I have been to the Wildlands before."

"Very well," the Overseer said. "The four of you should be enough."

"What about you, Papa?" Emilia asked.

"I have no desire to have a reunion with Spartacus, but I have faith in all of you. Come home soon."

Emilia and Caedus embraced Therion together. Emilia buried her face into her father's shoulder while Caedus grabbed him tight. Therion held back tears.

"I'm proud of both of you."

Alanna hugged Therion as well.

"So, young Caedus, your journey begins," Turog said with a wide smile. "I wish the three of you safe passage into the Wildlands."

"Thank you, Turog," Caedus said as he tried to smile. The left side of his face was still in a lot of pain. They shook hands, or what passed for shaking hands, considering the massive difference in the size of their hands.

"I wish you a safe journey, Alanna," Victor said as they hugged. "To you as well, Emilia." He hugged her as well. "And at last to you, Caedus." They locked forearms and pulled each other in for a one-armed hug. "Safe travels, my brother."

"Thank you, Victor," Caedus said as he patted Vic's back.

"The road ahead will be dangerous, and Spartacus will test you," Avaline said, leaning on her staff. "But I am confident in the three of you."

"Thank you, m'lady," the three of them said in unison.

"I can provide you with the provisions you need to get you as far as Lasgaroth, then you can purchase more supplies from them."

"Thank you, James, that's generous of you," Caedus said.

The Overseer squinted. "Don't think you can get away with calling me, James, young Caedus. It's still the Overseer to you."

Therion rolled his eyes behind the Overseer's back.

"As you say." Caedus slightly bowed his head.

The faed appeared from inside and requested for Avaline to accompany it back to Cresthill, the king requires her presence.

"I shall take my leave now. Good luck to all of you."

Everyone waved.

The faed opened a portal leading back to the city, and in a matter of seconds, they were gone.

"Wait…where is Giselle?" Alanna asked.

"And the other one, Reyna?" Therion asked.

"Last I saw they were still in the small section of forest over there." The Overseer pointed to the far side.

Regan ran toward the woods to see Reyna tied up by roots that came up from the ground. "By the goddess, I was right!"

"Giselle did this. We have to find her!" Victor yelled as he unsheathed his sword.

Caedus fell to one knee. "Oh no," he whispered.

"What's wrong?" Alanna asked.

"The dragon is gone. Giselle flew away on it, and she has the lightning blade." He punched the ground.

Alanna and Emilia grabbed his shoulders to attempt to comfort him. He closed his eyes and leaned into both of them.

"Can you call the lightning blade back to you?" the Overseer asked nervously.

Caedus shook his head. He was still too weak from the beating he took. He had to accept the fact that Lord Mathis was about to obtain the lightning blade and become even more powerful than he already was. The only choice he had was to find Spartacus and become strong enough to face Mathis.

EPILOGUE

L ORD MATHIS WALKED THROUGH THE dark hallways of his warded
area of the castle of Dulangar. He approached the red stone
floating in the middle of the room. He gently reached for it as it
levitated above his hand. He was nervous. Was this going to work?

Necromancy was the hardest form of magic to master, even he
couldn't do it. But transferring the power of the stone into Cedric's body
could, in theory, bring him back. There was only one way to find out.
He brought the stone to where Cedric's body was kept, on one of the
tables of his lab.

The stone began to levitate over the young man's body. After a few
seconds Mathis pushed the stone into the boy's chest. By doing so, it
began to cause damage to his own hand. Physical contact with the stone
was forbidden, but he wanted to bring Cedric back. He needed to. He
groaned in pain as his hand started burning, but what he was doing
was working. Bit by bit the stone began to dissolve and disperse into
Cedric's body.

He figured only half the stone was needed since it contained so
much power, and he was right. Cedric's eyes opened as he breathed in
deep. Mathis was relieved. It was never his intent to cause harm to the
boy. Cedric tried to stand, but Mathis held him down.

"Wha…where am I? What happened?" Cedric yelled out.

Mathis noticed his eyes were no longer yellow. They were blood red
like the stone.

"Calm yourself, boy! You're safe now." He let go of him to let him
stand up. "Rest up, because when your three companions come back,
we are going to war!"

CPSIA information can be obtained
at www.ICGtesting.com
Printed in the USA
LVHW040403130520
655431LV00001B/76